TALES OF
TERROR ON THE
HIGH SEAS

SHORT STORIES OF GHOSTLY
GALLEONS AND FEARFUL STORMS

FROM SOME OF THE FINEST WRITERS
SUCH AS EDGAR ALLAN POE
AND
SIR ARTHUR CONAN DOYLE

BY

VARIOUS AUTHORS

British Library Cataloguing-in-Publication Data
A catalogue record for this book is available from the
British Library

CONTENTS

TERROR FROM THE SEA

Eden Phillpotts

One August morning a West of England newspaper printed the following paragraphs in its columns:

'Since alcohol was banished from our tables and may no longer be drunk save under medical prescription, feats of imagination are not so common and do not win the respectful attention our ancestors were wont to give them; but of old, familiar spectres were accustomed to appear in the newspaper, when news ran short, and the Sea Serpent and Great Gooseberry usually adorned our pages during the holiday season. Imagination, however, being a thing of the past and flights of fancy long since relegated to the nursery, it is somewhat astounding to be reminded of these ancient aberrations at the present day. Old men no longer see visions, nor do young men dream dreams, so what shall be said of this preposterous story from a Devon strand? Whence its inspiration and how comes it that not less than five adult human beings stoudy cleave to it despite the laughter of their neighbours?

'Long-shore fisherfolk they are, who have their business in shallow waters with hook and line, net and lobster-pot. They operate from a strip of sand dunes and waste land a mile long which separates the estuarial waters of the river Exe from the sea and is known as Dawlish Warren. When men of old played ball games, golf links occupied this region; to-day it is derelict.

'Descending through these sand dunes at dawn to their boat, which lay upon the beach awaiting them, the fishers emerged upon the shore under the first grey of a still and cloudy morning. Light was as yet very dim, but the eastern sky began to mantle. Suddenly they saw a huge blot rising at the junction of sea and shore. It loomed large and dark against the peaceful dawn behind it and suggested to them the possibility that some small sloop, or coasting vessel, had lost her bearings and run aground by night.

'They were hastening to her when the keenest-eyed of the party stayed his mates and, as they all allege, saved their lives by doing so. The mass had moved. They stood still and, the light increasing, made a tremendous discovery. This great object at sea-level was alive, and the horrified spectators perceived that a marine crab confronted them. It resembled those they daily caught — the edible crab of commerce; but it was as large as an army tank, and they judged it must have weighed five hundred tons or more. Appalled and doubting their senses, the good fellows retreated backwards; but the monster had observed them. They declare that its large, black eyes were poised upon protruding stalks three feet long and moved in waving fashion to right and left as a flower blown by the wind upon its stem. They stood now two hundred yards from the creature, but it was evidendy aware of their presence, and our sailormen declare, as the next item in this nightmare, that from the shell of the crustacean above its head (if indeed crabs possess anything to be called a head) there shot suddenly a puff of vapour, as though a gas gun had been fired. And this was indeed what had happened! The crab had directed his discharge at them and a moment later they became conscious of the fact. The morning air grew thick with a heavy odour that none had ever known until then, and they ran away from it as fast as they might. One man fainted and his companions picked him up and continued their combined retreat into purer atmosphere. The sufferer swiftly returned to consciousness and the air about them grew sweet again. Their restricted breathing was restored and none suffered any ill effects from the discharge; but all are confident that, had they been nearer the giant, they must have perished. For a time they feared pursuit, but nothing further happened and, as dawn waxed and the light of day brightened the dunes, two of the fishermen crept back to the shore and, concealing themselves behind a ridge of sand and bent grass, spied upon the beach. They were just in time to see an upheaval of the sea and mark a disturbance of the placid tide as the intruder returned to its element. They waited an hour, saw no more of it and presendy, with what appears to us considerable courage, launched their boat and went about their business.

'It seems that they debated their weird experience and naturally hesitated to tell it; but since no less than five men were agreed as to the details of the adventure, it appeared to them worthy of credence.

'As our representative has conveyed this narrative to Professor Macmurdoch, principal of the great Marine Laboratory at Plymouth and the first living authority on the Crustacea, we are enabled to conclude our singular story with the learned gendeman's comment upon it.

' "That there are far larger decapods in the sea than ever came out of it," he admitted, "is exceedingly probable. Indeed submarine exploration has revealed their existence and at a mile beneath the surface of temperate and tropical oceans our diving chambers have reported the spider crab as large as a man, and often larger. It is not impossible that in those three-mile depths of the sea, as yet inadequately explored, there may dwell enormous crustaceans lighted, as are the deep sea fish, by their own electricity and created to resist the terrific weight of water above them. Science can offer no objections to such a possibility; but a crab weighing five hundred tons and armed with a gas gun upon his carapace must certainly be seen before it can be credited, and I for one should feel quite unprepared to accept the testimony of five mariners, or even five hundred. Such a chimera belongs to the days of fiction, when our forefathers still won pleasure from myth and legend, and human imagination played with fact, finding childish amusement in peopling the world with ogres and fairies and reading all manner of fanciful inventions, together with poetry and romance. But that time is past; fiction has disappeared; and the only interesting thing about this absurdity would be to learn by what trick, or freak of atavism, these simple fellows should have concocted or imagined such a piece of nonsense. That a solitary sailor of weak mind might have shown his ancient ancestry in this fashion, by imagining the thing that is not, one could easily understand; but that five fishermen tell the same story can, I fear, only be explained in one way. They desire to gain a little attention and possibly some pecuniary advantage from the tale. They have invented a new 'Rhyme of the Ancient Mariner'; and if you ask me what that might be, I shall tell you that it is a piece of poetry written in remote time by a British bard, whose name I forget, though men of letters might possibly remember it.

' "To sum up," concluded the professor, "I think we may

safely prophesy that we shall not hear of the Dawlish Warren crab again." '

But the expert proved mistaken, as experts are apt to be, and within one week of that Devonian experience, things began to happen that established the veracity of those English fishermen. Their little world had not done laughing at them before the world at large found itself faced with a growing problem of hideous complexity and the incursion of *Brychura Gigantea* began in earnest.

The great crab was reported from three places on the coast line of the Americas and from Newfoundland, while simultaneously solitary specimens appeared in South Africa, and on the African shore of the Red Sea. They occurred in the Yellow Sea also. One had visited Cyprus, another Malta, another Tripoli. The Baltic had seen them and Australia chronicled no less than nine upon her beaches. The accounts resembled each other and in one or two cases, supposing that the monsters were stranded by the tide, bodies of men had attacked them and perished under their poisonous discharge before the creatures returned unharmed to the sea. Only small arms had been employed on these occasions; but they failed to do any apparent injury.

The map of the world seemed to show that something like system and order attended the genesis of the crabs. Their pioneers and explorers were quartering out the earth, and a fact swifdy noted by science was this: that all seas appeared alike to them and they moved as freely in polar waters as around the temperate and tropical regions of ocean. The immediate objective was a capture, and Man assumed that so soon as he had slain or caught one of these formidable creatures, something as to its vulnerability might be learned. It was many weeks before actual fear appeared in the heart of humanity, together with those wild rumours and suspicions that fear is wont to breed; but anon a sense of real danger and doubt dawned before sensational news. In the Pacific something like concerted action began to be taken by Crab, and litde groups of islands were overrun by it. The lowly inhabitants, hemmed in on all sides, for the most part perished and the majority of their small vessels were also destroyed, but survivors, who had put to sea and escaped, made land elsewhere and reported the fate of their clans and families. They painted hideous pictures of the ruin and death created; they vouched for it that Crab was a Man-eater and devoured his victims after he had slain them with dreadful emanations from himself.

Science, measuring the significance of these stories, accepted the truth of them since it became no longer possible to doubt. The chemists pondered the gas which Crab was able to exude and the naturalists doubted not that this vapour, when discharged under sea, would secure the creatures their prey of great fishes. But such an elastic fluid was far more volatile and clearly operated at a far greater range when shot into the air. Its constituents soon became a matter of vital interest.

Brychura Gigantea waxed in size and in numbers. His Pacific depredations swiftly increased, so that the 'wireless' daily recorded new successes for him and television from Fiji enabled Europe actually to see him at work. Samoa was overrun by a prodigious invasion and thousands of mankind perished under it; while many of those who thought to escape by water also lost their lives, for Crab now attacked shipping and the disappearance of considerable tonnage was recorded. Futile signals of distress sounded upon all the Seven Seas and fishing fleets were destroyed, sometimes without a survivor to tell the tale. The creatures could encircle a steam trawler with ease, drag it under the surface and sink it without a trace. No wooden ships now existed and, under motive power, the average speed of all craft great and small had much increased; but Crab when afloat was able to wreck all save armoured vessels by impact with his own carcase. The weight and speed of ships had enormously increased, however, and against modern tonnage of any size he was powerless save to offer his floating hordes against them, stay their progress and labour under sea to pierce their hulls.

Curious facts of natural history appeared and it was found

that many small terrestrial species of the creatures, familiar to Man in the tropics and dwelling miles from the sea, were acting in unfamiliar fashion and operating in communion with their huge, marine compatriots. Observation revealed a connection, though its character could not be understood; but when the land crabs began to leave their mountain haunts and swarm seawards, many unhappy islanders knew that their turn had come. The sign could not be mistaken or the warning disregarded. In the West Indies thousands of white and coloured people were thus able to leave their homes by sea in time and reach Barbados, Jamaica and the larger islands now arming against incursion.

From these phenomena arose a dreadful theory that Crab was revealing something more than instinct, and science divided into two camps upon this question, the one holding that a measure of reason marked his operations, the other protesting against any hypothesis so terrible from a human standpoint, and declaring that *Brychura* operated mechanically and had only been drawn from die depths to seek unfamiliar light and air by some sudden accident of increase which multiplied his species abnormally. In any case no possibility existed of communicating with the creatures, or reaching such intelligence and comprehension as they might possess. No link could be forged and Man now perceived that death was the sole weapon to be used against them. But Crab increased by millions and his destruction in huge numbers, when compassed by explosives from the air, deterred him not at all. The danger zones widened; he increased his grip from the islands to the main lands; he penetrated the great river estuaries of North and South America; India and China began to swarm with him. At a thousand points, from North to South and upon every continent, Man found himself steadily driven back, and when fleets of bombing airplanes broke the crustacean ranks and slaughtered oncoming hosts, fresh legions surged out of the sea to devour their fallen and trample with hideous deliberation forward into all lands. Where individual pioneers from the horde had early been cut off and killed, Man was able to examine his foe scientifically and make important discoveries concerning his weapon and armour. The fighting lines had long been observed to consist of two species: the monstrous *Brychura* and the spider-crabs, their allies. The spiders were not larger, but far speedier, and they took the place of cavalry to the foot regiments of old. Spider Crab stood some twenty feet off the ground on lengthy legs as hard as steel and was the size of an average elephant. He could proceed over any sort of ground at forty miles an hour and he was responsible for appalling raids upon Man; but Spider proved more vulnerable than his massive companion, being as a cruiser to a battleship in naval terms.

Science discovered that the armour of the giant crabs was proof against anything but high explosives and of astounding and adamantine hardness. Nature had treated the lime of which it was composed to some formula beyond human ken and the substance of their skeletons could scarcely be scratched with anything less than diamond. Their gasometer was situated between the stalks of their eyes, with a sort of nozzle protruding beyond them and capable of being turned in any direction at the will of the operator. A cistern held the gas, which was created within the interior of the animal and stored in liquid form above. Chemistry analysed the constituents, and Man's history dated from that discovery the first ray of hope to shine through the darkness now crowding upon him.

Until this time no gas mask had proved able to resist the aerial poison distributed by Crab; while Man's counter-poisons ejected against the intruder had affected him not at all; but new experiments were made and defensive masks perfected, while meantime the great struggle continued under circumstances of increasing horror. Human hearts indeed were wrung to the limit, and thousands of men and women lost their senses, thousands committed suicide and slew their nearest and dearest as the remorseless monsters approached and no way of escape offered. Crab's numbers continued to be incalculable and the death of thousands strewed the air of Earth with a new pestilence that took its toll before their advance.

But all men were already operating as one. Though he fouled the air, Crab could not stay the Herzian waves from their steadfast flow, and the world, thanks to wireless communication, had long since become but a little place. Closest concert of action was therefore possible between her kingdoms; immense speeds were long since attained in air, and the great flying ships of all peoples flew at a thousand miles an hour. Thus concentrations against Crab became possible, and East and West, North and South, wherever Man suffered and fought, were closely linked in speech and understanding. The greatest sea vessels were also immune, and where Crab had proceeded, like the hordes of the locust, to destroy human food upon his march, the ranks of depleted men were succoured when possible from the ends of Earth.

The fighting technique of Crab did not improve and huge reverses failed to sharpen his instincts. Over many districts of Earth the unconscious monsters gave themselves into the hands of Man since their method of operations brought them in masses against his barriers and it became possible to destroy them in immense numbers from the air. Every seaside town and port was protected so far as it might be done, but vast tracts of continental coast had been conquered by the enemy and from these strongholds he swarmed inland.

Crab, however, lacked method and knew no means of commissariat. His pioneers plodded everywhere slaying and devouring, but thousands perished in the great deserts of Arabia and North Africa, where for generations afterwards their stony skeletons persisted — a perch for vulture and rendezvous for jackal — until the simoon hid them beneath the sand for ever. Some reaching great oases, wherein no power existed to oppose them, slew the inhabitants and laid the fertile regions waste.

The Foreign Legion battled with them but was worsted, for their terrible encounters had occurred before the gas mask came into being that could resist Crab. And still they gathered from the seas until many great islands had fallen; Greenland was gone with Iceland, Newfoundland promised soon to succumb. Air-planes now of huge size carried the inhabitants of many lost regions into safety and the conscious world was one, working with sole purpose to save dwindling humanity against the scourge. Thousands of young men found their life's work in the air and inflicted gigantic losses upon the enemy. A phenomenon appeared on the far flung battle front, for it seemed that a sort of reason did, after all, animate and direct Crab. He, too, acknowledged leaders and, in the third year of the attempted conquest, crustaceans of fabulous size came to the shore as commanders of the hosts, and about them the rank and file assembled. Man concentrated against these colossi — creatures that towered into the air like pyramids — and a fierce attack did shattering injury to one, where it had heaved up in the delta of Nile near Alexandria. But its companions crowded about it and the wounded mass was supported and conveyed into the Mediterranean beyond reach of further harm.

Man built a new submarine, for Crab was able to encompass and destroy the old type. But with a small and mobile vessel of immense resisting strength, heroes plumbed the depths and carried death to Crab in his own element. Exploratory work of these under-sea ships continued to report enormous reserves awaiting their turn to march upon Earth, and described creatures as great as the British cathedral of St Paul operating beneath.

Science suspected that a new genesis of Crab had occurred and, as the queen bee pours forth endless streams of life, so now Man's enemy must be breeding with a fecund profusion that no opposing forces were ever likely to limit.

Meantime the whole trend and purpose of human life became perforce changed and there was built a close intercommunion that brooked no interference of any sort. Such unsocial spirits as strove to benefit from the appalling crisis, or pluck personal advantage out of it, were destroyed and swept from humanity's path. The tangled business of commerce, the confusions of monetary exchange, the thousand cumbrous and intricate barriers that Man had raised between himself and his brother were swept into the melting pot. No longer might the secure make hard terms with those in peril; no longer might neutral nations stand at gaze and profit from the sufferings of their fellows. There was none secure, no neutrals to bargain, no kingdoms beyond reach of Crab.

Night and day were alike to the invader. He carried light with him; his huge, stalked eyes could see in the dark, and Man's flood-lighting showed the monsters trudging by thousands inland — ever inland — through the hours of night. The loss to humanity far transcended any computation and the race was beggared before the end. Beleaguered, surrounded, steadily driven in upon his great protected cities and lesser towns, he saw the work of his hands cast down and many monuments of art and industry destroyed.

Canada and the Americas began to lose heart at the beginning of the third year, for Crab had now penetrated to the Great Lakes and from them issued in mighty force both North and South. Out of the tropic regions of Brazil, from the Amazon and Orinoco, hordes poured North to join forces by way of Panama and Mexico; while the frontier State of Maine in the United States afforded, through its network of estuaries and great meres, abundant support and was in the enemy's claws. Japan and Australia were lost at this season also.

A tiny islet upon the western borders of Europe had long excited the admiration of Earth by the strength of its resistance, and now, nearly at its last gasp, from this little kingdom of the British Isles, a pharmaceutical chemist's assistant by name of Albert Mugg, emerged into the limelight of history and wakened new hope for his kind.

His discovery was by no means entirely responsible for a turn in the desperate affairs of Man, but it synchronised with other events and helped to reawaken hope long foundered. There is no doubt that, inspired by a passionate patriotism and devotion to his country, Albert Mugg sacrificed his own life to its preservation without any more extended ambition; but Earth was at a crisis when to save one nation from the onset was to hearten and help them all, and his discovery, probably animated by no grander desire than to rescue his native town from destruction, may be said to represent a tremendous and vital moment of the terrestrial conflict. He came from what was known as a fashionable watering-place of little moment, but his ancestors had dwelt here, his life was spent here; he possessed a wife and two children; and their home and welfare roused in this pharmaceutical chemist such a passionate genius that he devised means for the protection and release of Weston-Super-Mare from the adamant legions now closing in upon it. Germs without number had, indeed, already been scattered over Crab and every poison known as fatal to Man and beast pressed upon him without visible effect; but Albert Mugg, after numberless experiments, hit upon a combination and implored the local authority to let an experiment be made with it. Many flying machines were protecting the neighbouring city of Bristol, which was also sore beset, but there were none just then available at Weston and the whole question of aerial defence began to grow more and more impossible for Man. He still flew with petrol fuel and the supply was rapidly giving out. Already the demand far exceeded it and he was called to employ the spirit with infinite precautions.

An appeal, however, met with swift response, and a gyroscope appeared, landed in safety and ascended again with Mugg and his apparatus. It was simple enough and consisted of a gardener's syringe and a pail of chemicals. Mugg's inspiration arose from the conviction that in one spot alone Crab must prove vulnerable, and he suspected that if a poison could enter *Brychura*'s eye it would not only blind him but proceed through this channel to the enemy's brain and cause swift destruction. What was of no avail upon his armoured body might prove all-powerful if directed against the ebon eyes, that moved upon their stalks like huge black poppies above every enemy's head and directed its vision where it willed.

A great opportunity was offered to Mugg and his airman, for amid the encircling host that now only awaited nightfall for successful attack upon the little town, there towered one of the monsters — a spider crab so huge that he resembled the edifice of some insane architect and rose upon vast shanks to the height of the Eiffel Tower. This enormous thing was a leader and the centre of an army.

With courage won from a thousand encounters, the pilot launched Albert upon his ordeal, flew steadily at a height of five hundred feet above the giant, then, like a bird of prey, hovered in air and slowly sank until the creature beneath was in range. It lifted a prodigious claw above its head and ejected a spurt of venom upwards; but the airman had long learned how to keep out of danger and his mask made him safe enough. He poised at a height of fifty feet above the agitated giant beneath. Its eyes were pointed upwards now — black, lustrous circles with a diameter of a yard — and Mugg, filling his syringe and waiting for the sudden dart and swoop of the machine, discharged his metallic concoction full and fair into each of the great orbs uplifted upon him. Then the pilot mounted and stood off, while twenty thousand people behind the protections of Weston waited to behold what might come of their fellow townsman's experiment.

A stupendous spectacle rewarded them. When struck by high explosive Crab generally perished instantly, for a shattered carapace meant death. At a successful impact he tucked in his pincers and ceased to live. The mighty creature now stricken acted otherwise. No sound emerged from it, but the great erection tottered, its eyes, as though blasted, dropped helpless upon their stalks, it fell back supine and its legs rose into the air like a group of factory chimneys. The ground shook before this tremendous impact; but no motion followed until there rose a roar from watching human thousands. The mighty had fallen and probably the largest creature that Man had ever seen alive, he now saw dead. Crab, unable to understand the terrible fate which had overtaken his leader, stood for a moment helplessly staring into the sky and the air-plane swooped down again, while Albert once more operated upon the uplifted eyes beneath him until the last drop had fallen from his syringe. Ten more monsters met the discharge and incontinently perished. Then pilot and passenger returned to safety.

Within an hour Mugg's formula was despatched to the ends of the Earth and the genius himself had ceased to live, for his triumph brought death to a weakly frame and the chemist's heart was suddenly stilled by the thrill of joy awakened at his success.

Events of enormous significance quickly followed upon this local victory, and scientific observers, still watching and estimating every phase of Man's great challenge, were able to report that, for the first time, Crab's morale had been emphatically shaken by this reverse. Dimly but forcibly the monsters had perceived that Weston-Super-Mare possessed forces with which they could not reckon, and when night returned the expected struggle came not with it. There was only heard the ponderous din of Crab returning to the Severn Sea; and at dawn of day his dead alone remained in Somersetshire.

But Man was not yet quite at the end of his torment and the need for sleepless struggle still continued. Crab continued to hold on his dogged way and another mundane year of dire human tribulation needed to be faced and endured before the issue emerged without possibility of doubt.

For years after the great contest Crab still crept in lone valleys and amid the fastnesses of the lakes and mountains. He was hunted down as the wolf of old, and being now separated and scattered, only awaited discovery to meet his end. But the war was won and the beaten enemy at length conveyed his devastated hosts back again to the ocean. He lost many thousands more in the process, for the waves of every sea as they rolled in upon the land were now liberally drenched with metallic poison, and Crab found the gauntlet of the shallow waters hard to run. The crustaceans stood presently between two fatal forces, dying on shore and in every tide-way under the malign application of 'Albert

Mugg'. For no scientific and formidable name was ever given to the dead chemist's sublime synthesis. As 'Albert Mugg' it lived and the formula was preserved lest like peril should threaten Earth again.

So passed defeated Crab from the solid ground to his rightful and greater domain of the deep. No treaties or conferences marked the end of the encounter. Crab was not called to set his seal upon terms dictated by his conqueror; no demands impossible of fulfilment were heaped upon him; but memorials rose to commemorate the terrific event and every city and township of the least importance received a shell of Crab — to be set in their market places and central resorts for remembrance. Children played upon them and the herb of the field found foothold in their crannies, until they also disappeared, and *Brychura Gigantea* might only now be seen in his habit as he lived within the aisles of Earth's national museums.

THE DROWNED MAN

Guy de Maupassant

I

EVERYONE in Fécamp knew the story of old Mother Patin. She had undoubtedly been unhappy with her man, had old Mother Patin; for her man had beaten her during his lifetime, as a man threshes wheat in his barns.

He was owner of a fishing-smack, and had married her long ago because she was nice, although she was poor.

Patin, a good seaman, but a brute, frequented old Auban's tavern, where, on ordinary days, he drank four or five brandies, and on days when he had made a good catch, eight or ten, and even more, according how he felt, as he said.

The brandy was served to customers by old Auban's daughter, a pleasant-faced, dark-haired girl, who drew Custom to the house merely by her good looks, for no one had ever wagged a tongue against her.

When Patin entered the tavern, he was content to look at her and talk civilly to her, quiet, decent conversation. When he had drunk the first brandy, already he found her

26

nicer; at the second, he was winking at her; at the third, he was saying: "Miss Désirée, if you would only . . ." without ever finishing the sentence; at the fourth, he was trying to hold her by her petticoat to embrace her; and when he had reached the tenth, it was old Auban who served him with the rest.

The old wine-seller, who knew every trick of the trade, used to send Désirée round between the tables to liven up the orders for drinks; and Désirée, who was not old Auban's daughter for nothing, paraded her petticoat among the drinkers and bandied jests, with a smile on her lips, and a twinkle in her eye.

By dint of drinking brandies, Patin grew so familiar with Désirée's face that he thought of it even at sea, when he threw his nets into the water, out on the open sea, on windy nights and calm nights, on moonlit nights and black nights. He thought of it as he held the helm in the stern of his boat while his four companions slept with their heads on their arms. He saw her always smiling at him, pouring out the yellow brandy with a lift of her shoulders, then coming towards him, saying:

"There! Is this what you want?"

And by dint of treasuring her so in eye and mind, he reached such a pitch of longing to marry her that, unable to restrain himself longer, he asked her in marriage.

He was rich, owner of his boat, his nets and a house at the foot of the cliff, on the Retenue; while old Auban had nothing. He was, therefore, accepted eagerly, and the wedding took place as quickly as possible, both parties being, for different reasons, anxious to make it an accomplished fact.

But three days after the marriage was over, Patin was no longer able to imagine in the least how he had come to think Désirée different from other women. He must have been a rare fool to hamper himself with a penniless girl who had wheedled him with her cognac, so she had, with the cognac into which she had put some filthy drug for him.

And he went cursing along the shore, breaking his pipe between his teeth, swearing at his tackle; and having cursed heartily, with every term he could think of, everything he knew, he spat out the anger still left in his stomach on the fish and crabs that he drew one by one out of his nets, throwing them into the baskets to an accompaniment of oaths and foul words.

Then, returning to his house, where he had his wife, old Auban's daughter, within reach of his tongue and his hand, he soon began to treat her as the lowest of the low. Then, as she listened resignedly, being used to the paternal violence, he became exasperated by her calm, and one evening he beat her. After this, his home became a place of terror.

For ten years, nothing was talked of on the Retenue but

the beatings Patin inflicted on his wife, and his habit of cursing when he spoke to her, whatever the occasion. He cursed, in fact, in a unique way, with a wealth of vocabulary and a forceful vigour of delivery possessed by no other man in Fecamp. As soon as his boat reached the harbour mouth, back from fishing, they waited expectantly for the first broadside he would discharge on the pier, from his deck, the moment he saw the white bonnet of his other half.

Standing in the stern, he tacked, his glance fixed ahead and on the sheets when the sea was running high, and in spite of the close attention required by the narrow, difficult passage, in spite of the great waves running mountain-high in the narrow gully, he endeavoured to pick out — from the midst of the women waiting in the spray of the breakers for the sailors — his woman, old Auban's daughter, the pauper wench.

Then, as soon as he saw her, in spite of the clamour of waves and wind, he poured on her a volley of abuse with such vocal energy that every one laughed at it, although they pitied her deeply. Then, when his boat reached the quay, he had a way of discharging his ballast of civilities, as he said, while he unloaded his fish, which attracted round him all the rascals and idlers of the harbour.

It issued from his mouth, now like cannon-shots, terrible and short, now like thunderclaps that rolled for five minutes, such a tempest of oaths that he seemed to have in his lungs all the storms of the Eternal Father.

Then, when he had left his boat, and met among the curious spectators and fishwives, he fished up again from the bottom of the hold a fresh cargo of insults and hard words, and escorted her in such fashion to their home, she in front, he behind, she weeping, he shouting.

Then, alone with her, doors shut, he beat her on the least pretext. Anything was enough to make him lift his hand, and once he had begun, he never stopped, spitting in her face, all the time, the real causes of his hate. At each blow, at each thump, he yelled: "Oh, you penniless slut, oh, you gutter-snipe, oh, you miserable starveling, I did a fine thing the day I washed my mouth out with the firewater of your scoundrel of a father."

She passed her days now, poor woman, in a state of incessant terror, in a continuous trembling of soul and of body, in stunned expectation of insults and thrashings.

And this lasted for ten years. She was so broken that she turned pale when she talked to anyone, no matter who, and no longer thought of anything but the beatings that threatened her, and she had grown as skinny, yellow and dried up as a smoked fish.

II

ONE night when her man was at sea she was awakened by the noise like the growling of a beast which the wind makes when it gets up, like an unleashed hound. She sat up in bed, uneasy, then, hearing nothing more, lay down again; but almost at once, there was a moaning in the chimney that shook the whole house and ran across the whole sky as if a pack of furious animals had crossed the empty spaces panting and bellowing.

Then she got up and ran to the harbour. Other women were running from all sides with lanterns. Men ran up and every one watched the foam flashing white in the darkness on the crest of the waves out at sea.

The storm lasted fifteen hours. Eleven sailors returned no more, and Patin was among them.

The wreckage of his boat, the *Jeune-Amélie*, was recovered off Dieppe. Near Saint-Valéry, they picked up the bodies of his sailors, but his body was never found. As the hull of the small craft had been cut in two, his wife for a long time expected and dreaded his return; for if there had been a collision, it might have happened that the colliding vessel had taken him on board, and carried him to a distant country.

Then, slowly, she grew used to the thought that she was a widow, even though she trembled every time that a neighbour or a beggar or a tramping pedlar entered her house abruptly.

One afternoon, almost four years after the disappearance of her man, she stopped, on her way along the Rue aux Juifs, before the house of an old captain who had died recently, and whose belongings were being sold.

Just at that moment, they were auctioning a parrot, a green parrot with a blue head, which was regarding the crowd with a discontented and uneasy air.

"Three francs," cried the auctioneer, "a bird that talks like a lawyer, three francs."

A friend of Widow Patin jogged her elbow.

"You ought to buy that, you're rich," she said. "It would be company for you; he is worth more than thirty francs, that bird. You can always sell him again for twenty to twenty-five easy."

"Four francs, ladies, four francs," the man repeated. "He sings vespers and preaches like the priest. He's a phenomenon . . . a miracle!"

Widow Patin raised the bid by fifty centimes, and they handed her the hook-nosed creature in a little cage and she carried him off.

Then she installed him in her house, and as she was opening the iron-wire door to give the creature a drink, she got a bite on the finger that broke the skin and drew blood.

"Oh, the wicked bird," said she.

However, she presented him with hemp-seed and maize, then left him smoothing his feathers while he peered with a malicious air at his new home and his new mistress.

Next morning day was beginning to break, when Widow Patin heard, with great distinctness, a loud, resonant, rolling voice. Patin's voice, shouting: "Get up, slut."

Her terror was such that she hid her head under the bedclothes, for every morning, in the old days, as soon as he had opened his eyes, her dead husband shouted in her ears those three familiar words.

Trembling, huddled into a ball, her back turned to the thrashing that she was momentarily expecting, she murmured, her face hidden in the bed:

"God Almighty, he's here! God Almighty, he's here! He's come back, God Almighty!"

Minutes passed; no other sound broke the silence of her room. Then, shuddering, she lifted her head from the bed, sure that he was there, spying on her, ready to strike.

She saw nothing, nothing but a ray of sun falling across the window-pane, and she thought:

"He's hiding, for sure."

She waited a long time, then, a little reassured, thought:

"I must have been dreaming, seeing he doesn't show himself."

She was shutting her eyes again, a little reassured, when

right in her ears the furious voice burst out, the thunderous voice of her drowned man, shouting:

"Damn and blast it, get up, you bitch."

She leaped out of bed, jerked out by her instinctive obedience, the passive obedience of a woman broken in by blows, who still remembers, after four years, and will always remember, and always obey that voice. And she said:

"Here I am, Patin. What do you want?"

But Patin did not answer.

Then, bewildered, she looked round her, and searched everywhere, in the cupboards, in the chimney, under the bed, still finding no one, and at last let herself fall into a chair, distracted with misery, convinced that the spirit of Patin itself was there, near her, come back to torture her.

Suddenly, she remembered the loft, which could be reached from outside by a ladder. He had certainly hidden himself there to take her by surprise. He must have been kept by savages on some shore, unable to escape sooner, and he had come back, more wicked than ever. She could not doubt it; the mere tone of his voice convinced her.

She asked, her head turned towards the ceiling:

"Are you up there, Patin?"

Patin did not answer.

Then she went out, and in an utterable terror that set her heart beating madly, she climbed the ladder, opened the garret window, looked in, saw nothing, entered, searched, and found nothing.

Seated on a truss of hay, she began to cry; but while she was sobbing, shaken by an acute and supernatural terror, she heard, in the room below her, Patin telling his story. He seemed less angry, calmer, and he was saying:

"Filthy weather . . . high wind . . . filthy weather. I've had no breakfast, damn it."

She called through the ceiling:

"I'm here, Patin; I'll make you some soup. Don't be angry. I'm coming."

She climbed down at a run.

There was no one in her house.

She felt her body giving way as if Death had his hand on her, and she was going to run out to ask help from the neighbours, when just in her ear the voice cried:

"I've had no breakfast, damn it."

The parrot, in his cage, was watching her with his round, malicious, wicked eye.

She stared back at him in amazement, murmuring:

"Oh, it's you."

He answered, shaking his head:

"Wait, wait, wait, I'll teach you to idle."

What were her thoughts? She felt, she realized that this was none other than the dead man, who had returned and hidden himself in the feathers of this creature, to begin tormenting her again, that he was going to swear, as of old, all day, and find fault with her, and shout insults to attract their neighbours' attention and make them laugh. Then she flung herself across the room, opened the cage, seized the bird, who defended himself and tore her skin with his beak and his claws. But she held him with all her might, in both hands, and throwing herself on the ground, rolled on top of him with mad frenzy, crushed him, made of him a mere rag of flesh, a little, soft, green thing that no longer moved or spoke, and hung limp. Then, wrapping him in a dishcloth as a shroud, she went out, in her shift, bare-footed, crossed the quay, against which the sea was breaking in small waves, and shaking the cloth, let fall this small, green thing that looked like a handful of grass. Then she returned, threw herself on her knees before the empty cage, and utterly overcome by what she had done, she asked pardon of the good God, sobbing, as if she had just committed a horrible crime.

THE MEMOIRS OF HERR VON SCHNABELEWOPSKI

Heinrich Heine

It was a charming spring day when I first left Hamburg. I can still see how in the harbour the golden sunrays gleamed on the tarry bellies of the ships, and think I still hear the joyous, long-drawn *Ho-i-ho!* of the sailors. Such a port in spring-time has a pleasant similarity with the feelings of a youth who goes for the first time out into the world on the great ocean of life. All his thoughts are gaily variegated, pride swells every sail of his desires — *ho-i-ho!* But soon a storm rises, the horizon grows dark, the tempest howls, the planks crack, the waves break the rudder, and the poor ship is wrecked on romantic rocks, or stranded on damp, prosaic sandbanks; or perhaps, brittle and broken, with its masts gone, and without an anchor of hope, it returns to its old harbour, and there moulders away, wretchedly unrigged, as a miserable wreck.

But there are men who cannot be compared to common ships, because they are like steamboats. They carry a gloomy fire within, and sail against wind and weather; their smoky banner streams behind, like the black plume of the Wild Huntsman; their zigzagged wheels remind one of weighty spurs with which they prick the ribs of the waves, and the obstinate, resistant elements must obey their will like a steed; but sometimes the boiler bursts, and the internal fire burns us up!

But now I will escape from metaphor, and get on board a real ship bound from Hamburg to Amsterdam. It was a Swedish vessel, and besides the hero of these pages, was also loaded with iron, being destined probably to bring as a return freight a cargo of cod-fish to the aristocracy of Hamburg, or owls to Athens.

The banks of the Elbe are charming, especially so behind Altona, near Rainville. There Klopstock lies buried. I know of no place where a dead poet could more fitly rest. To exist there as a *living* poet is, of course, a much more difficult matter. How often have I sought thy grave, oh Singer of the Messiah, thou who hast sung with such touching truthfulness the sufferings of Jesus. But thou didst dwell long enough on the Königstrasse behind the Jungfernsteig to know how prophets are crucified.

On the second day we came to Cuxhaven, which is a colony from Hamburg. The inhabitants are subjects of the Republic, and have a good time of it. When they freeze in winter woollen blankets are sent to them, and when the summer is all too hot they are supplied with lemonade. A high or well-wise senator resides there as pro-consul. He has an income of twenty thousand marks, and rules over five thousand subjects. There is also a sea-bath, which has the great advantage over all others, that it is at the same time an Elbe-bath. A great dam, on which one can walk, leads to Ritzebuttel, which also belongs to Cuxhaven. The term is derived from the Phoenician, as *Ritze* and *Buttel* signify in it the mouth of the Elbe. Many historians maintain that Charlemagne only enlarged Hamburg, but that the Phoenicians founded it about the time that Sodom and Gomorrah were destroyed, and it is not unlikely that fugitives from these cities fled to the mouth of the Elbe. Between the Fuhlentwiete and the coffee factory men have found old money, coined during the reign of Bera XVI and Byrsa X. I believe that Hamburg is the old Tarsus whence Solomon received whole shiploads of gold, silver, ivory, peacocks, and monkeys. Solomon, that is, the king of Judah and Israel, always had a special fancy for gold and monkeys.

This my first voyage can never be forgotten. My old grand-aunt had told me many tales of the sea, which now rose to new life in my memory. I could sit for hours on the deck recalling the old stories, and when the waves murmured it seemed as if I heard my grand-aunt's voice. And when I closed my eyes I could see her before me, as she twitched her lips and told the legend of the *Flying Dutchman.*

I should have been glad to see some mermaids, such as sit on white rocks and comb their sea-green hair; but I only heard them singing.

However earnestly I gazed many a time down into the transparent waters, I could not behold the sunken cities, in which mortals enchanted into fishy forms lead a deep, a marvellous deep, and hidden ocean life. They say that salmon and old rays sit there, dressed like ladies, at their windows, and, fanning themselves, look down into the street, where cod-fish glide by in trim councillors' costume, and dandy young herrings look up at them through eye-glasses, and crabs, lobsters, and all kinds of such common crustaceans, swarm swimming about. I could never see so deep; I only heard the faint bells of the sunken cities peal once more their old melodious chime.

Once by night I saw a great ship with outspread blood-red sails go by, so that it seemed like a dark giant in a scarlet cloak. Was that the *Flying Dutchman?*

But in Amsterdam, where I soon arrived, I saw the grim Mynheer bodily, and that on the stage. On this occasion, in the theatre of that city, I also had an opportunity to make the acquaintance of one of those fairies whom I had sought in vain in the sea. And to her, as she was particularly charming,

I will devote a special section.

You certainly know the fable of the *Flying Dutchman*. It is the story of an enchanted ship which can never arrive in port, and which since time immemorial has been sailing about at sea. When it meets a vessel, some of the unearthly sailors come in a boat and beg the others to take a packet of letters home for them. These letters must be nailed to the mast, else some misfortune will happen to the ship — above all if no Bible be on board, and no horse-shoe nailed to the foremast. The letters are always addressed to people whom no one knows, and who have long been dead, so that some late descendant gets a letter addressed to a far away great-great-grandmother, who has slept for centuries in her grave. That timber spectre, that grim grey ship, is so called from the captain, a Hollander, who once swore by all the devils that he would get round a certain mountain, whose name has escaped me, in spite of a fearful storm, though he should sail till the Day of Judgement. The devil took him at his word, therefore he must sail for ever, until set free by a woman's truth. The devil in his stupidity has no faith in female truth, and allowed the enchanted captain to land once in seven years and get married, and so find opportunities to save his soul. Poor Dutchman! He is often only too glad to be saved from his marriage and his wife-saviour, and get again on board.

The play which I saw in Amsterdam was based on this legend. Another seven years have passed; the poor Hollander is more weary than ever of his endless wandering; he lands, becomes intimate with a Scottish nobleman, to whom he sells diamonds for a mere song, and when he hears that his customer has a beautiful daughter, he asks that he may wed her. This bargain also is agreed to. Next we see the Scottish home; the maiden with anxious heart awaits the bridegroom. She often looks with strange sorrow at a great, time-worn picture which hangs in the hall, and represents a handsome man in the Netherlandish-Spanish garb. It is an old heirloom, and according to a legend of her grandmother, is a true portrait of the Flying Dutchman as he was seen in Scotland a hundred years before, in the time of William of Orange. And with this has come down a warning that the women of the family must beware of the original. This has naturally enough had the result of deeply impressing the features of the picture on the heart of the romantic girl. Therefore, when the man himself makes his appearance, she is startled, but not with fear. He too is moved at beholding the portrait. But when he is informed whose likeness it is, he with tact and easy conversation turns aside all suspicion, jests at the legend, laughs at the Flying Dutchman, the Wandering Jew of the Ocean, and yet, as if moved by the thought, passed into a pathetic mood, depicting how terrible the life must be of one condemned to endure unheard-of tortures on a wild waste of waters — how his body itself is his living coffin, wherein his soul is terribly imprisoned — how life and death alike reject him, like an empty cask scornfully thrown by the sea on the shore, and as contemptuously repulsed again into the sea — how his agony is as deep as the sea on which he sails — his ship without anchor, and his heart without hope.

I believe that these were nearly the words with which the bridegroom ends. The bride regards him with deep earnestness, casting glances meanwhile at his portrait. It seems as if she had penetrated his secret; and when he afterwards asks, 'Katherine, wilt thou be true to me?' she answers, 'True to death.'

I remember that just then I heard a laugh, and that it came not from the pit but from the gallery of the gods above. As I glanced up I saw a wondrous lovely Eve in Paradise, who looked seductively at me, with great blue eyes. Her arm hung over the gallery, and in her hand she held an apple, or rather an orange. But instead of symbolically dividing it with me, she only metaphorically cast the peel on my head. Was it done intentionally or by accident? That I would know! But when I entered the Paradise to cultivate the acquaintance, I was not a little startled to find a white soft creature, a wonderfully womanly tender being, not languishing, yet delicately clear as crystal, a form of home-like propriety and fascinating amiability. Only that there was something on the left upper lip which curved or twined like the tail of a slipper gliding lizard. It was a mysterious trait, something such as is not found in pure angels, and just as little in mere devils. This expression comes not from evil, but from the *knowledge* of good and evil — it is a smile which has been poisoned or flavoured by tasting the Apple of Eden. When I see this expression on soft, full, rosy, ladies' lips, then I feel in my own a cramp-like twitching — a convulsive yearning — to kiss those lips: it is our Affinity.

I whispered into the ear of the beauty:

'Young lady, I will kiss thy mouth.'

'*Bei Gott, Mynheer!* that is a good idea,' was the hasty answer, which rang with bewitching sound from her heart.

But — no. I will here draw a veil over, and end the story or picture of which the Flying Dutchman was the frame. Thereby will I revenge myself on the prurient prudes who devour such narratives with delight, and are enraptured with them to their heart of hearts, *et plus ultra*, and then abuse the narrator, and turn up their noses at him in society, and decry him as immoral. It is a nice story, too, delicious as preserved pine-apple or fresh caviare or truffles in Burgundy, and would be pleasant reading after prayers; but out of spite, and to punish old offences, I will suppress it. Here I make a long dash ——————— Which may be supposed to be a black sofa on which we sat as I wooed. But the innocent must suffer with the guilty, and I dare say that many a good soul looks bitterly and reproachfully at me. However, unto these of the better kind I will admit that I was never so wildly kissed as by this Dutch blonde, and that she most triumphantly destroyed the prejudice which I had hitherto held against blue eyes and fair hair. *Now* I understand why an English poet has compared such women to frozen champagne. In the icy crust lies hidden the strongest extract. There is nothing more piquant than the contrast between external cold and the inner fire which, Bacchante-like, flames up and irresistibly intoxicates the happy carouser. Ay, far more than in brunettes does the fire of passion burn in many a sham-calm holy image with golden-glory hair, and blue angel's eyes, and pious lily hands. I knew a blonde of one of the best families in Holland who at times left her beautiful chateau on the Zuyder-Zee and went incognito to Amsterdam, and there in the theatre threw orange-peel on the head of any one who pleased her, and gave herself up to the wildest debauchery, like a Dutch Messalina! . . .

When I re-entered the theatre, I came in time to see the last scene of the play, where the wife of the Flying Dutchman on a high cliff wrings her hands in despair, while her unhappy

45

husband is seen on the deck of his unearthly ship, tossing on the waves. He loves her, and will leave her lest she be lost with him, and he tells her all his dreadful destiny, and the cruel curse which hangs above his head. But she cries aloud, 'I was ever true to thee, and I know how to be ever true unto death!'

Saying this she throws herself into the waves, and then the enchantment is ended. The Flying Dutchman is saved, and we see the ghostly ship slowly sink into the abyss of the sea.

The moral of the play is that women should never marry a Flying Dutchman, while we men may learn from it that one can through women go down and perish — under favourable circumstances!

THE TRUE FATE OF THE FLYING DUTCHMAN

George Griffith

There is nothing original about the following story as far as I am concerned, and therefore I cannot of course be expected to vouch for the truth of it. I merely retail it to you as nearly as possible as I had it from the man who gave it to me, an ancient shellback very much on his beam ends, as the nautical saying goes, to whom I once had an opportunity of doing a good turn, as a set-off to which, like the ancient mariner in Gilbert's burlesque of Coleridge's masterpiece, 'he spun me this painful yarn'.

'As I was telling you, Sir,' taking a fresh nip of the grog wherewith I had loosened his tongue, 'until three or four year ago, when I got laid by for good, I'd been following the sea, man and boy, for something going on for sixty years, and, as you rightly guessed, I've seen one or two queer sorts of things in my time.

'It's the fashion nowadays for folk to turn up their eddicated noses at things that isn't plain for 'em to see in all their bearings with the naked eye a fathom in front of them, but for all that there's things as true as any that ye reads in the papers, and a bit truer, some of 'em, that happens away out there in the big wide sea that few folks ever 'ears of, and when they do 'ear of 'em, as I say, they just turns their noses up at 'em in a superior sort of way and calls 'em lies.'

'Like the story of the *Flying Dutchman* for instance?' I said, drawing a sympathetic bow at a venture, and, as it happened, hitting the mark.

The old man's jaw dropped for a moment and the wrinkles round his still bright grey eyes contracted. Then he rapped gently on the table with the little blackened stump of a clay pipe that he was smoking, and said in a half-startled, half-dreamy sort of voice:

'You've hit it, Mister. I don't know how you've come to do it, but it's just about that that I'm going to spin you this yarn you asked for. It's no lie that story about Vanderdecken and the old galliot that he boxed about the Cape in for pretty near three hundred years, because, mister, as true as I'm sitting here' — and again he rapped on the table with his pipe — 'I've seen him, and, what's more, I believe I'm the only man living, ashore or afloat, that saw the last of him and his old broad-bottomed hooker, or what was left of him.'

To have expressed doubt at such a juncture would have been fatal, so I simply said:

'Then if that's so you must have as queer a yarn to spin as ever man told. Help yourself and reel it out.'

He accepted the invitation and got under weigh again.

'It's getting on for five-and-forty years now that I, a British-born boy hailing from Falmouth, had the bad luck to find myself cabin-boy and general knock-about on the *Prairie Flower*, a Yankee China tea-clipper, sailing out of Baltimore. I say "bad luck" because if ever a harmless, willing lad led a dog's life on board a floating workhouse that was me on the *Prairie Flower*.

'The Skipper, Dave Schuyler was his name, was a good seaman of the old driving sort, but as big a brute as ever thought himself the Lord Almighty because he had command of a smart ship. He was a half-Yankee, half-Dutchman, as you might guess from his name, and he was wicked enough to sink a ship twice the tonnage of the *Prairie Flower*.

'There was another boy on board beside me, a little fellow with a spirit of a lion and a body of a mouse, so to speak, and we hadn't been at sea a week before the skipper took a deadly hate against him because he answered him back once instead of cringing to him like a kicked dog as he expected everyone aboard the ship to do. After that he never lost a chance of hazing the poor lad — that's the sea term for 'sitting on him' you know, Sir — and at last one bitter cold night down in the Forties he found some fault with him and for a punishment

49

sent him up to the foretop-gallant yard and told him to stop there till he told him to come down.

'He never did come down, leastways not in the regular way, for when it got daylight there was no one on the yard and I was the only boy on board the ship. Of course the poor little chap had either been jerked off the yard by the rolling of the ship or else he'd got half-frozen and half-stupid with the cold and just dropped overboard. It was put down against his name in the log-book "Fallen overboard from aloft", and it was an accident for all anyone knew except the skipper and me and a young long-shoreman named Frank Peters, who had been sent by the owners as supercargo or ship's husband, as we used to call 'em in those days.

'The skipper didn't know that I knew anything about it; he didn't see that I wasn't below when he sent Slim Jim aloft to sit on the yard. If he had done I shouldn't have seen the end of the voyage, but Mr Peters heard him give the order and saw the kick that he helped him off the poop with, and the next morning when he was missing he up and told him that it was nothing less than manslaughter and he should report him at the first port the ship touched at. The skipper didn't say much, but he thought a lot, and what he thought wasn't very healthy for Mr Peters.

'We had a rough baddish lot in the fo'castle — just such a lot as yer might expect to sail with such a skipper — and as we had a lot of bad luck one way and another after the lad fell overboard, he hadn't much trouble in persuading them that the super-cargo was an out-and-out Jonah and was bringing all the bad time on to 'em. We hadn't got many days' runs behind us before poor Peters was hated fore and aft, and there were a good many of the chaps for'ard and who'd have helped him overboard for an extra tot of grog.

'We went hammering away down the Forties and at last got round the Cape, and one bright windy moonlight night the lookout sung out:

' "A sail on the starboard bow — and a queer one she looks too."

'Queer she did look, I can tell you, lying right in the track of the moon's light over the water, rising and falling to the waves with a slow heavy motion that showed she was a dull sailor, whatever else she was. You've seen those square-bowed square-sterned slab-sided Dutchmen that used to sail out of Rotterdam and Amsterdam a few years ago?

'Well, build up a great high sort of castle on the stern with galleries running out aft at the sides and big square lanterns like they have now in the streets stuck up at the corners, cut the bow down low, run the bowsprit up about as steep again as we have them now, and put a square sail underneath it on the martingale and rig the masts and yards in the most antediluvian style you can think of — and that's the sort of craft that we saw lying between us and the moonlight that night.

'There was a flag hanging half-mast high from his foremast and his sails were flapping about just as though there wasn't a catspaw of wind, and yet we were beating up under short sail against a ten-knot breeze from the nor'east. The skipper got his glass on him in a minute, and when he took it down from his eye he said with words that I won't repeat to you, Sir:

' "If that's not old Vanderdecken himself may I be drowned with my head in a slush bucket. Haul round the fore-yard there, and let her fall off a bit. We'll see if the old Dutchman has anything to say. P'raps he can tell us what to do with this ———— Jonah that we've got aboard."

'It wasn't a job that any man aboard the ship liked, but Dave Schuyler was in a mood that it wouldn't do to fool with. When the yards were round he called the boat's crew aft, ordered the steward to serve out a double tot of rum, and then told them to lower away the quarter-boat, as he wanted to take Jonah to pay a visit to Vanderdecken.

' "We'll send bad luck to bad luck, boys," he said, "and then p'raps we'll be rid of it. What do you say? He might be able to show old Vanderdecken the way into Table Bay."

'It was a horrible cruel ghastly sort of notion, but as soon as they'd got the grog into them the men jumped at it and went to clear away the boat, swearing that Jonah had better sink the Dutchman than them. The skipper had a word or two with the mate, nearly as big a brute and bully as himself, and by the time the boat was clear poor Peters was brought up on deck out of his bunk, and Schuyler showed him the queer craft that was bobbing about under half a mile from us and said in a mocking politeful sort of voice:

' "There, Mr Peters, Sir, allow me to introduce you to an old pal and countryman of mine, Philip Vanderdecken, better known as the Flying Dutchman. You've brought us a blamed sight of bad luck since you've been on board the *Prairie Flower*, and as I think we shall get to China better without you than with you I am going to take you aboard in the boat and ask Vanderdecken to give you a passage home."

'The poor chap looked at the strange uncanny craft abeam and then at the skipper in a mute beseeching sort of way. Then he lost his nerve, as any other man might have done in the same fix, and fell on his knees and started out to beg for mercy, but Schuyler wasn't that sort.

'He sung out to a couple of the chaps at the davits and they picked up poor Peters, whipped a line round his hands and feet and bundled him into the boat without any more fuss. Then he sent me down into the supercargo's cabin to fetch up some of his clothes, saying with a laugh that he might find it cold and want them before he got home. I went down and fetched up all I could lay my hands on.

'Now I ought to have said that this Peters was a Roman Catholic, and on his table I found a little silver crucifix with a silver chain to it. Something told me to take this up too, I thought it might sort of comfort him. When I got on deck the boat was in the water and the skipper pretty nearly frightened the life out of me by telling me to shin down the tackles and take the gentleman his clo'es, as he said.

'I had to go, though I think I'd sooner have jumped overboard than get into a boat going to that ghostly-looking ship; but when I got down and showed poor Peters his crucifix, his face lit up so that I was almost glad I'd come. He asked me to hang it round his neck, and I did.

'As we approached, the most awful-looking faces mortal eyes ever looked at showed themselves over the bulwarks, staring down at us, but there was never a word or a sound out of any of 'em. On the big high stern there was a tall figure with long white hair and a long ragged white beard, and he was dressed just like the sailors you see in some of the old pictures at Grinnidge Hospital.

'When we ran alongside under her high quarter the faces of the boat's crew were almost as white as the ghostly things that were looking at us over the side, but the skipper didn't seem to have a bit of fear about him. He stood up in the stern sheets and hailed in Dutch, and there came back something that sounded like the same language, only far away as though the voice had dropped from the clouds.

'The tall figure came down from the quarter-deck and then a crazy old rope ladder all covered with dried green slime, like the ship's sides were, tumbled out of the gangway port. All he could do the skipper couldn't persuade one of the men to go up that ladder. They told him straight they'd see him further first, only in a lot stronger words than that, and so he cursed them for a lot of white-livered chicken-hearted swabs and swarmed up himself.

'We held our breath and heard him saying something to the old fellow with the white hair and beard that we knew by this time must be Vanderdecken himself. Then he came to the gangway and slung a rope over and told us to make it fast round the supercargo's shoulders. The men wanted to be away again, and they did it without any more telling, in spite of the poor fellow's shrieks and prayers for mercy. Then the skipper, and maybe some of them on board, toiled on the rope and hauled poor Peters, struggling and yelling like a madman, up over the side. They had scarcely got him on deck when Schuyler called to me and told me to bring his clothes up.

'I was so struck with fright that I couldn't move, and when the skipper saw this he swore that if I didn't come up sharp he'd haul me up after Peters and leave me with him. Then one of the chaps in the boat told me to hurry up and hoist myself aboard, or they'd sling me up, for they didn't want to stop there all night, and the end of it was that I slung the bundle of Peter's clothes round my neck and swarmed up, feeling every moment as I should drop into the water again.

'It's no use telling you what I saw on deck, because if I did you wouldn't believe me. If ever there was a ghost-ship with real timbers, and cordage, and sails, and a crew of ghosts, that was her. The skipper had untied Peters's legs and arms and was just telling him that he might like to walk about a bit and get acquainted with his new shipmates as I reached the deck. Then he slung his bag of clothes at him with a horrible oath, knocking the poor chap over like a nine-pin he was that weak with fright, and after he'd done it he did what I couldn't have believed even he'd do if I hadn't seen it — he held out his hand to Vanderdecken's ghost and said what I expect was good-bye in Dutch.

'Vanderdecken took it, and said something in his queer, far-away voice that made Schuyler drop his hand as if it had been red-hot instead of ice-cold as I expect it was, and he was almost as white as Vanderdecken himself when he stumbled to the gangway and scrambled down the ladder as hard as he could go. I needn't tell you I followed him as sharp as I could, Peters cursing Schuyler from the bulwarks.

'As we were pulling away from the side those queer ghostly faces came and looked over at us, and among them was poor Peters's, and it was as white and ghostly as any of 'em, but they were quiet and he wasn't. He shook his fists above his head and screamed out words that were a lot awfuller than swearing from the way he said 'em, and the last words we heard were:

' "We'll meet again yet, David Schuyler, and when we do I'll take you with me to the judgment of God. Remember that."

'And then there came a long scream like the whistle of the wind through cordage in a living gale, and we all shut our eyes and the chaps at the oars pulled as if old Vanderdecken himself was coming after 'em to fetch 'em back.

'By the time we got to the ship again and had her under weigh the Dutchman had got all his sails drawing and was bumping away over the short seas to the nor'ard and west'ard heading straight for Table Bay. The *Prairie Flower* never got to China, but that's not in the story so I can make it short. We ran ashore on one of the islands in the Malacca Straights one dark night when it was blowing fit to blow the beard off a Turk. Not a soul of the crew were saved but the skipper and me.

'It was nearly fifteen years after we parted company that time that I saw Dave Schuyler again. It was on the wharf at Hoboken and he knew me at once, although I had grown from a boy to a man. He wasn't much changed except he looked a good bit soberer and quieter. He came and spoke to me quite friendly like and we soon got into conversation, and he told me he'd got converted and found religion, or something of that sort, and had repented of his past life and was doing very well.

'Then he told me that he had a great scheme on hand, that there was millions in it if it could only be worked proper like, and he asked me to go to his house that night and he'd tell me all about it. I was out of a job just then, although I'd got my master's certificate, and to tell you the truth I was mortal hard up. I'd almost forgotten, not the *Flying Dutchman*, but what took us on board of him, for I'd seen so many other queer things done at sea since then that it didn't seem anything particular, so I said yes, and when I got to Schuyler's house that evening he spread out a chart of the middle Atlantic on his table, clapped his fore-finger down on it and said:

' "There, Tom lad, that's where we're going."

'I looked down and saw that he'd put his finger on the big patch in the centre of the North Atlantic that's called the Sargasso Sea.

' "I never knew there were any millions in seaweed before," I said looking up at him with a bit of a grin.

' "No," he said, "no more there aren't, and it isn't seaweed we're goin' for. You know enough not to need me to tell you that's a patch of still water made by the meeting of a lot of currents. No ship ever goes there, leastways if it can help it, but lot's go there as can't help it. Don't yer see that pretty near all the derelicts and missing ships in the North Atlantic that don't go down there must get taken there by the currents some time or other? Some of 'em have good cargoes that won't spoil by water. Most of 'em have money and valuables aboard and some of 'em have hundredweights of specie and bullion — and that's what we're going after."

' "That looks as if there might be money in it," I said after thinkin' a bit quietly and really it did seem very reasonable when you came to look at it. "How are you goin' to get there?" I said, looking at it all practical like.

' "Well, I've had this scheme in my head some years and now I've got a little three-hundred-ton steamer and we're going to drive her slap into the middle, seaweed or no seaweed, and if you like to be first officer of that steamer, well you can be and you shall have your share of the plunder if there is any and good wages as well."

' "I'm with you, Schuyler," says I. And so it was settled.

'I needn't tell you how long we were getting the *Gold Seeker*

— that was the name of our steamer — into the middle of those hundreds of miles of seaweed or what day-and-night labour we had to shove her through it, for it was about time I was hauling in the slack of this yarn, so I'll get on to the end.

'Never did mortal eyes look on such a collection of old weather-battered hulks and rusty iron floating coffins as we found jammed up together in that patch of sea and weed. We sighted 'em first at night and for all the world they looked in the gloom like a lot of ghost-ships that had started out to sail to the other world and never got there.

'We lay to for the light, and when it came what should be the first ship that I clapped eyes on lying broad abeam of us and only two or three hundred yards away but old Vanderdecken's craft, the *Flying Dutchman*. He'd got round the Cape at last, and this was the end of his three-hundred-year voyage.

'There was no mistaking him, although the ropes and chains had rotted and rusted through, and the yards had fallen down on deck, and the fore and aft sails were falling in tatters, and the timbers were that full of worm holes that they might have been riddled with small shot. As I was standing looking at her Schuyler came up from below.

'I didn't turn to look at him; I daren't, but I felt a trembling hand laid on my shoulder and heard his voice say in a hoarse shaking whisper:

' "My God, Tom, that's her again! You remember what Peters said when we left him on board of her. I knew it'd come — I've dreamt of it and I've heard his voice calling to me when I've been broad awake. It's got to be and I've got to go. Lower the boat, Tom, and come with me."

'I tried to persuade him out of it but it was no good. He swore he'd jump overboard and swim to her; so at last I gave in, hoping that after all it might be some other old craft like the Dutchman that had got fastened up here for hundreds of years. We had the gig out with a couple of men to pull her, and in a few minutes we were once more standing on the deck where we'd left poor Peters.

'There was no mistake about it, it was the same ship, only there was this difference, there was no captain and no crew. A few grey crumbling bones were lying about the cracked curled up decks and that was all. Schuyler gave one look round and then made straight for the cabin under the high quarter-deck. I followed him, and there, sitting at each end of the table with their heads bent forward on their folded arms were the bodies of Philip Vanderdecken and poor Frank Peters.

'They were dried to mummies, but still horribly life-like, and round Frank's neck was hanging the little silver chain with the crucifix lying on the table in front of him.

We stared at 'em speechless with horror and then Schuyler gasped out:

' "I knew it, Tom, he's fetched me here and here I'll have to die. What's that?"

'As he spoke a shiver seemed to run through the old hulk and we heard a queer crackling creaking noise and the sound of something falling on deck. Then Schuyler turned to me and whispered, for fear hadn't left him any better voice:

' "Run, Tom, run for the boat! She's breaking up at last."

'I took him by the arm and tried to drag him out with me, but as soon as I got him to the door he broke away and ran back and threw himself on his knees at the table. Just then the old craft gave a heave and my own fear got the best of me and I ran on deck.

'The fellows in the boat were shouting for us and I shouted back to 'em to come and help me bring the Skipper out. But before one of 'em could get up the side the main-mast fell aft crashing through the rotten timbers of the quarter-deck and blocking the way to the cabin. Then a great split opened right across the deck and I bundled into the boat and we pulled away as fast as the weed would let us.

'We hadn't got twenty yards off when the old craft broke up as though a broadside of big guns had been fired into her. She seemed to go right to pieces where she lay and the last of her that we saw was the high stern heeling over and going down, dragging the weeds with it. That was the last that any man, saw or ever will see of the *Flying Dutchman*.'

'And what about the *Gold Seeker*?' I asked. 'Did you get your millions?'

'Yes. The men wouldn't go back when we'd taken so much trouble to get there, and in less than a fortnight we got tons of treasure; but it never did us any good. No ship ever sighted the *Flying Dutchman* and got back safe to port. We broke our shaft getting out of the weed and knocked about for a month under what sail we could carry, then we drifted into the hurricane area and the last of the *Gold Seeker* was that she was smashed to pieces on one of the Keys of the Bahamas. I was the only one of her crew that was saved, and that's why I'm the only man alive that knows the true story of the fate of the *Flying Dutchman*.'

SENTA

Sir Max Pemberton

The storm had menaced the ship since two bells of the first dog-watch; but its full fury was not to be experienced until darkness fell.

A fiery sun sank into clouds as black as thunder when the bells were heard; and anon, the wind came wailing from the west with such a note of utter melancholy that even the oldest among the sailors shuddered at their own prophecies; while the passengers of many nations lay huddled about the deck or sought the deep shelter of the profound cabin, where a crazy lamp but emphasised the darkness. There a Dutch pastor prayed that God would deliver them from the storm — while women clutched their children as though strong arms would protect them.

Now, this was a Dutch barque that had put out from Riga to sail to London; and among its passengers was a young musician with a lofty brow and a thinker's moods, who had set out from Russia to visit Paris, in the hope of having the first of his serious operas represented there.

Richard Wagner was twenty-six years old at that time. He had written much that was afterwards to be forgotten; had studied at Leipzig and at Vienna, where he composed the music of a romantic opera *Die Feen*, and subsequently heard that great singer, Schroder-Devrient, for whom he was to complete *Rienzi*, and so at last come into his own.

Unhappily, Germany did not yet know the genius in her midst — and poor, and at his wits' end for bread, the Master passed from one scene to another — always seeking a haven for his genius, but yet to find it. A post as musical director in the theatre at Riga did not satisfy him — and feeling that he was being too much influenced by the music of France and Italy, he conceived the idea that Paris might welcome him . . . and that, even from the least musical nation in Europe, the English, he might obtain a hearing.

He was very poor at that time, occupied a mean lodging in Riga and had the greatest difficulty in supporting himself and the wife, who subsequently was to suffer so much chagrin because of his infidelities.

But he managed, nevertheless, to secure a passage for them both upon the Dutch barque that was to sail for London — nor did he forget to take his Great Dane, Robber, who accompanied him at that time on all his voyages.

So the party set out and soon was faced by the difficulties of the passage.

A motley horde of Russians, Poles, Germans and Dutch crowded the mean ship to the point of danger. There were two or three English merchants, some sailors of the same race who had been shipwrecked on an island of the Baltic, a group of Jewish traders, and last, but by no means the least interesting to the romantic Master, there was Senta, the Norwegian girl, with her wide blue eyes and her plaintive songs and her weird stories of the sea, which the Vikings surely should have taught her in the great ages of adventure.

It was Robber, the Great Dane, who first discovered Senta, as she squatted by the round house amidships and recited her legends to the sailors. Somehow, the monster hound seemed a fit companion for the fragile little creature, whose mind was an index to the ages, but whose body was a mere wraith. He would curl up beside her and reward her ballads with no more than reproachful eyes — when her voice sank into the soft melancholy of some doleful fable of the sea, he would howl without shame and so rebuke her. Nevertheless, all felt that Senta was quite safe in the great dog's keeping — and when the captain, Darand, tried to make love to her, he cursed the day which brought such a ferocious beast aboard.

To a man of the romantic and amorous temperament of

Richard Wagner, his discovery of a blue-eyed prophetess was a godsend.

Often he would pace the deck with her until the early hours of the morning; and always in her talk he discovered that profound note of melancholy which the drear seas and ghostly Northern lands inspire. Nevertheless, it was not always of the sagas that she spoke, but sometimes of the more earthly passion of love.

'I am to marry Erik of Bergen when he returns from his next voyage,' she confessed to the Master one day — and no sooner had the words been uttered than she fell into a profound melancholy, as though the tidings were of sorrow and not of joy.

'Does not marriage mean very much to you, then?' the Master asked her. 'Are you not in love with this sailor lover of yours?'

Senta looked up with eyes that burned.

'I am so much in love with him that we shall sail the seas together when all here are in their graves and this ship is but rotting wood on a forgotten shore.'

Wagner was not at all surprised. He knew what Norse imagery was and would not mock it.

'A very old woman you will be then, Senta.'

'A very, very old woman, Master, who now has but a few days to live. We go into the world of shadows, Erik and I, and we sail these seas for ever. Thus has sadness come to me, I shall perish, but this ship may be saved at last. The voices tell me so, and they have never lied to me.'

'But Senta, why should the ship be in danger? Was there ever a calmer sea than this upon which we sail? And if a storm comes, are there not many havens? Come, come, let us think of Erik and of love. I will make a song for you, and you shall sing it. We will call it Erik the Steersman — for I also have written of your sagas and you shall hear my verses when there is nobody round about to hear us.'

She told him in return that she had known both of him and his music when she had been in Riga, and his proper vanity swelled at her prophecies of his future greatness.

'All the world will acknowledge you for its Master,' she said, 'but there will be weary years of waiting. Count nothing upon the city to which you are going, for it is through your own Germany that success will come. The English will not understand you, for they know no music; and in Paris they will not hear you. No, no, Master, it is to Germany that you must look if the ship is saved!'

'Then even your voices are not sure about that, Senta. They think there is danger for us.'

'There is great danger, Master, and it is coming out of the west. Some will perish but some will live — while I, I shall ride upon the storm with my lover through all eternity —

68

even as she who gave me her name and whose spirit hovers upon these waters even as we talk.'

She took up her guitar at the words and began to sing softly, as though addressing one unseen but waiting.

The Master, however, went back to his cabin wondering at this message of death and asking himself if the hour which should end all his dreams was at hand.

So the menace of the storm became apparent when the ship had rounded the North Cape and was heading to the south-west for the Port of Bergen.

The day had been fair enough with a clear light of an ungenerous sun and placid waters which were a solace to the emigrants. All, indeed, was life and laughter upon the crowded ship . . . and even Senta, the dreamer, could attune her song to the mood and remember the cry of her youth. They had all been dancing to her music when the dinner bell called them . . . and Richard Wagner himself was thinking in terms of a ballet, which, many years later on, was to ornament his opera of *Tannhäuser* as Paris first knew it. So the merry hours passed until the reddening sun sank beneath the ominous bank of the clouds and the dirge of the wind began to be heard in the rigging as a prelude to the dreadful night. Then, truly, Senta's laughter passed; and gathering the seamen about her, she told them stories of phantom ships and of shrieks from their stricken decks, above which the spirits hovered as the doomed vessels drove on to a penance of eternity.

'There was one named Darand, as this captain of yours is named,' she said, 'and he was in the southern seas, long, long years ago. There was also a wind such as blows upon us tonight . . . and the great Cape faced him and all his skill could not bring his ship into the western waters. Then he cared not for God or Devil, but called upon the spirits of evil to answer him, and they came up from the black waters and pestilence fell upon all that company, and it died horribly even while the storm was still raging. But the souls of those poor people came back again to Darand's barque from the blackness of death, and the steersman took his place at the wheel again, and now for ever the ship sails that southern sea and woe to those whose eyes look upon it, for they also shall surely perish.

So much and much more fell from the lips of the little prophetess as she gathered the seamen about her, and together they watched the oncoming storm.

Darand, their captain, a lusty fellow with the courage of a rabbit, did not hear his name thus taken in vain . . . and for long he refused to believe that the storm was more than a passing squall; while he averred that midnight would show them a fine heaven of stars with a breeze so favourable that they would be half-way to Bergen at the same hour of the morrow. At the same time, he continued to hope that fear might yet drive the pretty Senta to his cabin . . . and he fixed wanton eyes upon her while she sang her plaintive little songs to the sailors, and even carried her a pannikin of wine, like a gallant lover who thinks first of his Dulcinea, whatever the peril of the hour. When she drank it, however, her toast was 'the Phantom Ship,' and that so scared this sawdust Nelson that he turned as white as one of his own sails and began to question her closely.

'How — you talk of phantom ships. Who, then, has put that nonsense into your head, my pretty? There are no phantom ships in these waters, as every sailor knows. Why, then, speak of what does not exist?'

'I speak, Captain, of that which my eyes have seen. A ship sails yonder in the loom of the cloud, and its crew are not of this world. Be warned, then, for the danger is upon us and God alone knows if any of us will be alive when the new day breaks.'

She pointed with a hand no bigger than that of a child away to the west, and to the gold and the deep crimson of its horizon. There was no ship there — but so had she hypnotised the devil-fearing seamen about her that more than one cried — 'Yonder, yonder on the starboard bow — don't you see her — a fore-and-aft schooner — no, no, a brig — I tell you she's a barque . . . there's a man on the quarter deck — no, two and two more at the wheel . . . I tell you it's nothing at all, just the shadows, that's what it is . . . and the wind rising — my God, how long is the old man going to hold on like this . . . has he lost his senses then?'

Darand himself was at first too afraid to say anything at all, but presently he awoke to the realities and crying — 'All hands on deck to take in sail,' he began to prepare the ship for the ordeal which was upon her. In a twinkling, as it were, the topsails were down, the jibs bellowing on the boom, the mizzen lowered and the hatches battened down. All passengers were ordered below and sent there with little ceremony; and so it befell that Richard Wagner and Senta, neither of whom the Dutchman cared to provoke, sought the shelter of the cuddy beneath the quarter deck, where two men now stood at the wheel, and the great dog watched them as though his very presence might avail against the tempest.

'You spoke of a phantom ship,' said the Master presently. 'I saw none and there was none to see. Are these things then revealed to you in a vision, child, or do you desire to drive these good fellows crazy? That, surely, would not be worthy of you.'

She flushed at the rebuke, and for a little while did not know how to answer him.

'I see with my soul, but not with my eyes,' she said at

last, 'since my childhood, the visions have come to me and I have heard voices which tell me of things hidden from those about me. To-night, I can hear the voices of Evil which come from the Phantom Ship, and so I speak of it. It is a warning that many of these poor people must die — that God is about to judge their souls. Why, then, should I be silent when the voices bid me speak? Have I not told you already the things that are true?'

'You have said that I shall live when many perish.'

'It is true, true,' she cried . . . and then with a voice of woe, she added, 'but I shall die and go to my love, and we shall sail these seas for ever.'

For ever!

Richard Wagner looked out on the storm-ridden ocean and the terror of her prophecy appalled him.

What an irony of his destiny if all his dreams should perish in these dark waters! He believed that he had a master message to deliver to the people of all countries and that the first notes of it would soon be heard. Now the raging sea threatened to obliterate all that he had planned and desired with such an earnest hope . . . and he knew for a truth that his grave might be there amidst the tumult of the surf which now drove the barque headlong.

Yet his was not a superstitious mind, and although its images were of the shadow world of gods and sirens and sagas of the remote past, his faith was merely negative; and he no more believed the story of a phantom ship than of the devil knocking on Luther's door at Weimar. Squatting there upon the deck of the barque he had become a materialist, weighing but his personal chance of safety in the balance, and yet content, almost as one driven to any consolation, to listen to this little dreamer and to take comfort in her words.

He would live; but she would perish.

Her youth, her spirituality fascinated him . . . and he looked at her with profound sorrow as he thought that to-morrow the same beautiful eyes might be gazing sightless at the angry heaven . . . the voice hushed, the poetry of her thoughts unsung. Then, almost in the same mood, he could rid himself of the spell and come back to reality. The ship and all its people might perish despite her prophecies. And, indeed, it soon seemed that such must be their fate, and that the end truly was at hand.

It was black dark by this time and all their light came from the loom of the scudding cloud, where the lightning found its curtain and cast back great aureoles of light down upon the frenzied breakers. All the terror of the storm would be revealed at one instant, to be blotted out the next and left but a memory of a menacing revelation. And all the time the wind howled and screeched in the flying rigging; sails were torn to ribbons; the decks washed by huge waves; the lanterns extinguished . . . and those below terrified by the waters which poured in among them as the backwash of that Styx they presently must cross.

Anon, panic arose.

Russians mad with terror forced their way to the decks and shouted wildly at a captain whom fear had already deprived of his wits. Drink was got from the purser's store, and a keg of brandy broached in the waist of the barque. Soon, weird figures staggered to the slippery decks and shook impotent fists at the skies which mocked them. Men were swept overboard now as flies from a board which is washed and women died in men's arms for very fear. There came a crescendo of terrifying sounds out of the void and the thunders crashed as though a myriad devils were clamouring for souls, while there was no longer steerage way upon the barque, nor any thought of a haven. She had become the sport of the tempest, and her hours appeared to be numbered.

Throughout it all, Senta and the Master watched from the shelter of the lower deck and rarely ventured a word in the momentary intervals of storm. Once, indeed, it became again apparent that she saw some vision of the sea, and that some figure of her subjective mind appeared to her. When the musician dared to ask her what that figure was, she declared without hesitation that Erik, her lover, was calling to her, and that he had told her that the ship would be saved.

'But only,' she said with unutterable sadness, '- only if I go to him where he is waiting for me.'

'You do not fear to go, my dear — not to your lover, surely.'

'You do not understand,' she said, 'when Erik comes for me, then I must die. Oh, I know it, I know it!' and for the first time she began to weep, not for fear of the storm, but for the man's sake.

Wagner was well acquainted with moods such as this, and his own dreams were often the fruit of them.

Profound mysteries of the Unseen, the shadow-world peopled by unnumbered souls; gods fighting in the air and below the water, lovers who died because they had loved . . . of such fables were his mighty operas to be made. And here, surely, in this pathetic little oracle, whom the visions haunted, here, in truth, was just such a figure as he loved.

He believed no word of her story, it may be, and yet her words gave him consolation. The ship was to be saved, she said, though she might perish. He did not believe that she was to die, yet such argument as he could use seemed weak enough in view of his bias toward the dreamer.

'Believe no such thing,' he said, 'if this Erik of yours is the brave fellow I believe him to be, he will be the first to protect you — is he not a sailor also? I think that you have told me so, my dear. Then, surely, sailors do not come to do evil to those they love?'

The question intrigued her and turned her thoughts to other scenes.

'He is captain of the sloop *Christiana*,' she said, 'his father is the minister in the church of Molda. He was at Riga last year, and we spent many days together — such happy days they were, never to come again. We should have seen him this time at Bergen if God had let us go there. But now I know it must be in some other place . . . and if he finds me, it will be because he is sent to do so. Oh, do not think that I fear death with Erik — but we are both so young to leave the sunshine and the light; and at one time it seemed that we had many years before us. It cannot be now. I have seen the Phantom Ship, and none see it and live . . .'

'You think, then, that all these mad people who perished to-night, they all saw the vision with you?'

'I am sure of it. Did you not hear their words? "Yonder," they cried, and pointed at it. Then I knew how it would be with them — and you, Master, you have seen it happen with your own eyes.'

He had to confess that it was so.

The sea had claimed the price of folly and the dead already floated about the ship in the darkness.

It was the crisis of the storm; and none upon the barque

believed that she could live.

Darand, the captain, had long given up any hope of saving either vessel or cargo, and of his crew, few were sober. Some sang crazy songs of ancient mariners and of seamen who had gone to the devil; others lay about like logs, half insensible and wholly indifferent to the storm. Of them all but the Englishman, Barker, and the Scottish bo'sun, Atkinson, kept their wits, and did all that seamanship could do to keep the crazy ship afloat and the monster seas from engulfing her. Rousing such of the hands as were capable of any service at all, they got the torn jibs from the booms and stripped the aft rigging of all canvas. Almost under bare poles, the barque headed to the south-west and so toward that town of Bergen, which it now seemed impossible that she should ever see. And as though such courage merited reward, there was at last a breaking of the hurricane, a modulation in the raucous voices of winds and a sudden cleavage of the black cloud, which drove no longer across the heavens in unbroken mass but was riven to let the moon shine upon the raging water and to show them Ursa Major in all its majesty. Now, indeed, the mate began to tell them that there was hope . . . and as though to justify his words, the man at the wheel cried 'light on the port bow' — and instantly the whole company became alert as though this was the end of it and the port of their salvation already made.

Richard Wagner saw the light and Senta with him.

She knew that northern shore well, for she had often sailed it with the seamen who came to her father's house; and her lover Erik had spent the best part of his young life in trading with the villages of the fjords and in piloting strange ships into them.

So, no sooner had she seen the beacon than she declared it to be that of the Hammerfest, and that if they could weather the great cape which sheltered the fjord, then indeed were they as surely saved as though they had dropped anchor in the harbour of Bergen.

'I know the place,' she cried wildly. 'I have sailed there often with Erik when he was taking English people to the North Cape. There is another light, a red one, when you pass the point of the island, and after that you can see the houses of the town, a very little town with very poor people, but there is an inn there, and we can all shelter there. Did I not tell you that the ship would be saved? Was I not right from the beginning, dear Master?'

He told her that she was and rejoiced to see that her other words had seemingly been forgotten. The joy of hope and life was as sure for her as any upon the ship — and in the new excitement of deliverance, she stood by the side of the Englishman telling him that this or that was the course he must follow, explaining the situation both of the island

and the port and promising him water enough to float the greatest ship that ever sailed the seas.

'They say that the fjord is a mile deep even against the side of the mountain. I have seen Erik sail the *Christiana* so close to the rock that I could put my hand upon it. Now keep a little more to port and then you must put the helm hard over. Yes, yes, there is the red lantern, and those are the lights of the town. We are safe now and shall think of storm no more.'

The man obeyed, while Captain Darand, perceiving what had happened, came to his senses and again took charge of the barque.

Among the passengers, there was indescribable reaction. Women fainted for joy of their escape; men sang incoherently or danced about or remembered the unfinished bottles. And gradually, as the vessel was steered amid the jagged rocks upon which great waves still broke into fountains of foam and swirling waters, even Richard Wagner suffered an intense emotion which even he could not control.

Music now came to his aid, and all its magic inspiration.

He has told us how, at that moment, the scheme of *The Flying Dutchman* came to him. How the music possessed his soul and would be heard. The thunder of storm; the tragic love (if it were to be tragic) of the litde prophetess; the great crags towering up in the first light of the coming dawn — all contributed to that elation of the spirit by which alone great masterpieces are born.

Yet there remained the doubt.

As he watched the frail Senta standing triumphantly at the helmsman's side, he could ask, what of to-morrow.

Was the fable of her end but a fable, or had she been truly warned?

Time alone would tell him whether this child of the dreams had dreamed truly — whether she would die or live, prove her prophecies true or deny them gloriously.

The ship was anchored to the rock just as the day broke — and even at that early hour, some townsmen waited on the shore to offer help to a company so miraculously saved.

A dreadful night it had been, they declared. More than one good barque would sail the seas no more. Dead men's faces had been seen from the cliff head and wreckage had been washed up against the barrier reefs outside. Fortunate was this fellow Darand; fortunate those who sailed with him. He should go to the church, they said, and give thanks — and for that the church stood open, and there were candles lighted upon its altar.

A few obeyed this injunction; but more thought of the inn and of hot food and drink there to be prepared.

Soon a procession was formed, the lanterns of the welcomers still lighted though the day had come. The pious sang hymns; the impious laughed and shouted and patted upon their broad backs the good folk who welcomed them. It was natural at this time, that Richard Wagner should find himself walking side by side with Senta of the dark prophecies, and that he should wish to recall them to her. She, however, had the radiance of the new day upon her pretty face . . . and when it passed, it was some memory of the man Darand, and of his pursuit of her, which brought the cloud.

'I shall sail no more with him,' she said, 'you see how he insults me. It is well for him that Erik is not here. There would be no more Captain Darand, no surely,' and then with real anger she cried: 'But he shall yet repay — I will tell a tale of him at Bergen that many will hear — if ever I see Bergen again.'

'But, my dear, you don't doubt that now. What is to forbid you? We shall wait until the good weather comes, and then we shall sail — you cannot stop in a wild man's country like this. It might be months before any ship called to take you to your home.'

She laughed at that.

'They are my own people and none are kinder . . . I shall tell them how Darand has treated me, and they also may have something to say to him. I don't fear him here, and I will never sail with him again — even though I have seen the

Phantom Ship, and may not have many days to live.'

So back to her premonitions and to their sorrow. She had not forgotten the apparition, as Wagner hoped; and the old legend still could affright her.

'You must forget that,' the Master said, with a kindly hand laid upon her shoulder, 'think no more of it, Senta. I like to hear these old tales as well as anybody, but I know that they are all nonsense. They come out of the darkness of the blind ages when life was a terrible thing and men had no true perception of God or of His purpose. They are the fairy stories of people whose imagination dwelt often upon death because life itself was such a hazardous thing. We know that they are false now when we listen to them — and you are too wise to give them credence.'

She shook her head but was not convinced.

'I hope it may be so — I do not know,' she said, 'things have been revealed to me in dreams often, and I have never found them untrue. The days will tell us, Master, the days that are to come. If Erik comes here, then I shall know that all is true and that it is the end.'

He tried to laugh it away with kindly banter about her lover . . . and so they went to the hospitable inn and to the warm breakfast there prepared for them. Darand, the captain, it appeared had arrived there before them, and his stories of the adventure seemed to imply that his courage had been as high as the waves which so nearly overwhelmed them. Menacingly also, he declared that it all came of having a 'witch' woman aboard — and that true or false, he was convinced in his own mind that all their misfortunes had been brought upon them by a little strumpet, who pretended to see phantom ships and such like, and had frightened the seamen half out of their wits.

Ridiculous as these tales were, a lonely people listened to them with greedy ears. Many a superstition held its own triumphantly amid those dominating crags and angry seas, where life itself was a daily battle with want and darkness, and the loom of solitude. To such a hamlet no visitor was less welcome than one credited with occult powers, able to tell them of to-morrow and to prophesy of life and death. Senta, indeed, would have been thrust bodily out of the inn but for Wagner's presence and protection.

'You are fools to listen to any such stories,' he thundered, 'the child is to marry Erik of Bergen, and would he marry a witch? Ask that fellow Darand rather, how he has done his duty by her and then let us answer him. I will be responsible for her, good people. You need fear nothing while she is with me.'

That was well enough; but it was quite clear that no house in the little town would shelter her when night came again, and that she must, willy nilly, either sleep on the shore or go back to Darand and the ship. Wagner advised the latter course, being afraid of what would happen if she remained ashore. Indeed, he promised to accompany her, though much preferring a dry bed at the inn, and so they set out together at sundown and a fisherman rowed them back to the barque — almost deserted save for a few of its crew, and still showing shattered evidence of the storm.

The night was fair and the wind much moderated. Darand had not returned to the ship; and it appeared that he would not return; yet Senta was afraid to go to her cabin, and they made themselves snug in the old harbourage by the wheel house. A bribe to a somnolent cook brought them hot coffee from the galley, and afterwards there was the guitar for those songs which had so sure a hold upon the imagination of the seamen. Senta sang as sweetly as ever; but this time it was of the ancient heroes, of Vikings in armour who sailed the Southern seas and returned with women and booty as their prey. And while she sang, the tarry sailors gathered about her and tears of sentiment or of greed rolled down their unwashed cheeks.

Wagner found, as ever, this barbarous music much to his liking. The scheme of his life's work was already shaping in his mind, and he was preparing to abandon all those traditions of French and Italian art by which hitherto he had been bound. Soon he would teach the world the lessons it must learn and by those lessons his own fame would be won. So he listened patiently to Senta; and when at last she wearied and the sailors crept to their bunks, he still dwelt upon the immensity of his dream and all that realization would mean to him. Then sleep overtook him also — and the sunshine of a better day was shining when he awoke to hear a sailor tell him that Senta had left the ship and that the manner of her going had been miraculous.

'The ship passed us in the night — I saw the loom of her sails,' he said, '— a voice called out to her, and she sprang from yonder poop as the phantom went by us — in silence, sir, as a wisp of cloud that drifts down from the hills. No man will ever see or hear of her again, believe me. She has gone whence none return, and God deliver her soul.'

The Master thought upon it, pacing the deck in the chill air full of wonder at what he had heard.

Was the story of another world or of this?

Had Erik come after all in his ship the *Christiana*, and was her cry one of recognition as she leapt into the arms awaiting her? He believed it might be so — and yet, who shall fathom all the mystery of the sea and her phantoms?

One thing is sure.

The truth he never learned. Next day the barque set sail for London, and a few weeks after Richard Wagner was in Paris.

But he never forgot Senta nor her songs; *The Flying Dutchman* bore witness to that as all the world knows. He would never have written so great a masterpiece, he has confessed, but for the little prophetess, who believed that death awaited her and yet may have found life in her lover's arms.

AN ENCOUNTER WITH A GHOST

W. Clark Russell

It is a great many years now since the Phantom Ship was last sighted; so long indeed that one might fairly suppose Vanderdecken had got to windward at last, doubled the Cape, and settled down somewhere in his native land to enjoy a well-earned repose after his centuries of conflict with the Pacific gales. It turns out, however, that the poor old skipper is still afloat. His vessel has not only been sighted, but boarded — a quite unprecedented incident in the history of this marine apparition. The countenance of Vanderdecken has been surveyed by human eyes, and, what is of some importance, the vexed question of the rig of his craft has been set at rest once and for good. She is not a ship, it seems, but a brig with stump topgallantmasts and single topsail yards. The yarn of one of the crew of the barque who sighted the *Flying Dutchman* and boarded her is curious, rather graphic, and full of singular particulars. Perhaps were an engraving of the mariner who related the story to accompany this account the interest would be heightened

— for so queer a looking sailor I never before set eyes on. He is what the young ladies of Limehouse and Poplar would call a 'shell-back,' his shoulders being as round as the shell of a turtle; his hair hangs over his forehead and down the back of his neck in masses of minute ringlets; he broke the bridge of his nose when a youth by falling down the main hold of a ship, and that feature submits but little more to the eye than a pair of nostrils; his small eyes are lodged very deep, and twinkle in their caverns like glowworms, and under his chin stands a lump of coarse black hair. He masticated a large junk of tobacco as he gave me his story, which may have added a deeper note to his hoarse and wheezing voice. He began thus:

'The *Sally G.*'s an American barque; Captain Prodgers was the master, Mr Anderson chief mate, and there were sixteen hands. We was bound from Palermo to New London with a cargo of fruit, and on the 11th of April last we reckoned ourselves to be somewhere near about 1500 miles to the east'ards of Montauk Point. We was rather a mixed company. I'm an Englishman myself, and there was Tom, a Gravesend man. Us two made all the Englishmen aboard. But there was three Scotchmen and six Irishmen; so Britannia mustered middling strong. There was likewise a Swede, and chaps we call 'Dagos', Mediterranean scowbanks, the right word is, who'll pass for Portuguese, or Spaniards, or Hi-talians, just as they're wanted.

'The 11th of April was a werry fine morning: a light breeze from the south'ard and east'ard, sea calm, and sky blue. I was in the port watch, and came on deck at eight o'clock. The barque was under all plain sail; and soon after we had turned out, Mr Anderson, the chief mate, sings out to some of us to jump aloft and get the stun'sail booms rigged out. I lay aloft, and got on to the foretopsail yard; but, as I was stepping from the rigging on to foot-ropes, I caught sight of a bit of white shining upon the horizon about two points on the starboard bow. I turned my head and bawled down "Sail ho!" and pointed, and the mate crossed the deck to look; but he had to wait a bit to see her; for it required half-an-hour more of sailing to heave the stranger up wisible from the deck. You may reckon no one took much notice of the wessel ahead while she remained small. Having set the stun'sails, we went on quiedy with our different jobs, and the mate walked up and down the weather side o' the deck, sometimes squinting aloft, sometimes taking a look at the compass, and now and again casting his eyes upon the stranger. But the *Sally G.*'s a quick boat in smooth water; the stun'sails were helping her along, and we came up with the old sawed-off square wagon ahead as though she had been a lighthouse. I thought she'd h'ist her ensign as we came along, but she never showed no colours.

'When we was close enough to see her plain we all stood lookin' and wonderin'. I don't know as ever I saw a queerer-looking wessel. Her stern was up and down in the water; she'd a great sheer aft that made her look sagged: her sides were as rusty as an old kettle; her rigging was grey; she had short topgallant masts, and a man named Maloney told me the canvas was so thin that he could see the sky looking blue through it. This might ha'been, but I took no notice o' that myself, I saw the mate working away at the brig's stern with a spyglass, and then he turns to the captain, who had come on deck, and says, "Captain," says he, "I can't see no name." "Here, give me hold," says the captain, and he took the glass and looked himself, and then says, "No; there's no name. But I'll tell 'ee what, Mr Anderson, there's *bin* a name there, but the water's washed the letterin' away." "Well," says the mate, "I reckon she must be a diving job. They've fished her up out o' deep water, and ye may take her to be a showman's speculation, sir." The cook was standing near the pumps looking at her, and he says to me who was anigh him, "Bill," he says, "d'ye notice her deck-house is green?" "Yes," says I, "I see that, cook," I says. "That means, Bill," says he in a slow way, and looking strange, "that she's a Dutchman." "She ought to be," says I. "I don't know that we ought to be glad that we met her, Bill," says the cook. "I'd as lief be shipmates with a Fin as keep that wessel company." "Why,

91

what ails ye, cook?" says I. "What's the matter with the brig?" "Look at her," says he, shaking his head and speaking hollow like. I thought he wasn't worth while paying attention to. The cook, sir, was a man as believed in ghosts, and was a werry ignorant person. He couldn't read nor write, but he was extraordinary positive. He'd quote things wrong, and 'ud refuse to be corrected, saying he knew better, and that books was full o' lies. Yet he was a good cook, and there was more conscience in the duff he biled for the men than I can recollect meeting with in any sea-mess. Well, I let him shake his head, and stood watchin' the brig.

'As we came up with her she backed her main yards and lowered a boat. This was a pretty strong hint to us to stop; so we boom-ended our stun'sails, brought the barque to the wind, and hove her to. Two men got into the boat, and a man squatted hisself in the stern sheets, and the boat headed for us. It were difficult to guess what they could want, for the vessel looked right enough aloft, nothin' wanting up there, and if they was in distress it was queer they didn't signalize us in the morning, when we hove in sight.

'All hands knocked off work to see the Dutchman, as the cook called him, come aboard. The boat hooked on, and the man in charge of her climbed over the side. He was a shortish man with a werry Dutch face on him, and there was no getting at his age by staring. His skin had the greyish, washed-out look o' the brig's rigging. He'd got on a bell-shaped fur cap with a peak to it, that lay flat on his forehead, sea-boots, a round jacket, big breeches which he filled out handsomely, and the stem of a long Dutch pipe sticking out of his coat pocket werry strangely ornamented. I noticed a sort o' eagerness in the way some of our men — 'specially the Swede and two o' the Scotchmen — stared at him as if he wan't a wholesome sight. The cook never took his eyes off him for an instant.

'Arter gazing slowly round at us, he singled out the captain with ne're a man to tell him who was skipper, and going up to Captain Prodgers, he makes a long speech. While he talked, the captain and Mr Anderson twisted their heads about like hens trying to look aloft, first bringing one ear to bear and then another, but they couldn't understand him no more than if he had spoke Chinaman's lingo. He spoke to'em for ten minutes, never stoppin', goin' along slow and regular, without e'er a movement in his face, and his arms hanging up and down alongside of him without a stir. I see him now, and I likewise see the skipper and Mr Anderson a listenin' and lookin' just as they'd appear if they was trying to see into the bottom of a well. At last he stopped, and then nobody spoke, and all hands looked at each other, savin' the cook, who wouldn't take his eyes away from the Dutchman. Suddenly the skipper sings out, "Call the watch below on deck." I ran forward and bawled down the scuttle for the men to rouse up smartly, and presently all the crew were on deck looking at the Dutchman.

' "Look ye, men," says Captain Prodgers, "among you all there's enough of you, to make out seven languages; Irish, Scotch, English, Swedish Portugee, Spanish, and Hi-talian. Let all hands turn to and listen their hardest whilst I make this man say his speech over again. Now, then, fix your hattentions, bullies." And with that he signs to the Dutchman to begin again. He didn't seem to know what was wanted at first, but after the skipper and Mr Anderson had motioned and flourished to him like a pair of windmills for about five minutes, he gravely nods his head and goes through his speech, all hands listening hard, bobbing their noses together as they leans forward, and all o' them werry anxious to make out the man's meaning. In ten minutes he made an end; and then Captain Prodgers, looking at us, says, "Well?" Nobody answered. "Is it Irish?" says he. "No, it isn't Irish, sor," says Micky O'Connor. "Is it English or Scotch?" says he. "No, sir," says I. "Is it, Swedish?" says Captain Prodgers. The Swede says; "Not it," and the scowbanks said it wasn't Portuguese, nor Hi-talian, nor any lingo that's spoke down in their part o' Europe. "Then, what the deuce can it be?" says Captain Prodgers. "A languidge," answers the cook, in a faint voice, "as is buried and forgot."

'Well, sir, this being the sitiwation, what was to be done? Some skippers, I daresay, would ha'waved the Dutchman into his boat, filled the main topsail, and stood on. But Captain Prodgers is a humane man. "Look here, Mr Anderson," says he, "it's pretty clear that whatever may be the matter with that there brig, this Dutch sailor man, if so be he *is* a Dutchman, can't tell us what's wrong. So," says he, "get that starboard quarter boat manned and go aboard the brig yourself, and see if you can make out what's amiss."

'No sooner said than done. The boat was lowered, and me and two o' the scowbanks and one o' the Scotchmen, makin' four men, tumbled into her, and we rowed Mr Anderson on board the brig. I took notice of Mr Anderson looking and looking werry hard at the wessel as we went along, as a man might who didn't much fancy the job he was put upon. We had our backs to the brig, but when we threw in our oars and got alongside, I'm blessed if the sight o' that old hull and the queer appearance o' the rigging didn't give me a kind o' crawling sensation. It might ha' been what the cook had said, or it might ha' been the faded paint and the brig's sides, that looked like a man's face arter he's cured o' the smallpox, or like a bit of French cheese I once saw, that might ha' passed for a muffin. But whatever it was, I didn't like the feeling, and rather wished I had let Sammy Saunders shove in front of me and get my place when we all run to man the boat.

However, there I was, and bein' there I thought I might as well see all that was going to happen, so I followed the mate aboard, he taking no notice. Indeed, I reckon he wished me to come, not liking to be the only one o' us 'twixt the rails of that strange old brig.

'I took a look forward and saw four men standing together, and leaning against the side o' the galley, where the sun shone. I didn't like their appearance at all. They hung there like coves fairly wore out. They all seemed middlin' old, but for that matter their faces was just as puzzling as the Dutchman's who had boarded us; ye might ha' called them old or young as you please, and both 'ud ha' been right. They all stared at us as we got over the side, but barring this twisting of their eyes round they was quite lifeless, and a melancholy row of men they seemed. There was a dim and grey-lookin' old man at the tiller, and him that was the skipper stood at the gangway to meet Mr Anderson. Did ye ever see a dried apple — a werry old 'un, sir? Well, that skipper's face were like that. It was all brownness and wrinkles, with a bit of a withered nose amidships, and under it a slit that stood for a mouth, and a pair of eyes that I calculate 'ud shine red in the dark. He'd a fur cap on, and an old coat that came down to the calves of his legs, and I never see skinnier fingers nor legs with such a sheer at the joints as though his body stood on a hoop. His boots was like a pair of shovels. He bobbed to

the mate and smiled away like clockwork and then droppin'
his arms down as t'other Dutchman had done, he up and
spoke a speech that must ha' lasted eight minutes by any
man's watch.

'When he began to talk the mate looked round and was
glad enough to see me standing close astern of him, I believe;
he fell back a step to draw nearer to me, and listened with
his head dropped. But the strange bosh, sir, were harder to
follow than t'other man's had been; this old man's pipes were
cracked, and he made a noise like a saw. The men forrards
never moved; there they stood sunning themselves, and the
dim old cove as steered looked at nothin' but the leech o' the
topgallant sail, though the wessel was hove-to, mind.

'As soon as the skipper had done, Mr Anderson he says
in a loud strong voice, "Mister," says he, "all that you've bin
saying is no doubt past contradicting of, but I'm bound to
tell 'ee I don't understand your lingo. Yonder barque's the
Sally G., Captain Prodgers, and I'm her mate. If ye'll tell
me what you want, we'll try to do it for you;" and here he
stopped and looked at the little man, who made no answer,
but kept on smilin' away as if somebody was tickling of him.
"What's the name o' this wessel?" says Mr Anderson in a
werry powerful woice. The skipper only smiled. The mate
looked forrards at the men, and sings out sternly, "Anybody
understand me there?" Says he, "I say, what's the name o'

this wessel, and what d'ye want?" Ne'er a one took notice, and the skipper he kept on smiling. "Come you along with me," says Mr Anderson, after takin' a long look round, and speaking to me. "We'll overhaul his old sugar-box for ourselves, and see what's wrong."

'So away we went to the harness-cask, the old skipper arter us, smiling all the time, and we looks into it, and sees it full o' pieces of meat. The mate he smelt of these wittles, and says, "They're sweet enough. Nothin' wrong in here." Then we goes over to the scuttle-butts and drops the dipper in, and finds 'em full o' fresh water. "Well, they can't be in want o' water," says the mate. Then, stopping a minute, he pulls out a piece o' chalk and stoops down and writes down the latitood and longitood in big letters, and then gets up and points to the marks, looking at the skipper. But this wasn't it either, for the skipper, always smiling, shakes his head so quickly that I thought it would ha' dropped off. Then we sounded the well, but that was right enough; no water there to take notice of. "Come along with me," says the mate, and down we bundles into the cabin, the skipper behind us. A strange old place it was, with a smell of snuff about. It looked to me to be wisibly decayin'. It made me feel as a diver does when he finds hisself in the cabin of a wessel that's been under water for years and years. I wondered to see no barnacles. We opens a door or two until we comes to the pantry, looks in, and sees plenty o' grub knocking about the shelves. "Well, they ain't starvin'," says the mate. "An' there's no water comin' in," says I. "And they don't want our reckonin'," says the mate. "Perhaps they've got the cholera aboard," says I. "Let's go forrard and see," says the mate.

'We went up the companion steps, the skipper followin' of us like a shadder, and walks to the fore hatch, and drops into the forecastle. A rummier place even than the cabin: full of ancient bunks covered with a wild flourish o' carving, and scores o' cockroaches blackening the timbers, with three or four sea-chests and an odd boot or two, and the likes o' that. "If the cholera's aboard," says the mate, "it ain't in this fo'cs'le, for there's nobody here." With that we scrambles on deck again. The skipper lay in wait for us at the fore scuttle, and when he sees us he falls a-smiling. "Capt'en," says Mr Anderson, "we've overhauled your wessel fore and aft, and can't find anything wrong. There's plenty o' meat and water aboard, the wessel's tight, ye don't want our reckonings, and there ain't no disease perceptible. That bein' so, I don't see what good we can do by stopping."

'The skipper looked at him narrowly and smilingly as he said this, and when he were done, he began another speech; but this Mr Anderson cut short by saying that there was nothing to thank him for, and that what we had done wasn't worth mentioning, and then calling to me, we drops into our boat and returns to the *Sally G.* None of us spoke as we rowed back, no man feelin' comfortable. On reaching the barque, I went forrard, followed by all hands, who wanted to know what we had seen; but their questions was stopped by the order being given to swing the main yards and get the stunsails on her agin.

'No sooner was this done than the cook tailed on to me and wouldn't let me go. "What did ye see?" says he. "A brig," says I. "And what else," says he. "Four strange men standing in the sun," says I, "and a dim old man at the tiller, and a skipper like a marmozeet," says I. "And what was his langwidge," says the cook. "Unbeknown," says I. "Bill," says he, in a low woice, which made the others, who stood listening, lean forrards to hear, "Bill," says he, "I'm sorry for you," says he, "I don't want to alarm you, Bill, but you've been aboard the *Flying Dutchman*," says he, "and take notice of what I'm going to say," says the cook; "and if I'm wrong I'll give any man leave to bile me in my own coppers. There'll be a gale o' wind," he says, "within the next twenty-four hours."

'D'ye see this hand, sir,' said the mariner who favoured me with this narrative, laying his large paw upon his knee, with the tar-stained palm uppermost. 'Well, as true as that there hand of mine is a-lying on my leg at this minute, did a wiolent gale o' wind bust down upon us heighteen hours arter we parted company with that Dutch brig. It blew from the west'ards, and drove us one hundred mile out o' our course. So there ye have it, sir. That's the naked truth. I don't ask you to mind what the cook said. You may forget him. Here's a fact to speak for itself. Heighteen hours arter we left that brig, a hurricane bust down upon us. If that ain't conclusive there's nothin' more to say'.'

THE STORY OF THE HAUNTED SHIP

Wilhelm Hauff

My father kept a small shop at Balsora. He was neither poor nor rich, and one of those people who are afraid of venturing anything lest they should lose the little they possess. He brought me up plainly and virtuously, and soon I was enabled to assist him in his trade. Scarcely had I reached my eighteenth year, and hardly had he made his first large speculation, when he died, probably from grief at having confided a thousand pieces of gold to the sea.

I could not help thinking him lucky afterwards on account of his death, for a few weeks later the news arrived that the ship to which my father had entrusted his goods had sunk. This mishap, however, did not curb my youthful courage. I converted everything that my father had left into money, and set forth to try my fortune abroad, accompanied only by my father's old servant, who from long attachment would not separate himself from me and my fate.

We took ship at Balsora and left the haven with a favourable wind. The ship in which we embarked was bound for India.

When we had sailed some fifteen days over the ordinary track, the Captain predicted a storm. He looked very serious, for it appeared that he was not sufficiently acquainted with the course in these parts to await a storm with composure. He had all sail furled, and we drifted along quite gently. The night had fallen. It was cold and clear, and the Captain began to think he had been deceived by false indications of the storm. All at once a ship which we had not observed before drove past at a little distance from our own. Wild shouts and cheers resounded from her deck; at which, in such an anxious hour before a tempest, I wondered not a little. The Captain, who stood by my side, turned as pale as death. 'My ship is doomed!' he cried; 'yonder sails death.' Before I could question him as to the meaning of this strange exclamation, the sailors came running towards us, howling and crying. 'Have you seen it?' they cried. 'It is all over with us.'

But the Captain caused some consolatory verses to be read out of the Koran, and placed himself at the helm. All in vain! Visibly the storm increased in fury, and before an hour had passed the ship crashed and stuck fast. The boats were lowered, and scarcely had the last sailors saved themselves, when the ship sank before our eyes, and I was launched on the sea, a beggar. Further miseries yet awaited us. The storm raged more furiously, our boat became unmanageable. I had clasped my old servant tightly, and we vowed never to part from one another. At length day broke. But at the first dawn of morning a squall caught the boat in which we were seated and capsized it. I never saw my shipmates again. I was stunned by the shock; and when I awoke, I found myself in the arms of my old and faithful servant, who had saved himself on the overturned boat and dragged me after him. The tempest had subsided. Nothing more was seen of our ship. We discovered, however, not far from us another ship, towards which the waves were drifting us. As we drew near I recognized it as the same ship that had dashed past us on the preceding night, and which had terrified our Captain so much. I was inspired with a singular horror at the sight of this vessel. The expression of the Captain which had been so terribly fulfilled, the desolate aspect of the ship, on which, near as we were and loudly as we shouted, no one appeared, frightened me. However, this was our only means of safety, therefore we praised the Prophet who had so wonderfully preserved us.

Over the ship's bow hung a long cable. We paddled with hands and feet towards it in order to grasp it. At length we succeeded. Loudly I raised my voice, but all was silent on board. We then climbed up by the rope, I as the youngest going first. Oh, horror! What a spectacle met my gaze as I stepped upon the deck! The planks were reddened with blood; twenty or thirty corpses in Turkish dresses lay on the deck. Close to the mainmast stood a man, richly attired, a sabre in his hand, but with features pale and distorted; a great nail driven through his forehead pinning him to the mainmast. He also was dead.

Terror shackled my steps. I scarcely ventured to breathe. At last my companion had also come up. He too was struck at the sight of the deck, on which nothing living was to be seen, only so many frightful corpses. After a time we ventured, after having invoked the aid of the Prophet in anguish of heart, to go forward. At each step we glanced around expecting to discover something new and yet more terrible. But all was the same. Far and wide nothing was living but ourselves and the ocean. We dared not even speak aloud, lest the dead Captain spitted to the mast should turn his ghastly eyes upon us, or one of the corpses move its head. At last we reached a hatchway which led to the ship's hold. There we both stopped, involuntarily, and looked at each other, for neither dared to speak his thoughts.

'O Master,' said my faithful servant, 'something awful has happened here! Yet, though the hold below be full of murderers, I would rather give myself up to their mercy than remain here any longer among these corpses.' I thought the same. We grew bold and, full of expectation, descended. But here likewise all was still as death, and only our steps sounded on the ladder. We stood at the door of the cabin. I placed my ear against it and listened. Nothing could be heard. I opened it, and the cabin presented a disorderly appearance. Dresses, weapons; and other things lay in confusion. Everything was out of its place. The crew, or at least the Captain, must have been carousing not long since, for all was still lying about.

We went from place to place and from cabin to cabin, and everywhere found splendid stores of silk, pearls, sugar, and the like. I was beside myself with joy at this sight, for since no one was on board, I thought I had a right to appropriate all to myself; but Ibrahim reminded me that we were doubtless far from land, which we could never reach without the help of man.

We refreshed ourselves with the meats and drinks, of which we found an ample supply, and finally ascended again to the deck. But here we shuddered at the sight of the ghastly corpses. We resolved upon freeing ourselves from them by throwing them overboard. But how awful was the dread which we felt when we found that not one could be moved from his position! So firmly fixed were they to the flooring, that we should have had to take up the planks of the decks in order to remove them, and for this purpose we had not tools. Neither could we loose the Captain from the mainmast, nor wrest his sabre from his rigid grasp.

We passed the day in sad contemplation of our position, and when night began to fall I allowed old Ibrahim to lie down to sleep, while I kept watch on deck spying for some means of deliverance. But when the moon had come out, and I reckoned by the stars that it was about eleven o'clock, such an irresistible sleep took possession of me that I involuntarily fell behind a cask that stood on the deck. However, this was more stupefaction than sleep, for I distinctly heard the sea beating against the side of the ship, and the sails creaking and whistling in the wind. All of a sudden I thought I heard voices and men's footsteps on the deck. I endeavoured to get up to see what it was, but an invisible power held my limbs fettered; I could not even open my eyes. The voices, however, grew more distinct, and it appeared to me as if a merry crew was rushing about on the deck. Now and then I thought I heard the sonorous voice of a commander, and also distinctly the hoisting and lowering of cordage and sails. But by degrees my senses left me, I sank into a deeper sleep, in which I only thought I could hear a clatter of arms, and only awoke when the sun was far above the horizon and scorching my face.

I stared about in astonishment. Storm, ship, the dead, and what I had heard during the night, appeared to me like a dream, but when I glanced around I found everything as on the previous day. Immovable lay the dead, immovable stood the Captain spitted to the mast. I laughed over my dream, and rose up to seek the old man.

He was seated, absorbed in reflection in the cabin. 'Oh, Master,' he exclaimed, as I entered. 'I would rather lie at the bottom of the sea than pass another night in this bewitched ship.' I inquired the cause of his trouble, and he thus answered me: 'After I had slept some hours, I awoke and heard people running about above my head. I thought at first it was you, but there were at least twenty, rushing to and fro, aloft, and I also heard calling and shouting. At last heavy steps came down the cabin. Upon this I became insensible, and only now and then my consciousness returned for a few moments, and then I saw the same man who is nailed to the mast overhead, sitting there at that table, singing and drinking, while the man in the scarlet dress, who is close to him on the floor, sat beside him and drank with him.' Such was my old servant's narrative.

Believe me, my friends, I did not feel at all at ease, for it was no illusion. I had also heard the dead men quite plainly. To sail in such company was gruesome to me. My Ibrahim, however, relapsed into profound meditation. 'I have just hit it!' he exclaimed at last. He recalled a little formula, which his grandfather, a man of experience and a great traveller, had taught him, which was a charm against ghosts and sorcery. He likewise affirmed that we might ward off the unnatural sleep during the coming night, by diligently saying verses from the Koran.

The proposal of the old man pleased me. In anxious expectation we saw the night approach. Adjoining the cabin was a narrow berth, into which we resolved to retire. We bored several holes through the door, large enough to overlook the whole cabin; we then locked the door as well as we could inside, and Ibrahim wrote the name of the Prophet in all four corners. Thus we awaited the terrors of the night. It might be about eleven o'clock when I began to feel very drowsy. My companion therefore advised me to say some verses from the Koran, which indeed helped me. All at once everything grew animated above, the cordage creaked, feet paced the deck, and several voices became clearly heard. We had thus sat for some time in intense expectation, when we heard something descending the steps of the cabin stairs. The old man on hearing this commenced to recite the formula which his grandfather had taught him against ghosts and sorcery:

If you are spirits from the air,
Or come from depths of sea,
Have in dark sepulchres your lair,
Or if from fire you be.
Allah is your God and Lord,
All spirits must obey His word.

I must confess I did not quite believe in this charm, and my hair stood on end as the door opened. In stepped that tall majestic man whom I had seen nailed to the mainmast. The nail still passed through his skull, but his sword was sheathed. Behind him followed another person less richly dressed; him also I had seen stretched on deck. The Captain, for there was no doubt it was he, had a pale face, a large black beard and fiery eyes, with which he looked around the whole cabin. I could see him quite distinctly as he passed our door; but he did not seem to notice the door at all, which hid us. Both seated themselves at the table which stood in the middle of the cabin, speaking loudly and almost shouting to one another in an unknown tongue. They grew more and more hot and excited, until at last the Captain brought his fist down upon the table, so that the cabin shook. The other jumped up with a wild laugh and beckoned the Captain to follow him. The latter rose, tore his sabre out of its sheath, and both left the cabin.

After they had gone we breathed more freely, but our alarm was not to terminate yet. Louder and louder grew the noise on deck. We heard rushing backwards and forwards, shouting, laughing and howling. At last a most fiendish noise was heard, so we thought the deck together with all its sails was coming down on us, clashing of arms and shrieks — and suddenly a dead silence followed. When, after many hours, we ventured to ascend, we found everything as before; not one had shifted his place; all lay as stiff as wood.

Thus we passed many days on board this ship, and constantly steered on an eastern course, where according to my calculation land should be found; but although we seemed to cover many miles by day, yet at night it seemed to go back, for we were always in the same place at the rising of the sun. We could not understand this, except that the dead crew each night navigated the ship in a directly opposite course with full sails. In order to prevent this, we furled all the sails before night fell, and employed the same means as we had used on the cabin door. We wrote the name of the prophet, and the formula prescribed by Ibrahim's grandfather upon a scroll of parchment, and wound it round the furled sails. Anxiously we awaited the result in our berths. The noise now seemed to increase more violently than ever; but behold, on the following morning, the sails were still furled, as we had left them. By day we only hoisted as many sails as were needed to carry the ship gently along, and thus in five days we covered a considerable tract.

At last on the sixth morning we discovered land at a short distance, and thanked Allah and his Prophet for our miraculous deliverance. This day and on the following night we sailed along a coast, and on the seventh morning we thought at a short distance we saw a town. With much difficulty we dropped our anchor, which at once struck ground, lowered a little boat, which was on deck, and rowed with all our strength towards the town. After the lapse of half-an-hour we entered a river which ran into the sea, and landed. On entering the gate of the town we asked the name of it, and learnt that it was an Indian town, not far from where I had intended to land at first. We went towards a caravanserai and refreshed ourselves after our adventurous journey. I also inquired there after some wise and intelligent man, intimating to the landlord that I wished to consult one on matters relating to sorcery. He led me to some remote street to a mean-looking house and knocked. I was allowed to enter, and simply told to ask for Muley.

In the house I met a little old man, with a grey beard and a long nose, who asked me what I wanted. I told him I desired to see the wise Muley, and he answered me that he was Muley. I now asked his advice what I should do with the corpses, and how I was to set about to remove them from the ship. He answered me that very likely the ship's crew were spell-bound on the ocean on account of some crime; and he believed the charm might be broken by bringing them on land, which, however, could only be done by taking up the planks on which they lay. The ship, together with all its goods, by divine and human law belonged to me, because I had, as it were, found it. I was, however, to keep all very secret, and make him a little present of my abundance in return for which he and his slaves would assist me in removing the dead. I promised to reward him richly, and we set forth followed by five slaves provided with saws and hatchets. On the road the magician Muley could not sufficiently laud the happy thought of tacking the Koran verses upon the sails. He said that this had been the only means of our deliverance.

It was yet early morning when we reached our vessel. We all set to work immediately, and in an hour four lay already in the boat. Some of the slaves had to row them to land to bury them there. They related on their return that the corpses had saved them the trouble of burial, for hardly had they been put on the ground when they crumbled into dust. We continued sawing off the corpses, and before evening all had been removed to land except one, namely he who was nailed to the mast. In vain we endeavoured to draw the nail out of the wood. Every effort could not displace it a hair's-breadth. I did not know what to do, for it was impossible to cut down the mast to bring him to land. Muley, however, devised an expedient. He ordered a slave quickly to row to land, in order to bring him a pot filled with earth. When it was brought, the magician pronounced some mystic words over it, and emptied the earth upon the head of the corpse. Immediately he opened his eyes, heaved a deep sigh, and the wound of the nail in his forehead began to bleed. We now extracted the nail easily, and the wounded man fell into the arms of one of the slaves.

'Who has brought me hither?' he said, after having slightly recovered. Muley pointed to me, and I approached him. 'Thanks be to thee, unknown stranger, for thou hast rescued me from a long martyrdom. For fifty years has my corpse been floating upon these waves, and my spirit was condemned to reanimate it each night; but now earth having touched my head, I can return to my fathers reconciled.' I begged him to tell us how he had fallen into this awful condition, and he answered: 'Fifty years ago I was a man of power and rank, and lived in Algiers. The longing after gain induced me to fit out a vessel in order to engage in piracy. I had already carried on this business for some time, when one day I took on board at Zante a Dervish, who asked for a free passage. My companions and myself were wild fellows, and paid no respect to the sanctity of the man, but rather mocked him. But one day, when he had reproached me in his holy zeal with my sinful mode of living, I became furious at night, after having drunk a great deal with my steersman in my cabin. Enraged at what a Dervish had told me, and what I would not even allow a Sultan to tell me, I rushed upon deck, and plunged my dagger in his breast. As he died, he cursed me and my crew, that we might neither live nor die till our heads should touch the earth. The Dervish died, and we threw him into the sea, laughing at his menaces; but in the very same night his words were fulfilled.

'Some of my crew mutinied against me. We fought with insane fury until my adherents were defeated, and I was nailed to the mainmast. But the mutineers also expired of their wounds, and my ship soon became but an immense tomb. My eyes also grew dim, my breathing ceased, I thought I was dying. But it was only a kind of numbness that seized me. The very next night, and at the precise hour that we had thrown the Dervish into the sea, I and all my companions awoke, we were alive, but we could only do and say what we had said and done on that night. Thus we have been sailing these fifty years unable to live or die: for how could we reach land? It was with a savage joy that we sailed many times with full sail in the storm, hoping that at length we might strike some rock, and rest our wearied heads at the bottom of the sea. We did not succeed. But now I shall die. Thanks once more, to my unknown deliverer, and if treasures can reward thee, accept my ship as a mark of my gratitude.'

After having said this, the Captain's head fell upon his breast, and he expired. Immediately his body also, like the crew's, crumbled to dust. We collected it in a little urn and buried him on shore. I engaged, however, workmen from the town, who repaired my ship thoroughly. After having bartered the goods which I had on board for others at a great profit, I collected a crew, rewarded my friend Muley handsomely, and set sail towards my native place. I made, however, a detour, and landed on many islands and countries where I sold my goods. The Prophet blessed my enterprise. After a lapse of nine months, twice as wealthy as the dying Captain had made me, I reached Balsora. My fellow citizens were astonished at my riches and my fortune, and did not believe anything else but that I must have found the diamond valley of the celebrated traveller Sinbad. I left their belief undisturbed, but henceforth the young people of Balsora, when they were scarcely eighteen years old, were obliged to go out into the world in order like myself to seek their fortune. But I lived quietly and peacefully, and every five years undertook a journey to Mecca, in order to thank the Lord for His blessing at this sacred shrine, and pray for the Captain and his crew that He might receive them into His Paradise.

THE CAPTAIN OF THE *POLE-STAR*

[BEING AN EXTRACT FROM THE SINGULAR JOURNAL OF JOHN M'ALISTER RAY, STUDENT OF MEDICINE.]

SEPTEMBER II—Lat. 81 degrees 40' N.; long. 2 degrees E. Still lying-to amid enormous ice fields. The one which stretches away to the north of us, and to which our ice-anchor is attached, cannot be smaller than an English county. To the right and left unbroken sheets extend to the horizon. This morning the mate reported that there were signs of pack ice to the southward. Should this form of sufficient thickness to bar our return, we shall be in a position of danger, as the food, I hear, is already running somewhat short. It is late in the season, and the nights are beginning to reappear.

This morning I saw a star twinkling just over the fore-yard, the first since the beginning of May. There is considerable discontent among the crew, many of whom are anxious to get back home to be in time for the herring season, when labour always commands a high price upon the Scotch coast. As yet their displeasure is only signified by sullen countenances and black looks, but I heard from the second mate this afternoon that they contemplated sending a deputation to the Captain to explain their grievance. I much doubt how he will receive it, as he is a man of fierce temper, and very sensitive about anything approaching to an infringement of his rights. I shall venture after dinner to say a few words to him upon the subject. I have always found that he will tolerate from me what he would resent from any other member of the crew. Amsterdam Island, at the north-west corner of Spitzbergen, is visible upon our starboard quarter—a rugged line of volcanic rocks, intersected by white seams, which represent glaciers. It is curious to think that at the present moment there is probably no human being nearer to us than the Danish settlements in the south of Greenland—a good nine hundred miles as the crow flies. A captain takes a great responsibility upon himself when he risks his vessel under such circumstances. No whaler has ever remained in these latitudes till so advanced a period of the year.

9 P.M.—I have spoken to Captain Craigie, and though the result has been hardly satisfactory, I am bound to say that he listened to what I had to say very quietly and even deferentially. When I had finished he put on that air of iron determination which I have frequently observed upon his face, and paced rapidly backwards and forwards across the narrow cabin for some minutes. At first I feared that I had

seriously offended him, but he dispelled the idea by sitting down again, and putting his hand upon my arm with a gesture which almost amounted to a caress. There was a depth of tenderness too in his wild dark eyes which surprised me considerably. "Look here, Doctor," he said, "I'm sorry I ever took you—I am indeed—and I would give fifty pounds this minute to see you standing safe upon the Dundee quay. It's hit or miss with me this time. There are fish to the north of us. How dare you shake your head, sir, when I tell you I saw them blowing from the masthead?"—this in a sudden burst of fury, though I was not conscious of having shown any signs of doubt. "Two-and-twenty fish in as many minutes as I am a living man, and not one under ten foot.[4] Now, Doctor, do you think I can leave the country when there is only one infernal strip of ice between me and my fortune? If it came on to blow from the north tomorrow we could fill the ship and be away before the frost could catch us. If it came on to blow from the south—well, I suppose the men are paid for risking their lives, and as for myself it matters but little to me, for I have more to bind me to the other world than to this one. I confess that I am sorry for you, though. I wish I had old Angus Tait who was with me last voyage, for he was a man that would never be missed, and you—you said once that you were engaged, did you not?"

"Yes," I answered, snapping the spring of the locket

which hung from my watch-chain, and holding up the little vignette of Flora.

"Curse you!" he yelled, springing out of his seat, with his very beard bristling with passion. "What is your happiness to me? What have I to do with her that you must dangle her photograph before my eyes?" I almost thought that he was about to strike me in the frenzy of his rage, but with another imprecation he dashed open the door of the cabin and rushed out upon deck, leaving me considerably astonished at his extraordinary violence. It is the first time that he has ever shown me anything but courtesy and kindness. I can hear him pacing excitedly up and down overhead as I write these lines.

I should like to give a sketch of the character of this man, but it seems presumptuous to attempt such a thing upon paper, when the idea in my own mind is at best a vague and uncertain one. Several times I have thought that I grasped the clue which might explain it, but only to be disappointed by his presenting himself in some new light which would upset all my conclusions. It may be that no human eye but my own shall ever rest upon these lines, yet as a psychological study I shall attempt to leave some record of Captain Nicholas Craigie.

A man's outer case generally gives some indication of the soul within. The Captain is tall and well-formed, with dark, handsome face, and a curious way of twitching his limbs, which may arise from nervousness, or be simply an outcome of his excessive energy. His jaw and whole cast of countenance is manly and resolute, but the eyes are the distinctive feature of his face. They are of the very darkest hazel, bright and eager, with a singular mixture of recklessness in their expression, and of something else which I have sometimes thought was more allied with horror than any other emotion. Generally the former predominated, but on occasions, and more particularly when he was thoughtfully inclined, the look of fear would spread and deepen until it imparted a new character to his whole countenance. It is at these times that he is most subject to tempestuous fits of anger, and he seems to be aware of it, for I have known him lock himself up so that no one might approach him until his dark hour was passed. He sleeps badly, and I have heard him shouting during the night, but his cabin is some little distance from mine, and I could never distinguish the words which he said.

This is one phase of his character, and the most disagreeable one. It is only through my close association with him, thrown together as we are day after day, that I have observed it. Otherwise he is an agreeable companion, well-read and entertaining, and as gallant a seaman as ever trod a deck. I shall not easily forget the way in which he handled the ship when we were caught by a gale among the loose ice at the beginning of April. I have never seen him so cheerful, and even hilarious, as he was that night, as he paced backwards and forwards upon the bridge amid the flashing of the lightning and the howling of the wind. He has told me several times that the thought of death was a pleasant one to him, which is a sad thing for a young man to say; he cannot be much more than thirty, though his hair and moustache are already slightly grizzled. Some great sorrow must have overtaken him and blighted his whole life. Perhaps I should be the same if I lost my Flora—God knows! I think if it were not for her that I should care very little whether the wind blew from the north or the south tomorrow.

There, I hear him come down the companion, and he has locked himself up in his room, which shows that he is still in an unamiable mood. And so to bed, as old Pepys would say, for the candle is burning down (we have to use them now since the nights are closing in), and the steward has turned in, so there are no hopes of another one.

SEPTEMBER 12—Calm, clear day, and still lying in the same position. What wind there is comes from the south-east, but it is very slight. Captain is in a better humour, and apologised to me at breakfast for his rudeness. He still looks somewhat distrait, however, and retains that wild look in his eyes which in a Highlander would mean that he was "fey"—at least so our chief engineer remarked to me, and he has some reputation among the Celtic portion of our crew as a seer and expounder of omens.

It is strange that superstition should have obtained such mastery over this hard-headed and practical race. I could not have believed to what an extent it is carried had I not observed it for myself. We have had a perfect epidemic of it this voyage, until I have felt inclined to serve out rations of sedatives and nervetonics with the Saturday allowance of grog. The first symptom of it was that shortly after leaving Shetland the men at the wheel used to complain that they heard plaintive cries and screams in the wake of the ship, as if something were following it and were unable to overtake it. This fiction has been kept up during the whole voyage, and on dark nights at the beginning of the seal-fishing it was only with great difficulty that men could be induced to do their spell. No doubt what they heard was either the creaking of the rudder-chains, or the cry of some passing sea-bird. I have been fetched out of bed several times to listen to it, but I need hardly say that I was never able to distinguish anything unnatural.

The men, however, are so absurdly positive upon the subject that it is hopeless to argue with them. I mentioned the matter to the Captain once, but to my surprise he took it very gravely, and indeed appeared to be considerably disturbed by what I told him. I should have thought that he at least would have been above such vulgar delusions.

All this disquisition upon superstition leads me up to the fact that Mr. Manson, our second mate, saw a ghost last night—or, at least, says that he did, which of course is the same thing. It is quite refreshing to have some new topic of conversation after the eternal routine of bears and whales which has served us for so many months. Manson swears the ship is haunted, and that he would not stay in her a day if he had any other place to go to. Indeed the fellow is honestly frightened, and I had to give him some chloral and bromide of potassium this morning to steady him down. He seemed quite indignant when I suggested that he had been having an extra glass the night before, and I was obliged to pacify him by keeping as grave a countenance as possible during his story, which he certainly narrated in a very straight-forward and matter-of-fact way.

"I was on the bridge," he said, "about four bells in the middle watch, just when the night was at its darkest. There was a bit of a moon, but the clouds were blowing across it so that you couldn't see far from the ship. John M'Leod, the harpooner, came aft from the foe sle-head and reported a strange noise on the starboard bow.

"I went forrard and we both heard it, sometimes like a

bairn crying and sometimes like a wench in pain. I've been seventeen years to the country and I never heard seal, old or young, make a sound like that. As we were standing there on the foc'sle-head the moon came out from behind a cloud, and we both saw a sort of white figure moving across the ice field in the same direction that we had heard the cries. We lost sight of it for a while, but it came back on the port bow, and we could just make it out like a shadow on the ice. I sent a hand aft for the rifles, and M'Leod and I went down on to the pack, thinking that maybe it might be a bear. When we got on the ice I lost sight of M'Leod, but I pushed on in the direction where I could still hear the cries. I followed them for a mile or maybe more, and then running round a hummock I came right on to the top of it standing and waiting for me seemingly. I don't know what it was. It wasn't a bear any way. It was tall and white and straight, and if it wasn't a man nor a woman, I'll stake my davy it was something worse. I made for the ship as hard as I could run, and precious glad I was to find myself aboard. I signed articles to do my duty by the ship, and on the ship I'll stay, but you don't catch me on the ice again after sundown."

That is his story, given as far as I can in his own words. I fancy what he saw must, in spite of his denial, have been a young bear erect upon its hind legs, an attitude which they often assume when alarmed. In the uncertain light this would bear a resemblance to a human figure, especially to a man whose nerves were already somewhat shaken. Whatever it may have been, the occurrence is unfortunate, for it has produced a most unpleasant effect upon the crew. Their looks are more sullen than before, and their discontent more open. The double grievance of being debarred from the herring fishing and of being detained in what they choose to call a haunted vessel, may lead them to do something rash. Even the harpooners, who are the oldest and steadiest among them, are joining in the general agitation.

Apart from this absurd outbreak of superstition, things are looking rather more cheerful. The pack which was forming to the south of us has partly cleared away, and the water is so warm as to lead me to believe that we are lying in one of those branches of the gulfstream which run up between Greenland and Spitzbergen. There are numerous small Medusse and seale-mons about the ship, with abundance of shrimps, so that there is every possibility of "fish" being sighted. Indeed one was seen blowing about dinner-time, but in such a position that it was impossible for the boats to follow it.

SEPTEMBER 13—Had an interesting conversation with the chief mate, Mr. Milne, upon the bridge. It seems that our Captain is as great an enigma to the seamen, and even to the owners of the vessel, as he has been to me. Mr. Milne tells me that when the ship is paid off, upon returning from a voyage, Captain Craigie disappears, and is not seen again until the approach of another season, when he walks quietly into the office of the company, and asks whether his services will be required. He has no friend in Dundee, nor does anyone pretend to be acquainted with his early history. His position depends entirely upon his skill as a seaman, and the name for courage and coolness which he had earned in the capacity of mate, before being entrusted with a separate command. The unanimous opinion seems to be that he is not a Scotchman, and that his name is an assumed one. Mr. Milne thinks that he has devoted himself to whaling simply for the reason that it is the most dangerous occupation which he could select, and that he courts death in every possible manner. He mentioned several instances of this, one of which is rather curious, if true. It seems that on one occasion he did not put in an appearance at the office, and a substitute had to be selected in his place. That was at the time of the last Russian and Turkish war. When he turned up again next spring he had a puckered wound in the side of his neck which he used to endeavour to conceal with his cravat. Whether the mate's inference that he had been engaged in the war is true or not I cannot say. It was certainly a strange coincidence.

The wind is veering round in an easterly direction, but

is still very slight. I think the ice is lying closer than it did yesterday. As far as the eye can reach on every side there is one wide expanse of spotless white, only broken by an occasional rift or the dark shadow of a hummock. To the south there is the narrow lane of blue water which is our sole means of escape, and which is closing up every day. The Captain is taking a heavy responsibility upon himself. I hear that the tank of potatoes has been finished, and even the biscuits are running short, but he preserves the same impassible countenance, and spends the greater part of the day at the crow's nest, sweeping the horizon with his glass. His manner is very variable, and he seems to avoid my society, but there has been no repetition of the violence which he showed the other night.

7.30 P.M.—My deliberate opinion is that we are commanded by a madman. Nothing else can account for the extraordinary vagaries of Captain Craigie. It is fortunate that I have kept this journal of our voyage, as it will serve to justify us in case we have to put him under any sort of restraint, a step which I should only consent to as a last resource. Curiously enough it was he himself who suggested lunacy and not mere eccentricity as the secret of his strange conduct. He was standing upon the bridge about an hour ago, peering as usual through his glass, while I was walking up and down the quarterdeck. The majority of the men were below at their tea, for the watches have not been regularly kept of late. Tired of walking, I leaned against the bulwarks, and admired the mellow glow cast by the sinking sun upon the great ice fields which surround us. I was suddenly aroused from the reverie into which I had fallen by a hoarse voice at my elbow, and starting round I found that the Captain had descended and was standing by my side. He was staring out over the ice with an expression in which horror, surprise, and something approaching to joy were contending for the mastery. In spite of the cold, great drops of perspiration were coursing down his forehead, and he was evidently fearfully excited.

His limbs twitched like those of a man upon the verge of an epileptic fit, and the lines about his mouth were drawn and hard.

"Look!" he gasped, seizing me by the wrist, but still keeping his eyes upon the distant ice, and moving his head slowly in a horizontal direction, as if following some object which was moving across the field of vision. "Look! There, man, there! Between the hummocks! Now coming out from behind the far one! You see her—you MUST see her! There still! Flying from me, by God, flying from me—and gone!"

He uttered the last two words in a whisper of concentrated agony which shall never fade from my remembrance. Clinging to the ratlines he endeavoured to climb up upon the top of the bulwarks as if in the hope of obtaining a last glance at the departing object. His strength was not equal to the attempt, however, and he staggered back against the saloon skylights, where he leaned panting and exhausted. His face was so livid that I expected him to become unconscious, so lost no time in leading him down the companion, and stretching him upon one of the sofas in the cabin. I then poured him out some brandy, which I held to his lips, and which had a wonderful effect upon him, bringing the blood back into his white face and steadying his poor shaking limbs. He raised himself up upon his elbow, and looking round to see that we were alone, he beckoned to me to come and sit beside him.

"You saw it, didn't you?" he asked, still in the same subdued awesome tone so foreign to the nature of the man.

"No, I saw nothing."

His head sank back again upon the cushions. "No, he wouldn't without the glass," he murmured. "He couldn't. It was the glass that showed her to me, and then the eyes of love—the eyes of love.

"I say, Doc, don't let the steward in! He'll think I'm mad. Just bolt the door, will you!"

I rose and did what he had commanded.

He lay quiet for a while, lost in thought apparendy, and then raised himself up upon his elbow again, and asked for some more brandy.

"You don't think I am, do you, Doc?" he asked, as I was putting the bottle back into the after-locker. "Tell me now, as man to man, do you think that I am mad?"

"I think you have something on your mind," I answered, "which is exciting you and doing you a good deal of harm."

"Right there, lad!" he cried, his eyes sparkling from the effects of the brandy. "Plenty on my mind—plenty! But I can work out the latitude and the longitude, and I can handle my sextant and manage my logarithms. You couldn't prove me mad in a court of law, could you, now?" It was curious to hear the man lying back and coolly arguing out the question of his own sanity.

"Perhaps not," I said, "but still I think you would be wise to get home as soon as you can, and settle down to a quiet life for a while."

"Get home, eh?" he muttered, with a sneer upon his face. "One word for me and two for yourself, lad. Settle down with Flora—pretty little Flora. Are bad dreams signs of madness?"

"Sometimes," I answered.

"What else? What would be the first symptoms?"

"Pains in the head, noises in the ears flashes before the eyes, delusions—"

"Ah! what about them?" he interrupted. "What would you call a delusion?"

"Seeing a thing which is not there is a delusion."

"But she WAS there!" he groaned to himself. "She WAS there!" and rising, he unbolted the door and walked with slow and uncertain steps to his own cabin, where I have no doubt that he will remain until tomorrow morning. His system seems to have received a terrible shock, whatever it may have been that he imagined himself to have seen. The man becomes a greater mystery every day, though I fear that the solution which he has himself suggested is the correct one, and that his reason is affected. I do not think that a guilty conscience has anything to do with his behaviour. The idea is a popular one among the officers, and, I believe, the crew; but I have seen nothing to support it. He has not the air of a guilty man, but of one who has had terrible usage at the hands of fortune, and who should be regarded as a martyr rather than a criminal.

The wind is veering round to the south tonight. God help us if it blocks that narrow pass which is our only road to safety! Situated as we are on the edge of the main Arctic pack, or the "barrier" as it is called by the whalers, any wind from the north has the effect of shredding out the ice around us and allowing our escape, while a wind from die south blows up all the loose ice behind us and hems us in between two packs. God help us, I say again!

SEPTEMBER 14—Sunday, and a day of rest. My fears have been confirmed, and the thin strip of blue water has disappeared from the southward. Nothing but the great motionless ice fields around us, with their weird hummocks and fantastic pinnacles. There is a deathly silence over their wide expanse which is horrible. No lapping of the waves now, no cries of seagulls or straining of sails, but one deep universal silence in which the murmurs of the seamen, and the creak of their boots upon the white shining deck, seem discordant and out of place. Our only visitor was an Arctic fox, a rare animal upon the pack, though common enough upon the land. He did not come near the ship, however, but after surveying us from a distance fled rapidly across the ice. This was curious conduct, as they generally know nothing of man, and being of an inquisitive nature, become so familiar that they are easily captured. Incredible as it may seem, even this little incident produced a bad effect upon the crew. "Yon puir beastie kens mair, ay, an' sees mair nor you nor me!" was the comment of one of the leading harpooners, and the others nodded their acquiescence. It is vain to attempt to argue against such puerile superstition. They have made up their minds that there is a curse upon the ship, and nothing will ever persuade them to the contrary.

The Captain remained in seclusion all day except for about half an hour in the afternoon, when he came out upon the quarterdeck. I observed that he kept his eye fixed upon the spot where the vision of yesterday had appeared, and was quite prepared for another outburst, but none such came. He did not seem to see me although I was standing close beside him. Divine service was read as usual by the chief engineer. It is a curious thing that in whaling vessels the Church of England Prayer-book is always employed, although there is never a member of that Church among either officers or crew. Our men are all Roman Catholics or Presbyterians, the former predominating. Since a ritual is used which is foreign to both, neither can complain that the other is preferred to them, and they listen with all attention and devotion, so that the system has something to recommend it.

A glorious sunset, which made the great fields of ice look like a lake of blood. I have never seen a finer and at the same time more weird effect. Wind is veering round. If it will blow twenty-four hours from the north all will yet be well.

SEPTEMBER 15—Today is Flora's birthday. Dear lass! it is well that she cannot see her boy, as she used to call me, shut up among the ice fields with a crazy captain and a few weeks' provisions. No doubt she scans the shipping list in the Scotsman every morning to see if we are reported from Shetland. I have to set an example to the men and look cheery and unconcerned; but God knows, my heart is very heavy at times.

The thermometer is at nineteen Fahrenheit today. There is but little wind, and what there is comes from an unfavourable quarter. Captain is in an excellent humour; I think he imagines he has seen some other omen or vision, poor fellow, during the night, for he came into my room early in the morning, and stooping down over my bunk, whispered, "It wasn't a delusion, Doc; it's all right!" After breakfast he asked me to find out how much food was left, which the second mate and I proceeded to do. It is even less than we had expected. Forward they have half a tank full of biscuits, three barrels of salt meat, and a very limited supply of coffee beans and sugar. In the after-hold and lockers there are a good many luxuries, such as tinned salmon, soups, haricot mutton, &c., but they will go a very short way among a crew of fifty men. There are two barrels of flour in the storeroom, and an unlimited supply of tobacco. Altogether there is about enough to keep the men on half rations for eighteen or twenty days—certainly not more. When we reported the state of things to the Captain, he ordered all hands to be piped, and addressed them from the quarterdeck. I never saw him to better advantage. With his tall, well-knit figure, and dark animated face, he seemed a man born to command, and he discussed the situation in a cool sailor-like way which showed that while appreciating the danger he had an eye for every loophole of escape.

"My lads," he said, "no doubt you think I brought you into this fix, if it is a fix, and maybe some of you feel bitter against me on account of it. But you must remember that for many a season no ship that comes to the country has brought in as much oil-money as the old Pole-Star, and everyone of you has had his share of it. You can leave your wives behind you in comfort while other poor fellows come back to find their lasses on the parish. If you have to thank me for the one you have to thank me for the other, and we may call it quits. We've tried a bold venture before this and succeeded, so now that we've tried one and failed we've no cause to cry out about it. If the worst comes to the worst, we can make the land across the ice, and lay in a stock of seals which will keep us alive until the spring. It won't come to that, though, for you'll see the Scotch coast again before three weeks are out. At present every man must go on half rations, share and share alike, and no favour to any. Keep up your hearts and you'll pull through this as you've pulled through many a danger before." These few simple words of his had a wonderful effect upon the crew. His former unpopularity was forgotten, and the old harpooner whom I have already mentioned for his superstition, led off three cheers, which were heartily joined in by all hands.

SEPTEMBER 16—The wind has veered round to the north during the night, and the ice shows some symptoms of opening out. The men are in a good humour in spite of the short allowance upon which they have been placed. Steam is kept up in the engine-room, that there may be no delay should an opportunity for escape present itself. The Captain is in exuberant spirits, though he still retains that wild "fey" expression which I have already remarked upon. This burst of cheerfulness puzzles me more than his former gloom. I cannot understand it. I think I mentioned in an early part of this journal that one of his oddities is that he never permits any person to enter his cabin, but insists upon making his own bed, such as it is, and performing every other office for himself. To my surprise he handed me the key today and requested me to go down there and take the time by his chronometer while he measured the altitude of the sun at noon. It is a bare little room, containing a washing-stand and a few books, but little else in the way of luxury, except some pictures upon the walls. The majority of these are small cheap oleographs, but there was one watercolour sketch of the head of a young lady which arrested my attention. It was evidently a portrait, and not one of those fancy types of female beauty which sailors particularly affect. No artist could have evolved from his own mind such a curious mixture of character and weakness. The languid, dreamy

137

eyes, with their drooping lashes, and the broad, low brow, unruffled by thought or care, were in strong contrast with the clean-cut, prominent jaw, and the resolute set of the lower lip. Underneath it in one of the corners was written, "M. B., aet. 19." That anyone in the short space of nineteen years of existence could develop such strength of will as was stamped upon her face seemed to me at the time to be well-nigh incredible. She must have been an extraordinary woman. Her features have thrown such a glamour over me that, though I had but a fleeting glance at them, I could, were I a draughtsman, reproduce them line for line upon this page of the journal. I wonder what part she has played in our Captain's life. He has hung her picture at the end of his berth, so that his eyes continually rest upon it. Were he a less reserved man I should make some remark upon the subject. Of the other things in his cabin there was nothing worthy of mention—uniform coats, a campstool, small looking-glass, tobacco-box, and numerous pipes, including an oriental hookah—which, by-the-bye, gives some colour to Mr. Milne's story about his participation in the war, though the connection may seem rather a distant one.

11.20 P.M.—Captain just gone to bed after a long and interesting conversation on general topics. When he chooses he can be a most fascinating companion, being remarkably well-read, and having the power of expressing his opinion forcibly without appearing to be dogmatic. I hate to have my intellectual toes trod upon. He spoke about the nature of the soul, and sketched out the views of Aristotle and Plato upon the subject in a masterly manner. He seems to have a leaning for metempsychosis and the doctrines of Pythagoras. In discussing them we touched upon modern spiritualism, and I made some joking allusion to the impostures of Slade, upon which, to my surprise, he warned me most impressively against confusing the innocent with the guilty, and argued that it would be as logical to brand Christianity as an error because Judas, who professed that religion, was a villain. He shortly afterwards bade me good-night and retired to his room.

The wind is freshening up, and blows steadily from the north. The nights are as dark now as they are in England. I hope tomorrow may set us free from our frozen fetters.

SEPTEMBER 17—The Bogie again. Thank Heaven that I have strong nerves! The superstition of these poor fellows, and the circumstantial accounts which they give, with the utmost earnestness and self-conviction, would horrify any man not accustomed to their ways. There are many versions of the matter, but the sum-total of them all is that something uncanny has been flitting round the ship all night, and that Sandie M'Donald of Peterhead and "lang" Peter Williamson of Shetland saw it, as also did Mr. Milne on the bridge—so, having three witnesses, they can make a better case of it than the second mate did. I spoke to Milne after breakfast, and told him that he should be above such nonsense, and that as an officer he ought to set the men a better example. He shook his weatherbeaten head ominously, but answered with characteristic caution, "Mebbe aye, mebbe na, Doctor," he said. "I didna ca' it a ghaist. I canna' say I preen my faith in sea-bogles an' the like, though there's a many as claims to ha' seen a' that and waur. I'm no easy feared, but maybe your ain bluid would run a bit cauld, mun, if instead o' speerin' aboot it in daylicht ye were wi' me last night, an' seed an awfu' like shape, white an' gruesome, whiles here, whiles there, an' it greetin' and ca'ing in the darkness like a bit lambie that hae lost its mither. Ye would na' be sae ready to put it a' doon to auld wives' clavers then, I'm thinkin'." I saw it was hopeless to reason with him, so contented myself with begging him as a personal favour to call me up the next time the spectre appeared—a request to which he acceded with many ejaculations expressive of his hopes that such an opportunity might never arise.

As I had hoped, the white desert behind us has become broken by many thin streaks of water which intersect it in all directions. Our latitude today was 80 degrees 52' N, which shows that there is a strong southerly drift upon the pack. Should the wind continue favourable it will break up as rapidly as it formed. At present we can do nothing but smoke and wait and hope for the best. I am rapidly becoming a fatalist. When dealing with such uncertain factors as wind and ice a man can be nothing else. Perhaps it was the wind and sand of the Arabian deserts which gave the minds of the original followers of Mahomet their tendency to bow to kismet.

These spectral alarms have a very bad effect upon the Captain. I feared that it might excite his sensitive mind, and endeavoured to conceal the absurd story from him, but unfortunately he overheard one of the men making an allusion to it, and insisted upon being informed about it. As I had expected, it brought out all his latent lunacy in an exaggerated form. I can hardly believe that this is the same man who discoursed philosophy last night with the most critical acumen and coolest judgment. He is pacing backwards and forwards upon the quarterdeck like a caged tiger, stopping now and again to throw out his hands with a yearning gesture, and stare impatiently out over the ice. He keeps up a continual mutter to himself, and once he called out, "But a little time, love—but a little time!" Poor fellow, it is sad to see a gallant seaman and accomplished gentleman reduced to such a pass, and to think that imagination and delusion can cow a mind to which real danger was but the salt of life. Was ever a man in such a position as I, between a demented captain and a ghost-seeing mate? I sometimes think I am the only really sane man aboard the vessel—except perhaps the second engineer, who is a kind of ruminant, and would care nothing for all the fiends in the Red Sea so long as they would leave him alone and not disarrange his tools.

The ice is still opening rapidly, and there is every probability of our being able to make a start tomorrow morning. They will think I am inventing when I tell them at home all the strange things that have befallen me.

12 P.M.—I have been a good deal startled, though I feel steadier now, thanks to a stiff glass of brandy. I am hardly myself yet, however, as this handwriting will testify. The fact is, that I have gone through a very strange experience, and am beginning to doubt whether I was justified in branding everyone on board as madmen because they professed to have seen things which did not seem reasonable to my understanding. *Pshaw!* I am a fool to let such a trifle unnerve me; and yet, coming as it does after all these alarms, it has an additional significance, for I cannot doubt either Mr. Manson's story or that of the mate, now that I have experienced that which I used formerly to scoff at.

After all it was nothing very alarming—a mere sound, and that was all. I cannot expect that anyone reading this, if anyone ever should read it, will sympathise with my feelings, or realise the effect which it produced upon me at the time. Supper was over, and I had gone on deck to have a quiet pipe before turning in. The night was very dark—so dark that, standing under the quarter-boat, I was unable to see the officer upon the bridge. I think I have already mentioned the extraordinary silence which prevails in these frozen seas. In other parts of the world, be they ever so barren, there is some slight vibration of the air—some faint hum, be it from the distant haunts of men, or from the leaves of the trees, or the wings of the birds, or even the faint rustle of the grass that covers the ground. One may not actively perceive the sound, and yet if it were withdrawn it would be missed. It is only here in these Arctic seas that stark, unfathomable stillness obtrudes itself upon you in all its gruesome reality. You find your tympanum straining to catch some little murmur, and dwelling eagerly upon every accidental sound within the vessel. In this state I was leaning against the bulwarks when there arose from the ice almost directly underneath me a cry, sharp and shrill, upon the silent air of the night, beginning, as it seemed to me, at a note such as prima donna never reached, and mounting from that ever higher and higher until it culminated in a long wail of agony, which might have been the last cry of a lost soul. The ghastly scream is still ringing in my ears. Grief, unutterable grief, seemed to be expressed in it, and a great longing, and yet through it all there was an occasional wild note of exultation. It shrilled out from close beside me, and yet as I glared into the darkness I could discern nothing. I waited some little time, but without hearing any repetition of the sound, so I came below, more shaken than I have ever been in my life before. As I came down the companion I met Mr. Milne coming up to relieve the watch. "Weel, Doctor," he said, "maybe that's auld wives' clavers tae? Did ye no hear it skirling? Maybe that's a supersteetion? What d'ye think o't noo?" I was obliged to apologise to the honest fellow, and acknowledge that I was as puzzled by it as he was. Perhaps tomorrow things may look different. At present I dare hardly write all that I think. Reading it again in days to come, when I have shaken off all these associations, I should despise myself for having been so weak.

SEPTEMBER 18—Passed a restless and uneasy night, still haunted by that strange sound. The Captain does not look as if he had had much repose either, for his face is haggard and his eyes bloodshot. I have not told him of my adventure of last night, nor shall I. He is already restless and excited, standing up, sitting down, and apparently utterly unable to keep still.

A fine lead appeared in the pack this morning, as I had expected, and we were able to cast off our ice-anchor, and steam about twelve miles in a west-sou'-westerly direction. We were then brought to a halt by a great floe as massive as any which we have left behind us. It bars our progress completely, so we can do nothing but anchor again and wait until it breaks up, which it will probably do within twenty-four hours, if the wind holds. Several bladder-nosed seals were seen swimming in the water, and one was shot, an immense creature more than eleven feet long. They are fierce, pugnacious animals, and are said to be more than a match for a bear. Fortunately they are slow and clumsy in their movements, so that there is little danger in attacking them upon the ice.

The Captain evidently does not think we have seen the last of our troubles, though why he should take a gloomy view of the situation is more than I can fathom, since everyone else on board considers that we have had a miraculous escape, and are sure now to reach the open sea.

"I suppose you think it's all right now, Doctor?" he said, as we sat together after dinner.

"I hope so," I answered.

"We mustn't be too sure—and yet no doubt you are right. We'll all be in the arms of our own true loves before long, lad, won't we? But we mustn't be too sure—we mustn't be too sure."

He sat silent a little, swinging his leg thoughtfully

backwards and forwards. "Look here," he continued, "it's a dangerous place this, even at its best—a treacherous, dangerous place. I have known men cut off very suddenly in a land like this. A slip would do it sometimes—a single slip, and down you go through a crack, and only a bubble on the green water to show where it was that you sank. It's a queer thing," he continued with a nervous laugh, "but all the years I've been in this country I never once thought of making a will—not that I have anything to leave in particular, but still when a man is exposed to danger he should have everything arranged and ready—don't you think so?"

"Certainly," I answered, wondering what on earth he was driving at.

"He feels better for knowing it's all settled," he went on. "Now if anything should ever befall me, I hope that you will look after things for me. There is very little in the cabin, but such as it is I should like it to be sold, and the money divided in the same proportion as the oil-money among the crew. The chronometer I wish you to keep yourself as some slight remembrance of our voyage. Of course all this is a mere precaution, but I thought I would take the opportunity of speaking to you about it. I suppose I might rely upon you if there were any necessity?"

"Most assuredly," I answered, "and since you are taking this step, I may as well—"

146

"You! you!" he interrupted. "YOU'RE all right. What the devil is the matter with YOU? There, I didn't mean to be peppery, but I don't like to hear a young fellow, that has hardly began life, speculating about death. Go up on deck and get some fresh air into your lungs instead of talking nonsense in the cabin, and encouraging me to do the same."

The more I think of this conversation of ours the less do I like it. Why should the man be settling his affairs at the very time when we seem to be emerging from all danger? There must be some method in his madness. Can it be that he contemplates suicide? I remember that upon one occasion he spoke in a deeply reverent manner of the heinousness of the crime of self-destruction. I shall keep my eye upon him, however, and though I cannot obtrude upon the privacy of his cabin, I shall at least make a point of remaining on deck as long as he stays up.

Mr. Milne pooh-poohs my fears, and says it is only the "skipper's little way." He himself takes a very rosy view of the situation. According to him we shall be out of the ice by the day after tomorrow, pass Jan Meyen two days after that, and sight Shetland in little more than a week. I hope he may not be too sanguine. His opinion may be fairly balanced against the gloomy precautions of the Captain, for he is an old and experienced seaman, and weighs his words well before uttering them.

The long-impending catastrophe has come at last. I hardly know what to write about it.

The Captain is gone. He may come back to us again alive, but I fear me—I fear me. It is now seven o'clock of the morning of the 19th of September. I have spent the whole night traversing the great ice-floe in front of us with a party of seamen in the hope of coming upon some trace of him, but in vain. I shall try to give some account of the circumstances which attended upon his disappearance. Should anyone ever chance to read the words which I put down, I trust they will remember that I do not write from conjecture or from hearsay, but that I, a sane and educated man, am describing accurately what actually occurred before my very eyes. My inferences are my own, but I shall be answerable for the facts.

The Captain remained in excellent spirits after the conversation which I have recorded. He appeared to be nervous and impatient, however, frequently changing his position, and moving his limbs in an aimless choreic way which is characteristic of him at times. In a quarter of an hour he went upon deck seven times, only to descend after a few hurried paces. I followed him each time, for there was something about his face which confirmed my resolution of not letting him out of my sight. He seemed to observe the effect which his movements had produced, for he endeavoured by an over-done hilarity, laughing boisterously at the very smallest of jokes, to quiet my apprehensions.

After supper he went on to the poop once more, and I with him. The night was dark and very still, save for the melancholy soughing of the wind among the spars. A thick cloud was coming up from the northwest, and the ragged tentacles which it threw out in front of it were drifting across the face of the moon, which only shone now and again through a rift in the wrack. The Captain paced rapidly backwards and forwards, and then seeing me still dogging him, he came across and hinted that he thought I should be better below—which, I need hardly say, had the effect of strengthening my resolution to remain on deck.

I think he forgot about my presence after this, for he stood silently leaning over the taffrail, and peering out across the great desert of snow, part of which lay in shadow, while part glittered mistily in the moonlight. Several times I could see by his movements that he was referring to his watch, and once he muttered a short sentence, of which I could only catch the one word "ready." I confess to having felt an eerie feeling creeping over me as I watched the loom of his tall figure through the darkness, and noted how completely he fulfilled the idea of a man who is keeping a tryst. A tryst with whom? Some vague perception began to dawn upon me as

I pieced one fact with another, but I was utterly unprepared for the sequel.

By the sudden intensity of his attitude I felt that he saw something. I crept up behind him. He was staring with an eager questioning gaze at what seemed to be a wreath of mist, blown swiftly in a line with the ship. It was a dim, nebulous body, devoid of shape, sometimes more, sometimes less apparent, as the light fell on it. The moon was dimmed in its brilliancy at the moment by a canopy of thinnest cloud, like the coating of an anemone.

"Coming, lass, coming," cried the skipper, in a voice of unfathomable tenderness and compassion, like one who soothes a beloved one by some favour long looked for, and as pleasant to bestow as to receive.

What followed happened in an instant. I had no power to interfere.

He gave one spring to the top of the bulwarks, and another which took him on to the ice, almost to the feet of the pale misty figure. He held out his hands as if to clasp it, and so ran into the darkness with outstretched arms and loving words. I still stood rigid and motionless, straining my eyes after his retreating form, until his voice died away in the distance. I never thought to see him again, but at that moment the moon shone out brilliantly through a chink in the cloudy heaven, and illuminated the great field of ice. Then I saw his dark figure already a very long way off, running with prodigious speed across the frozen plain. That was the last glimpse which we caught of him—perhaps the last we ever shall. A party was organised to follow him, and I accompanied them, but the men's hearts were not in the work, and nothing was found. Another will be formed within a few hours. I can hardly believe I have not been dreaming, or suffering from some hideous nightmare, as I write these things down.

7.30 P.M.—Just returned dead beat and utterly tired out from a second unsuccessful search for the Captain. The floe is of enormous extent, for though we have traversed at least twenty miles of its surface, there has been no sign of its coming to an end. The frost has been so severe of late that the overlying snow is frozen as hard as granite, otherwise we might have had the footsteps to guide us. The crew are anxious that we should cast off and steam round the floe and so to the southward, for the ice has opened up during the night, and the sea is visible upon the horizon. They argue that Captain Craigie is certainly dead, and that we are all risking our lives to no purpose by remaining when we have an opportunity of escape. Mr. Milne and I have had the greatest difficulty in persuading them to wait until tomorrow night, and have been compelled to promise that we will not under any circumstances delay our departure longer than that. We propose therefore to take a few hours' sleep, and then to start upon a final search.

SEPTEMBER 20, EVENING—I crossed the ice this morning with a party of men exploring the southern part of the floe, while Mr. Milne went off in a northerly direction. We pushed on for ten or twelve miles without seeing a trace of any living thing except a single bird, which fluttered a great way over our heads, and which by its flight I should judge to have been a falcon. The southern extremity of the ice field tapered away into a long narrow spit which projected out into the sea. When we came to the base of this promontory, the men halted, but I begged them to continue to the extreme end of it, that we might have the satisfaction of knowing that no possible chance had been neglected.

We had hardly gone a hundred yards before M'Donald of Peterhead cried out that he saw something in front of us, and began to run. We all got a glimpse of it and ran too. At first it was only a vague darkness against the white ice, but as we raced along together it took the shape of a man, and eventually of the man of whom we were in search. He was lying face downwards upon a frozen bank. Many little crystals of ice and feathers of snow had drifted on to him as he lay, and sparkled upon his dark seaman's jacket. As we came up some wandering puff of wind caught these tiny flakes in its vortex, and they whirled up into the air, partially descended again, and then, caught once more in the current, sped rapidly away in the direction of the sea. To my eyes it seemed but a snowdrift, but many of my companions averred that it started up in the shape of a woman, stooped over the corpse and kissed it, and then hurried away across the floe. I have learned never to ridicule any man's opinion, however strange it may seem. Sure it is that Captain Nicholas Craigie had met with no painful end, for there was a bright smile upon his blue pinched features, and his hands were still outstretched as though grasping at the strange visitor which had summoned him away into the dim world that lies beyond the grave.

We buried him the same afternoon with the ship's ensign around him, and a thirty-two-pound shot at his feet. I read the burial service, while the rough sailors wept like children, for there were many who owed much to his kind heart, and who showed now the affection which his strange ways had repelled during his lifetime. He went off the grating with a dull, sullen splash, and as I looked into the green water I saw him go down, down, down until he was but a little flickering patch of white hanging upon the outskirts of eternal darkness. Then even that faded away, and he was gone. There he shall lie, with his secret and his sorrows and his mystery all still buried in his breast, until that great day when the sea shall give up its dead, and Nicholas Craigie come out from among the ice with the smile upon his face, and his stiffened arms outstretched in greeting. I pray that his lot may be a happier one in that life than it has been in this.

I shall not continue my journal. Our road to home lies plain and clear before us, and the great ice field will soon be but a remembrance of the past. It will be some time before I get over the shock produced by recent events. When I began this record of our voyage I little thought of how I should be compelled to finish it. I am writing these final words in the lonely cabin, still starting at times and fancying I hear the quick nervous step of the dead man upon the deck above me. I entered his cabin tonight, as was my duty, to make a list of his effects in order that they might be entered in the official log. All was as it had been upon my previous visit, save that the picture which I have described as having hung at the end of his bed had been cut out of its frame, as with a knife, and was gone. With this last link in a strange chain of evidence I close my diary of the voyage of the Pole-Star.

[NOTE by Dr. John M'Alister Ray, senior.—I have read over the strange events connected with the death of the Captain of the Pole-Star, as narrated in the journal of my son. That everything occurred exactly as he describes it I have the fullest confidence, and, indeed, the most positive certainty, for I know him to be a strong-nerved and unimaginative man, with the strictest regard for veracity. Still, the story is, on the face of it, so vague and so improbable, that I was long opposed to its publication. Within the last few days, however, I have had independent testimony upon the subject which throws a new light upon it. I had run down to Edinburgh to attend a meeting of the British Medical Association, when I chanced to come across Dr. P—, an old college chum of mine, now practising at Saltash, in Devonshire. Upon my telling him of this experience of my son's, he declared to me that he was familiar with the man, and proceeded, to my no small surprise, to give me a description of him, which tallied remarkably well with that given in the journal, except that he depicted him as a younger man. According to his account, he had been engaged to a young lady of singular beauty residing upon the Cornish coast. During his absence at sea his betrothed had died under circumstances of peculiar horror.]

4A whale is measured among whalers not by the length of its body, but by the length of its whalebone.

The Sea-Maiden
*J. F. **Campbell***

There was ere now a poor old fisher, but on this year he was not getting much fish. On a day of days, and he fishing, there rose a sea-maiden at the side of his boat, and she asked him if he was getting fish. The old man answered, and he said that he was not. 'What reward wouldst thou give me for sending plenty of fish to thee?' 'Ach!' said the old man, 'I have not much to spare.' 'Wilt thou give me the first son thou hast?' said she. 'It is I that would give thee that, if I were to have a son; there was not, and there will not be a son of mine,' said he, 'I and my wife are grown so old.' 'Name all thou hast.' 'I have but an old mare of a horse, an old dog, myself and my wife. There's for thee all the creatures of the great world that are mine.' 'Here, then, are three grains for thee that thou shalt give thy wife this very night and three others to the dog, and these three to the mare, and these three likewise thou shalt plant behind thy house, and in their own time thy wife will have three sons, the mare three foals, and the dog three puppies, and there will grow three trees behind thy house, and the trees will be a sign, when one of the sons dies, one of the trees will wither. Now, take thyself home, and remember me when thy son is three years of age, and thou thyself wilt get plenty of fish after this.' Everything happened as the sea-maiden said, and he himself was getting plenty of fish; but when the end of the three years was nearing, the old man was growing sorrowful, heavy hearted, while he failed each day as it came. On the namesake of the day, he went to fish as he used, but he did not take his son with him.

The sea-maiden rose at the side of the boat, and asked, 'Didst thou bring thy son with thee hither to me?' 'Och! I did not bring him. I forgot that this was the day.' 'Yes! yes! then,' said the sea-maiden; 'thou shalt get four other years of him, to try if it be easier for thee to part from him. Here thou hast his like age,' and she lifted up a big bouncing baby. 'Is thy son as fine as this one?' He went home full of glee and delight, for that he had got four other years of his son, and he kept on fishing and getting plenty of fish, but at the end of the next four years sorrow and woe struck him, and he took not a meal, and he did not a turn, and his wife could not think what was ailing him. This time he did not know what to do, but he set it before him, that he would not take his son with him this time either. He went to fish as at the former times, and the sea-maiden rose at the side of the boat, and she asked him, 'Didst thou bring thy son hither to me?' 'Och! I forgot him this time too,' said the old man. 'Go home then,' said the sea-maiden, 'and at the end of seven years after this, thou art sure to remember me, but then it will not be the easier for thee to part with him, but thou shalt get fish as thou used to do.'

The old man went home full of joy; he had got seven other years of his son, and before seven years passed, the old man thought that he himself would be dead, and that he would see the sea-maiden no more. But no matter, the end of those seven years was nearing also, and if it was, the old man was not without care and trouble. He had rest neither day nor night. The eldest son asked his father one day if any one were troubling him? The old man said that some one was, but that belonged neither to him nor to any one else. The lad said he *must* know what it was. His father told him at last how the matter was between him and the sea-maiden. 'Let not that put you in any trouble,' said the son; 'I will not oppose you.' 'Thou shalt not; thou shalt not go, my son, though I should not get fish for ever.' 'If you will not let me go with you, go to the smithy, and let the smith make me a great strong sword, and I will go to the end of fortune.' His father went to the smithy, and the smith made a doughty sword for him. His father came home with the sword. The lad grasped it and gave it a shake or two, and it went in a hundred splinters. He asked his father to go to the smithy and get him another sword in which there should be twice as much weight; and so did his father, and so likewise it happened to the next sword — it broke in two halves. Back went the old man to the smithy; and the smith made a great sword, its like he never made before. 'There's thy sword for thee,' said the smith, 'and the fist must be good that plays this blade.' The old man gave the sword to his son, he gave it a shake or two. 'This will do,' said he; 'it's high time now to travel on my way.' On the next morning he put a saddle on the black horse that the mare had, and he. put the world under his head,* and his black dog was by his side. When he went on a bit, he fell in with the carcass of a sheep beside the road. At the carrion were a great dog, a falcon, and an otter. He came down off the horse, and he divided the carcass amongst the three. Three third shares to the dog, two third shares to the otter, and a third share to the falcon. 'For this,' said the dog, 'if swiftness of foot or sharpness of tooth will give thee aid, mind me, and I will be at thy side.' Said the otter, 'if the swimming of foot on the ground of a pool will loose thee, mind me, and I will be at thy side.' Said the falcon, 'if hardship comes on thee, where swiftness of wing or crook of a claw will do good, mind me, and I will be at thy side.' On this he went onward till he reached a king's house, and he took service to be a herd, and his wages were to be according to the milk of the cattle. He went away with the cattle, and the grazing was but bare. When lateness came (in the evening), and when he took (them) home they had not much milk, the place was so bare, and his meat and drink was but spare this night.

On the next day he went on farther with them; and at

last he came to a place exceedingly grassy, in a green glen, of which he never saw the like.

But about the time when he should go behind the cattle, for taking homewards, who is seen coming but a great giant with his sword in his hand. 'Hiu! Hau! Hogaraich!!!' says the giant. 'It is long since my teeth were rusted seeking thy flesh. The cattle are mine; they are on my march; and a dead man art thou.' 'I said, not that,' says the herd; 'there is no knowing, but that may be easier to say than to do.'

To grips they go — himself and the giant. He saw that he was far from his friend, and near his foe. He drew the great clean-sweeping sword, and he neared the giant; and in the play of the battle the black dog leaped on the giant's back. The herd drew back his sword, and the head was off the giant in a twinking. He leaped on the black horse, and he went to look for the giant's house. He reached a door, and in the haste that the giant made he had left each gate and door open. In went the herd, and that's the place where there was magnificence and money in plenty, and dresses of each kind on the wardrobe with gold and silver, and each thing finer than the other. At the mouth of night he took himself to the king's house, but he took not a thing from the giant's house. And when the cattle were milked this night there *was* milk. He got good feeding this night, meat and drink without stint, and the king was hugely pleased that he had caught such a herd. He went on for a time in this way, but at last the glen grew bare of grass, and the grazing was not so good.

But he thought he would go a little further forward in on the giant's land; and he sees a great park of grass. He returned for the cattle, and he puts them into the park.

They were but a short time grazing in the park when a great wild giant came full of rage and madness. 'Hia! Haw! Hogaraich!!!' said the giant. 'It is a drink of thy blood that quenches my thirst this night.' 'There is no knowing,' said the herd, 'but that's easier to say than to do.' And at each other went the men. *There* was the shaking of blades! At length and at last it seemed as if the giant would get the victory over the herd. Then he called on his dog, and with one spring the black dog caught the giant by the neck, and swiftly the herd struck off his head.

He went home very tired this night, but it's a wonder if the king's cattle had not milk. The whole family was delighted that they had got such a herd.

He followed herding in this way for a time; but one night after he came home, instead of getting 'all hail' and 'good luck' from the dairymaid, all were at crying and woe.

He asked what cause of woe there was this night. The dairymaid said that a great beast with three heads was in the loch, and she was to get (some) one every year, and the lots had come this year on the king's daughter, 'and in the middle of the day (tomorrow) she is to meet the Uile Bheist at the upper end of the loch, but there is a great suitor yonder who is going to rescue her.'

'What suitor is that?' said the herd. 'Oh, he is a great General of arms,' said the dairymaid, 'and when he kills the beast, he will marry the king's daughter, for the king has said, that he who could save his daughter should get her to marry.'

But on the morrow when the time was nearing, the king's daughter and this hero of arms went to give a meeting to the beast, and they reached the black corrie at the upper end of the loch. They were but a short time there when the beast stirred in the midst of the loch; but on the General's seeing this terror of a beast with three heads, he took fright, and he slunk away, and he hid himself. And the king's daughter was under fear and under trembling with no one at all to save her. At a glance, she sees a doughty handsome youth, riding a black horse, and coming where she was. He was marvellously arrayed, and full armed, and his black dog moving after him. 'There is gloom on thy face, girl,' said the youth. 'What dost thou here?' 'Oh! that's no matter,' said the king's daughter. 'It's not long I'll be here at all events.' 'I said not that,' said he. 'A worthy fled as likely as thou, and not long since,' said she. 'He is a worthy who stands the war,' said the youth. He lay down beside her, and he said to her, if he should fall asleep,

162

she should rouse him when she should see the beast making for shore. 'What is rousing for thee?' said she. 'Rousing for me is to put the gold ring on thy finger on my little finger.' They were not long there when she saw the beast making for shore. She took a ring off her finger, and put it on the little finger of the lad. He awoke and to meet the beast he went with his sword and his dog. But there was the spluttering and splashing between himself and the beast! The dog was doing all he might, and the king's daughter was palsied by fear of the noise of the beast. They would now be under, and now above. But at last he cut one of the heads off her. She gave one roar RAIVIC, and the son of earth, MACTALLA of the rocks (echo), called to her screech, and she drove the loch in spindrift from end to end, and in a twinkling she went out of sight. 'Good luck and victory that were following thee, lad!' said the king's daughter. 'I am safe for one night, but the beast will come again, and for ever, until the other two heads come off her.' He caught the beast's head, and he drew a withy through it, and he told her to bring it with her there tomorrow. She went home with the head on her shoulder, and the herd betook himself to the cows, but she had not gone far when this great General saw her, and he said to her that he would kill her, if she would not say that 'twas he took the head off the beast. 'Oh!' says she, ' 'tis I will say it, who else took the head off the beast but thou!' They reached the king's house, and the head was on the General's shoulder. But here was rejoicing, that she should come home alive and whole, and this great captain with the beast's head full of blood in his hand. On the morrow they went away, and there was no question at all but that this hero would save the king's daughter.

They reached the same place, and they were not long there when the fearful Uile Bheist stirred in the midst of the loch, and the hero slunk away as he did on yesterday, but it was not long after this when the man of the black horse came, with another dress on. No matter, she knew that it was the very same lad. 'It is I am pleased to see thee,' said she. 'I am in hopes thou wilt handle thy great sword today as thou didst yesterday. Come up and take breath.' But they were not long there when they saw the beast steaming in the midst of the loch.

The lad lay down at the side of the king's daughter, and he said to her, 'if I sleep before the beast comes, rouse me.' 'What is rousing for thee?' 'Rousing for me is to put the ear-ring that is in thine ear in mine.' He had not well fallen asleep when the king's daughter cried, 'rouse! rouse!' but wake he would not; but she took the ear-ring out of her ear, and she put it in the ear of the lad. At once he woke, and to meet the beast he went, but *there* was Tloopersteich and Tlaperstich, rawceil s'tawceil, spluttering, splashing, raving and roaring on the beast! They kept on thus for a long time, and about the mouth of night, he cut another head off the beast. He put it on the withy, and he leaped on the black horse, and he betook himself to the herding. The king's daughter went home with the heads. The General met her, and took the heads from her, and he said to her, that she must tell that it was he who took the head off the beast this time also. 'Who else took the head off the beast but thou?' said she. They reached the king's house with the heads. Then there was joy and gladness. If the king was hopeful the first night, he was now sure that this great hero would save his daughter, and there was no question at all but that the other head would be off the beast on the morrow.

About the same time on the morrow, the two went away. The officer hid himself as he usually did. The king's daughter betook herself to the bank of the loch. The hero of the black horse came, and he lay at her side. She woke the lad, and put another ear-ring in his other ear and at the beast he went. But if rawceil and tawceil, roaring and raving were on the beast on the days that were passed, this day she was horrible. But no matter, he took the third head off the beast; and if he did, it was not without a struggle. He drew it through the withy, and she went home with the heads. When they reached the king's house, all were full of smiles, and the General was to marry the king's daughter the next day. The wedding was going on, and every one about the castle longing till the priest should come. But when the priest came, she would marry but the one who could take the heads off the withy without cutting the withy. 'Who should take the heads off the withy but the man that put the heads on?' said the king.

The General tried them, but he could not loose them; and at last there was no one about the house but had tried to take the heads off the withy, but they could not. The king asked if there were any one else about the house that would try to take the heads off the withy? They said that the herd had not tried them yet. Word went for the herd; and he was not long throwing them hither and thither. 'But stop a bit, my lad,' said the king's daughter, 'the man that took the heads off the beast, he has my ring and my two ear-rings.' The herd put his hand in his pocket, and he threw them on the board. 'Thou art my man,' said the king's daughter. The king was not so pleased when he saw that it was a herd who was to marry his daughter, but he ordered that he should be put in a better dress; but his daughter spoke, and she said that he had a dress as fine as any that ever was in his castle; and thus it happened. The herd put on the giant's golden dress, and they married that same night.

They were now married, and everything going on well. They were one day sauntering by the side of the loch, and there came a beast more wonderfully terrible than the other, and takes him away to the loch without fear, or asking. The king's daughter was now mournful, tearful, blind-sorrowful for her married man; she was always with her eye on the loch. An old smith met her, and she told how it had befallen her married mate. The smith advised her to spread everything that was finer than another in the very same place where the beast took away her man; and so she did. The beast put up her nose, and she said, 'Fine is thy jewellery, king's daughter.' 'Finer than that is the jewel that thou tookest from me,' said she. 'Give me one sight of my man, and thou shalt get any one thing of all these thou seest.' The beast brought him up. 'Deliver him to me, and thou shalt get all thou seest,' said she. The beast did as she said. She threw him alive and whole on the bank of the loch.

A short time after this, when they were walking at the side of the loch, the same beast took away the king's daughter. Sorrowful was each one that was in the town on this night. Her man was mournful, tearful, wandering down and up about the banks of the loch, by day and night. The old smith met him. The smith told him that there was no way of killing the Uile Bheist but the one way, and this is it — 'In the island that is in the midst of the loch is Eillid Chaisfhion — the white footed hind, of the slenderest legs, and the swiftest step, and though she should be caught, there would spring a hoodie out of her, and though the hoodie should be caught, there would spring a trout out of her, but there is an egg in the mouth of the trout, and the soul of the beast is in the egg, and if the egg breaks, the beast is dead.'

Now, there was no way of getting to this island, for the beast would sink each boat and raft that would go on the loch. He thought he would try to leap the strait with the black horse, and even so he did. The black horse leaped the strait, and the black dog with one bound after him. He saw the Eillid, and he let the black dog after her, but when the black dog would be on one side of the island, the Eillid would be on the other side. 'Oh! good were now the great dog of the carcass of flesh here!' No sooner spoke he the word than the generous dog was at his side; and after the Eillid he took, and the worthies were not long in bringing her to earth. But he no sooner caught her than a hoodie sprang out of her. ' 'Tis now, were good the falcon grey, of sharpest eye and swiftest wing!' No sooner said he this than the falcon was after the hoodie, and she was not long putting her to earth; and as the hoodie fell on the bank of the loch, out of her jumps the trout. 'Oh, that thou wert by me now, oh otter!' No sooner said than the otter was at his side, and out on the loch she leaped, and brings the trout from the midst of the loch; but no sooner was the otter on shore with the trout than the egg came from his mouth. He sprang and he put his foot on it. 'Twas then the beast let out a roar, and she said, 'Break not the egg, and thou gettest all thou askest.' 'Deliver to me my wife!' In the wink of an eye she was by his side. When he got hold of her hand in both his hands he let his foot (down) on the egg and the beast died.

The beast was dead now, and now was the sight to be seen. She was horrible to look upon. The three heads were off her doubtless, but if they were, there were heads under and heads over head on her, and eyes, and five hundred feet. But no matter, they left her there, and they went home, and there was delight and smiling in the king's house that night. And till now he had not told the king how he killed the giants. The king put great honour on him, and he was a great man with the king.

Himself and his wife were walking one day, when he noticed a little castle beside the loch in a wood; he asked his wife who was dwelling in it? She said that no one would be going near that castle, for that no one had yet come back to tell the tale, who had gone there.

'The matter must not be so,' said he; 'this very night I will see who is dwelling in it.' 'Go not, go not,' said she; 'there never went man to this castle that returned.' 'Be that as it pleases,' says he. He went; he betakes himself to the castle. When he reached the door, a little flattering crone met him standing in the door. 'All hail and good luck to thee, fisher's son; 'tis I myself am pleased to see thee; great is the honour for this kingdom, thy like to become into it — thy coming in is fame for this little bothy; go in first; honour to the gentles; go on, and take breath.' In he went, but as he was going up, she drew the Slachdan druidhach on him, on the back of his head, and at once — there he fell.

On this night there was woe in the king's castle, and on the morrow there was a wail in the fisher's house. The tree is seen withering, and the fisher's middle son said that his brother was dead, and he made a vow and oath, that he would go, and that he would know where the corpse of his brother was lying. He put saddle on a black horse, and rode after his black dog; (for the three sons of the fisher had a black horse and a black dog), and without going hither or thither he followed on his brother's step till he reached the king's house.

This one was so like his elder brother, that the king's daughter thought it was her own man. He stayed in the castle. They told him how it befell his brother; and to the little castle of the crone, go he must — happen hard or soft as it might. To the castle he went; and just as befell the eldest brother, so in each way it befell the middle son, and with one blow of the Slachdan druidhach, the crone felled him stretched beside his brother.

On seeing the second tree withering, the fisher's youngest son said that now his two brothers were dead, and that he must know what death had come on them. On the black horse he went, and he followed the dog as his brothers did, and he hit the king's house before he stopped. 'Twas the king who was pleased to see him; but to the black castle (for that was its name) they would not let him go. But to the castle he must go; and so he reached the castle. 'All hail and good luck to thyself, fisher's son: 'tis I am pleased to see thee; go in and take breath,' said she (the crone). 'In before me thou crone: I don't like flattery out of doors; go in and let's hear thy speech.' In went the crone, and when her back was to him he drew his sword and whips her head off; but the sword flew out of his hand. And swift the crone gripped her head with both hands, and puts it on her neck as it was before. The dog sprung on the crone, and she struck the generous dog with the club of magic; and there he lay. But this went not to make the youth more sluggish. To grips with the crone he goes; he got a hold of the Slachdan druidhach, and with one blow on the top of the head, she was on the earth in the wink of an eye. He went forward, up a little, and he sees his two brothers lying side by side. He gave a blow to each one with the Slachdan druidhach and on foot they were, and there was the spoil! Gold and silver, and each thing more precious than another, in the crone's castle. They came back to the king's house, and then there was rejoicing! The king was growing old. The eldest son of the fisherman was crowned king, and the pair of brothers stayed a day and a year in the king's house, and then the two went on their journey home, with the gold and silver of the crone, and each other grand thing which the king gave them; and if they have not died since then, they are alive to this very day.

*Took the world for his pillow. Editor's note.

THE FINISH OF THE 'FLYING DUTCHMAN'

C.J. Cutcliffe Hyne

'That brass belaying-pin you're handling,' said Mr McTodd, 'came from the main fife-rail of Captain George Vanderdecken's ship, *Flying Dutchman*. I helped myself to it. I now use it, as you see, as a paper weight on my desk.'

The wireless had been playing *Fliegende Holländer*, as we discovered from the programme in *The Scotsman*, and I suppose it was the tune and my action in using his paper weight to stamp out the smoulder from a pipe-dottel of his Ballindrochater grocer's abominable tobacco in the ash-tray, where it was smelling noisily, that brought the subject into conversation. Certainly the belaying-pin was of brass; it was extremely battered; it was of ancient vintage; and it was stamped G. van V. in ancient lettering.

'I do not,' said Mr McTodd, sitting back in his red plush chair, 'I do not see the connection between that tune and the windjammer our Chief boarded off San Thomé and which the old man said was the *Flying Dutchman*. Not that I ought to grumble, seeing that the Chief didn't come back to our packet, and being second, I was given the engine-room, though I'll admit I don't carry a Chief's ticket.' Mr McTodd poured whisky for himself, had an idea of passing me the bottle, but thought better of it. 'I'm a fully qualified engineer, ye'll understand, and was the pride of the Clydebank shops where I'd served my time, but when it comes to written examinations, the Board of Trade always dislikes my spelling.'

At this point the ex-mess-room steward, who was buder, cook, housemaid and general factotum of Mr McTodd's establishment, announced dinner, and we stepped across the room, swung our chairs on their pivots, and swivelled in to face our food. The table, which was of enduring mahogany, had a coaming round its edge, and was bolted sturdily to the floor; so were the chairs; and the mahogany panelling of the room was (as the furnishing people say) *en suite*. The whole scheme of the room was reminiscent of marine engineers' quarters afloat, and indeed had been bought, ready to install, from the shipbreakers' yard at Morecambe. It was built on the purest mid-Victorian lines, and though re-upholstered by its new owner in the richest red plush, still carried out its original scheme of offensive solidity.

We started dinner with some good rasping pea-soup, fragrant of the salt pork which formed its basis. Course number two was a rhombohedron of the salt pork, the aforesaid, garnished with boiled suet dumplings that would have pierced armour plate, and assisted by potatoes and tinned beans. A virgin Dutch cheese followed, blushing with rude health, but as it seemed a pity to cut into it when there were only two of us, we didn't.

A jar of pickled onions, hospitably uncorked, stood on the table's white oilcloth cover within easy fork reach of both of us, as did also a bottle of Mr McTodd's home-made whisky. But though I, like my host, strongly object to being robbed by the excise parasites of my country to the tune of eight-and-six a bottle, the McTodd brew is a few degrees above my capacity. I am a Sassenach, and lack the copper stomach of the hardy Scot.

'Three years this pork's been in barrel,' said the engineer. 'Fine stuff. If you'll pour a little of the pickle vinegar on to it with your onions, you'll find it brightens the flavour. Watch me.'

Part of the Vanderdecken yarn I had already picked up from Brabazon, who at the time had been master of the tramp S.S. *Betty Bedford*, from East India ports for Liverpool with rice cargo. Captain Brabazon did not call Mr McTodd blessed, but admitted that he was capable. His chief engineer, Mr Augustus Pighills, a member of the well-known Goole marine engineering family, was a trial.

'Pighills,' Captain Brabazon told me, 'could not be relied

175

on to go straight any of the time, and could be guaranteed to go crooked most of the time. The way that fat man soaked the chandlers for cumshaw on his engine-room stores was chronic, and the rake-off he got on bunkers made me blush. He wouldn't hand out my share, either. He was a dour, hard-hearted teetotaller on the top of it all, and boasted that when he was back on the beach at Goole he'd a good practice as a Methody Dick. He was the one and only inventor, so he said, of the Converted Engineer's Revivalist Mission. He told me there was far more in that than he bagged in royalties for his patent davit and releasing gear. Now I came across another of the Pighills engineering crowd that was chief on a little coaster in West Scotland, that was a decent man, barring that he carried a weak stomach. The *Bride of Dunvegan* she was, 183 tons —'

'Yes, but Augustus?' said I. 'The yarn goes that he transhipped from your *Betty Bedford* to Captain Vanderdecken's *Flying Dutchman*. You've told me just now I was no sailor when I said I thought the gyroscopic compass was a good idea, but you admitted I seemed to have an interest in the sea and sailormen. Just get back, skipper, please, to plump Mr Chief Engineer Augustus Pighills.'

Captain Brabazon twisted a length of string into the bore of his pipe, and drew out horrors. 'The fellow was pushed on to me by the shore superintendent, and I said

176

from the moment I clapped eyes on him he'd never make a comfortable shipmate. But he'd all the proper certificates, and testimonials, and office pull, and what not, and so they signed him on in spite of me. Little tubby chap he was, and I disliked him in the engine-room from the minute we cast off our wires from the quay in Bramley Moor dock. I may not be fond of the Scotch, but they've a right over ship's engine-rooms, and you feel unhomey when you've a foreigner like a Kelly from Cork or a Pighills from Goole taking their places. At least I am, and I never feel safe with them either. They bring in gadgets of their own, and inventions they want to try out, and before you're seven days at sea there's a tube burst, or a gauge-glass blown, and a half-boiled fireman for the old man and the steward to mend. He treated us to one of his smashes just after I'd brought up to an anchor off San Thomé.'

'Why disturb the San Thomé sea floor? Had you put in there to make sure the equator was carrying on with its job?'

Captain Brabazon regarded me with a sour eye. 'I'd gone in there to pick up a cable, as per instructions. That was before the days of wireless, and the charterers naturally wouldn't make up their minds till the last moment where my rice cargo was going to. Very tricky thing the rice market. Beats rubber, so they say. I pushed off to the beach myself. I always like San Thomé.'

'That's a very splendid building, the old amber-coloured Portuguese cathedral.'

'Well, Mister, my pub's round the North corner of it, and I tell you the lady who runs it is just fifteen-stone of all right, though I'll admit she does lay on that blue face powder too thick, and it's apt to get into your mouth. Teresa her name is, as you'll remember, though as I'm an old friend she answers to Tessa. My trouble was that our Mr Augustus Pighills came off to collect me. You see, there had been a delay in getting the reply cable, and my mate was a bit young, and —'

'Captain Brabazon, I OK every word of it. The cable station is disgustingly slow, and in my case there was a bad beach when the message did come through, and the surf-boat couldn't get off for another twenty-four hours. Besides, whatever else may be wrong with the equator since Einstein tampered with it, even the Astronomer Royal can't deny it raises a thirst.'

'It's pleasant not to be misunderstood for once. Our Mr Pighills had a song about a shark or a barracouta or something like that jammed in the weed filter of his condensers, and thought he'd like a couple more days for repairs. But I know my duty to owners as well as any shipmaster afloat, and naturally told him off in style, and in three hours it was up-hook from San Thomé bay, and off. But did that beastly mechanic clear his tubes, or whatever it was, and give me my lawful eight knots? He did not. He kept throttling down, presumably to pick chunks of fish out of his machinery, and then just as an ugly water-spout was bearing down on me, up comes one of his dirty coal heavers, chewing his sweat-rag, and giving me "Chief's comps, sir, and in three minutes main engines is going to stop for a three-hours repair." Now I ask you?'

'Probably genuine-to-goodness Act o' God, skipper. You mustn't book it all up to Goole. Besides, you had one Scot with your machinery, and whatever else N. A. McTodd may be, he's a capable engineer.'

'He is, Mister, though thirsty. But he and Pighills had been having a disagreement over a professional matter, connected with the thrust blocks, and Augustus had hit first with a cast-iron slush-lamp, and had sent the remains to his room. The slush-lamp I saw by the repairs-list was entered as "smashed — useless." But McTodd was put to sleep for eight hours.'

'Very creditable to Goole, if you come to think of it. I'll pull Mr McTodd's leg about that some day.'

'That wobble-kneed water-spout cruised down on us in style, and I tell you, with no weigh on I was frightened. The spout looked like delivering the goods fair on our starboard quarter. But it took a sheer, and swung astern, and then the top half sucked up into the black cloud above, and the bottom end boiled down, and away came a number-one-topside tornado, slewing around North-East-South before I could get my awnings furled.

'Well, of course, that was a sort of thing that might happen to anybody. But wait a minute. The air was that full of spindrift you could hardly see number two hatch from the upper bridge, and just then I heard a hand on the foredeck hailing that there was a wind-jammer trying to run us down. My eyes were feeling like pickled onions that had been well-chewed, but I slewed round to windward, and just caught the look of her. She was a rum-looking craft, barque-rigged, with single topsails, and (I'll trouble you) a lateen mizzen. She'd a high poop with funny kind of street lamps at the butt end of it, and forrard she'd a beak and a bowsprit stuck up at an angle of forty-five, with a pocket handkerchief of a square-s'l pulling like a bull-dog on the under side of it. She was pierced for about a dozen guns, but they were all in-board, and well-secured. She was steered by a tiller, and had four hands on the relieving taykles, regular Drake, and kids' books, and Armada style. Of course Mister, you'll say she couldn't have been, and I'd not got over that San Thomé jag at Teresa's. But there she was, blowing through it, slap athwart my bows, at a good nine-point-five, pushing her old bows into it to above the knight-heads.'

'One does meet funny kind of craft south of the line,' I admitted. 'There are similar nautical survivals up White Sea way.'

'Let me get a word in edgeways, Mister. This prehistoric freak cleared us to leeward, and then I'm hanged if she didn't go about, and flatten her sheets, and come sailing back again nearer to the wind's eye than a racing cutter. A great clumsy apple-bowed tub she was, just like one of those Armada pictures, and if you'd asked me, never went to windward in her life without the help of a tug and a tow rope. She rolled like a palm oil puncheon being hauled off a surf beach.

'Mark you it was blowing too; the wind was an equatorial tornado, running all-out; and it had eased my *Betty Bedford* of both quarterboats, all awnings, and everything else that would shift. Old-fashioned single-topsails she had, as I told you, and they went out when I was a boy. But she'd both fore and main set, and courses with never a reef tied down, and her big lateen mizzen was pushing away on the poop with the yard bending and whipping like a fishing rod. I tell you the quartermaster was nearly kicked away from her tiller at every second, but the four blokes on the relieving taykle knew their job, and amongst them they steered her as cleverly as those sharps in the fancy jerseys you see racing at Cowes.'

'Fine sailor-men, Captain.'

'The best that are left outside the churchyards,' Captain Brabazon admitted. 'Well, the old galleon, or whatever she was, made a short board of it, and rounded up and hove-to, main topsail aback, and then I'm hanged if hands didn't lay aloft, and rig whips to her yardarms, and start to hoist out a clumsy tub of a boat she carried in chocks on her deck amidships.

'It's my belief if they'd got her into the water she'd have blown away like a chip, but the breeze began to ease then, as is the way with these tropical blows, and though of course a hell of a sea got up in no time, that didn't seem to worry the ancient mariners worth a cent. Whiskers they had, all of them, most yellow-white, and they wore short P-jackets, and petticoats, and high sea-boots like the parties in the kid's pirate yarns I've been telling you about. The sour smell of her came down to us in waves: it was like the frowst in the bird-house in the Antwerp Zoo, Mister, if you've ever tried that.

'They hove up their boat off the chocks, bowsted her overside, and dropped her into the water. A clumsy clinker-built brute she was, a bit on the North Sea trawler's dinghy lines, only more so, and I don't suppose she'd have stove-in if she'd hit Mount Ararat. Four of those whiskered mariners tumbled in to her off the starboard main channels, and then an officer who looked a thousand went aboard and shipped a steering sweep. He'd pistols in his belt. All five of them had cutlasses strapped on. They were got up in regular kid-book buccaneer rig as I keep on telling you. But they were boatmen: I give them that. I'd no hands aboard the *Betty Bedford* that could have kept even one of my lifeboats afloat in a sea like what was running then.

'Then up on to the top of the fiddley climbs my fat Mr Pighills to see about a ventilator that had jammed, and "My Christmas!" says he. "Captain, but that's the *Flying Dutchman*."

' "I thought," said I, "you were teetotal."

'He didn't even trouble to answer that. He just climbed over on to my upper bridge without invitation. "Man, Captain," says he, "here's a legend come true. That boat's coming off to ask you to take letters to Holland. Don't take 'em. It means big danger, and the old *Betty* will sink soon enough without your helping her. She's just rotten. The main condensers are a comic opera, and though I called our Mr McTodd a liar over what he said about our thrust-block holding down bolts, I'll admit to you that half of them are stripped. But that packet of Captain Vanderdecken's immortal — up to a point, and if I can board her, and bring her people round to the True Faith, and let their weary bodies die comfortable like, I've got the best point any Revivalist Missionary ever had in this competitive world. Man, Captain, it's a thing I can retire on into a house of my own, with an institute attached, and very likely a two-seater. If you'll help me and don't balk things, I'll see you have your proper rake-off. Captain, think: this chance may mean a ten-pun note to you, or at the lowest seven pounds five".'

'Seems to be a man who was used to big figures, your stout Mr Augustus Pighills,' said I.

'Well, Mister, money continues to talk, and the master of an old 800-ton tramp like the *Betty Bedford* sees mighty little of it. I guess I fell to our Mr Pighills' blan-dish-what-you-calls like a Krooboy fades to gin. I ordered the mate to rig a guess-warp, but to put over no ladder, and Captain Vanderdecken, if that was old white whiskers at the steer oar, comes alongside like a *pukka* sailor, and bawls up to me in what was perhaps Dutch.

' "No savvy," I sang down to him. "Can do dago or pigeon".'

' "Can do," said he, and spouted a stream of what I recognised was French. But his Dutch accent was beyond me, mine, being the pure Marseilles variety. Then our Mr McTodd came out on deck and took over. He was still a bit what the doctors call whambly from that bash on the head with the cast-iron slush-lamp, but he'd the gift of tongues all right, though it struck me most was cross-bred Coocaddens and Clydebank.

' "Here you Dutchman, Captain Vanderdecken!" said McTodd. "Whit d'ye mean by being in these latitudes? You were doomed to roam in the Indian Ocean because you swore you'd tack board and board off the Cape till you weathered it on the passage westward, or hell froze over. You guaranteed to carry on along those lines, Captain, and that's why you were allowed to become a ghost. But now you have brought your packet round the bottom corner of Africa, and are doing naval manoeuvres off San Thomé. Captain, you've dirtied your ghost's ticket, and it's my idea you've been disrated, and are once more plain meat and bones seaman. That may not be the best Free Kirk theology, which my father who was minister of that body in Ballindrochater tried to ram into my heid. But it's common sense, which is a thing even the Churches in these modern times have to accept. Get me?"

' "Ja," said old hairy at the boat's steering sweep, and rather drooped, "Ja, *Mynheer*, I bin feel a change."

' "You'll not, during the time you been ghosts, have broached many stores, Captain?"

' "No," says Cappy Vanderdecken, "we don' eat nothing. Don' seem to have no appetite."

' "Nor drink?" says McTodd, sort of what you might call prophetic and eager.

' "Well, *Mynheer*, I keep the key of the spirit room hung to this chain round my neck — *so* — and so de schnaps ha'n't been touched."

' "Salt beef gone to mahogany," says McTodd. "Salt pork soaked into the barrel staves, hard-bread mere weevil-dust, but schnaps as bright as ever. Does schnaps improve like Madeira, Captain, by being carried round the Cape in a windjammer? I've never tried any; I've taken most of my spiritual refreshments hot from the still; but it shall never be said of me that I'm above being lairned. Couldn't you bring us off an anker of that old matured schnaps for this packet to drink your health in?"

' "Eet is cargo, and I could not in faith to my owners geef it to another."

' "Of course you couldn't, Cappie. My mistake. But I take it yours isn't a long ship?"

' "Pardon, but I do not get?"

' "Long ship: craft where it's a long time between drinks."

' "No, *Mynheer*. I am old, if you like, but I am Hollander, and in my country we keep the guest's cup full."

' "Man," said McTodd, "you almost persuade me to change my nationality. I'm Scotch, myself, though I'm sure you'd never guess it of me. Hand that boat along the guess-warp a bit further aft, and I'll board her through the well-deck gangway!" '

Captain Brabazon's account of proceedings was fairly good up to this, but faded off afterwards into wishes that he had accepted Teresa's invitation, and settled down in a partnership in the little restaurant at the back of the ivory-coloured cathedral in equatorial San Thomé. So after that sumptuous and succulent dinner in Mr McTodd's house at Ballindro-chater, I applied to him for further details. I used tact, and avoided any reference to the slush-lamp, which would have hurt his professional feelings. 'You were in your room, I believe, with a dose of malaria, when old Captain Vanderdecken came alongside the *Betty Bedford*?'

'Malaria was the currse, with all its distressing symptoms. But the emergency re-recuperated me. I'm a scientific observer, ye'll mind. I felt I'd a mission to note conditions, sanitary and otherwise, in that pre-historic windjammer, and so I tumbled into the boat, and told the hands to let go the guess-warp, and push off home. Unfortunately Pighills, who had been misrated as our packet's chief, insisted on coming also. The man was a poor engineer, with the most faulty theories on the lubricants needed for steam engines that have ever drifted to sea, and he was also a schismatic of the most poisonous school. He was worse than a UP. I warned him that trouble would come of it if he insisted on boarding the old windjammer, and sure enough as we were being ferried across, a six-inch flying fish shot out of the water, and bobbed into his fat mouth which he had open for convenience in cursing me. But, like a good many other unbelievers, he wouldn't be told. *Hinc* — you'll pardon me: I meant that — *hinc lachrimae.*

'For the sake of experience, and no' because I was forced, ye'll understand, I've signed on in some of the worst engine-rooms that have been carried across the wa'er. But never have I set foot on a worse sea-ruin than yon *Flying Dutchman*. She'd not a bit of wire on her. Her rigging was all hemp, stretched to the limit, and with the tar bleached out till it was white as a laundry show. Her decks had spewed their oakum, and were like sponge to the foot, and she hadn't a winch or a windlass about her. She'd capstans and pulley-haul taykles from her heavy lifts, and enough brass pins in her fiferails to make teeth for a saw. Think on to make me tell you about those belaying pins later. You've seen one of them.'

'I'm going to crack some of your walnuts with it now,' said I. '*G. van V.* are the initials on it, I see.'

'Well, Mister, teetotallers I hear drink port with walnuts. You stick to the sound home-brewed whisky you'll find in that bottle, and you'll live longer. Help 'self. G.W.V. stands for George William Vanderbilt, the party that had the extravagant yacht with the silver door-handles which old Pirrie bought and then sold to the breaking yard at

Morecambe. I had thought of buying some of her cabin fixtures to add to the furniture of this room. But when it came to the point, I looked around me, and refrained. It's pairfect, just pairfect, as it stands: best engineer's mess-room style: and if you can tell me people with better taste, I'd like to hear about them. That yacht stuff, when you came to look it over next morning, was a wee meretricious —'

'Was old Cappie Vanderdecken's packet a dry ship after all? Or perhaps you weren't invited below?'

'Invited? Lord help you, Mister, a quartermaster and one of the mates did the hall-porter business of bowing me to the door in the poop half-deck that led to the main cabin, and inside there was a steward with bunches of ragged riband at the knees of his plus-fours that nearly did a curtsey at the sight of me. That fat little Augustus Pighills came puffing along in my wake, but I suppose they'd got used to the look of sea-going engineers by then, because they took little enough notice of him.

'There was only five foot of head-room except between deck beams, which were frequent, so once inside I stayed sat, and that, Mister, as you'll know for yourself, is a bad observation point for a gentleman who is apt at times to exceed his high co-efficient of absorption. The schnaps when it came was a thing to make hymns about. Bit varnishy, of course, like all those Hollander drinks, but smooth as best tinned milk, and milk as a virgin's prayer. There are whiles, ye'll note, I drop into poetry. A ship-mate I sailed with, one Kettle, had the habit, and I caught it of him.

'The schnaps was in none of your nasty little bottles; the old Father Christmas steward in his doddering plus-fours with the swanky-bows served it out of a wicker-covered demi-john, no less, and though we supped it from horns that carried the taste of the last eighteen drinks they'd been used for, I doff my hat to Cappie Vanderdecken's cellar.

'Pighills was the blot on the cabin. Pighills is teetotal, and like all his breed always had to go around shouting about it. I personally dislike the Hun liver sausage; it always provides me with returrns; but do I make a song and dance about it? I do not, and put out my fork into the next dish as a gentleman should. Old Captain Vanderdecken was a gentleman, and forgave much to a guest. But I could see his mossy whiskers begin to bristle and twist at Pighills' cant and clack about the sin of swigging schnaps and the advantages of his conventicle down Goole way.

'But Pighills, with his two elbows locked in the standing fiddles of the black oak table, preached away without a break, and I just carried on with the wicker-covered demi-john to prevent further waste. Man, it was sinful to think of that beautiful schnaps being carried all those years uselessly about the stormy oceans.

'The row came when Cappie Vanderdecken produced his packet of letters. There must have been forty of them in the bundle, which was lashed up with spun-y'n. They were yellow and sea-stained, and tattered at the angles, ye'll mind that according to the histories they'd been hunting a mail-boat for 200 years.

'Mossy whiskers had got tired of being the pleasant landlord, and was now all captain. He tackled me first. "You," he said, "will take charge of these letters to our friends at home in Holland, and see that they are delivered."

'I disliked his tone. It had the regular deck bark that we in the engine-room always get narky over. But he was an old, old man, and I was grateful for his beautiful schnaps, and it had maybe softened some of my asperities. So I just said, "Captain, I'm not a postman. Moreover, mail carrying is a monopoly of the Government, and ships' officers on pain of keel-hauling and a fine not exceeding £1 sterling and costs are forbidden to carry other folks' letters. See 7 Vic. cap 22 *et seq.* Ye'll see my attitude?"

'My Law talk, translated into Dutch, was a wee above his heid, which was my intention. It was a pairfect bit of tact. The Old Man waved me back to the demi-john, and tackled Pighills, and there was an opportunity to Pighills' taste. I've always disliked the English in engine-rooms, especially when they are preachers, and Captain Vanderdecken shared my dislike.

'I can't report how the dispute went on, for after the first five minutes of it I slept. We'd been having a strenuous time on the *Betty*'s machinery since leaving San Thomé, nothing of course out of the way to a highly skilled engineer like myself, but I'll admit tiring. So I slept, with my head jammed down in the fiddle that held that wicker-covered gallon bottle.

'I was woke by a man falling over my back. Nothing in that, you'll say, Mister. It's a thing, as *you* know, that's happening every day in seaports all over the world. But this man started to cuff me over the heid on a spot where a few hours before I'd had a wee abrasion from a lump of cast iron. That woke me, and I found myself scrapping with that octogenarium in the plus-fours and the ribbon-bunches who had been acting pot-man. I'd respect for his years, and put him to the deck with a touch an angel might have envied.

'But that steward carried a bo's'n's whistle, which by sea law he'd no right to, and he put it in his gums, and blew as loud a call as a man with teeth could manage. All the petticoated sea-booted ship's company came pouring into the cabin off the main deck, smelling noisily, and I saw we were in for one of those little disturbances which you and I know so well, Mister.

'Pighills and Captain Vanderdecken were having a private

dog-fight of their own on the floor, and, being a Scottish gentleman, of course I didn't interfere with them. But that frowsty Dutch crew started attending to me; they looked really mean and ugly; and that low-roofed cabin with only five-foot head room under the deck beams was no place for a man who knows how to use his hands to get in real artistic work. So I broke through — and left casualties.

'For a windjammer of some 300 tons to-day, even with single topsails if you can imagine such freaks doing work on the seas now, we'd have a skipper and a mate and perhaps three deckhands. The cook would be on the head sheets. *Flying Dutchman* must have had seventy of a crew, and where they stowed below, the good Lord, who had presumably the freedom of the forecastle, knows. I was not invited there, and am ignorant of the way it was packed. The deck area was cluttered with gun carriages and chicken crates, and every kind of dunnage, and those Dutch could not all get on to me at once. But enough did, and they must have been bonny fighting men 200 years earlier. You may think tiredness and the malaria I told you about handicapped me, and perhaps they did a bit. But the three-quarter gallon of that pairfect schnaps that I'd put under hatches merely made me vivacious. Still, I'm free to admit to you, Mister, that I picked a brass belaying pin out of the main fife-rail to help put in the proper accents on my conversations. The pin's the one you're now stopping down the tobacco in your pipe with — and I always like to see friends load freely when they use my pouch. It's marked *G. van V.* Don't mind leaning back in that chair. The antimacassar will keep the grease in your heid from spoiling my red plush seating.'

'So they hove you overboard?' I suggested.

'Well,' said Mr McTodd thoughtfully, 'as the late Lord Balfour said in his *Essay on Philosophic Doubt*, weight tells. The Earl was a man who lived near Ballindrochater when he wasn't away earning his living in Parliament. I always wanted to meet him over a dram and drum into him my views on Empire politics, but I'll never have the opportunity now — in this world at any rate. It will be a satisfaction to him at this moment, if he's listening in from wherever he may be, to lairn that he's the weight of my opinion, based, mark you, on experience, on the theory of this thesis being correct. As a convinced metaphysician myself —'

'I tapped the table with the brass belaying pin. 'Drop politics, man, and get back to *Der Fliegende Holländer*.'

'I didn't know you'd the gift of tongues like that, Mister. But I wish you'd stop beating up my furniture. That last bat dinged the coaming. Better try a stand-easy on the home-brewed. This timber's best bay-wood mahogany as specified by the Shore Superintendents for marine engineers' mess-rooms. As regards those Dutch deck hands, as I've admitted already, numbers told. I can tackle seven any day and enjoy the job. But offer seventy, and you see me beat. I put in some good useful work with that brass pin you're handling, and brought it home with me. *Spolia opima*, and it's not one professional soldier out of a thousand that can point to those on his walls. But at last they hove me neck and crop into their clumsy clinker-built dinghy that was bumping against the old ship's bilge-streak, and it took thairty-seven of it to do the job. Also I'll admit that thairty of them had picked out those brass belaying pins, and each had given me the maximum bat over the heid permitted to his years.

'You've said, Mister, most injuriously, that in your opinion I'm all bone above the ears. But for that ancestral protection my brain would have been spread like a ham sandwich on my shoulder blades after the way those *Flying Dutchman* deck-hands battered at me. With the — the reinforcement aforesaid, and possibly a skinful of that pairfectly matured schnaps acting as a resilient, I escaped with nothing worse than a concussion, which, added on to the bat with the cast-iron — as-you-were — added on to the malarial symptoms I have spoken about already, made me a very interesting subject for enquiry for any young coroner who was whipping up a practice. Luckily the *Betty Bedford's* old man, Brabazon his name was, had seen similar cases previously in his sea career. He had me picked out of the old windjammer's quarter-boat when it blew in against his packet, and taken to my room, and laid out on my bunk, and covered with two blankets. He omitted the restorative of a second-mate's tot of whisky as by Board of Trade ordained for those apparently knocked-out. If I've not mentioned it before, I'll state now, the skipper was English, and therefore by nature thrifty about such important matters.

'What? No, Mister, I didn't see our Mr. Augustus Pighills again. He and Cappie Vanderdecken were enjoying a dog-fight on the cabin floor when I pulled out from that department for the more spacious main deck, and the last I saw was Cappie trying to ram his tattered packet of yellow mail with the spun-y'n lashing on it down the neck of my chief's dungaree overalls. He may have done it. I suspect he did, because getting someone to take off their mail was the one way of breaking the curse which lay on the *Flying Dutchman*; and even whilst I was enjoying that scrap I was telling you about on the main deck, with my back to the fife-rail I couldn't help but see that at every roll she brought up a bit lower in the water than she did the roll before.

'Of course, with Pighills "missing: believed drowned" the Old Man was pairfectly correct in promoting me Chief, though I'll admit that, thanks to the Board of Trade's beastly requirement in the way of spelling, I've never bothered to take out a Chief's ticket. The *Betty* didn't carry a third, so the donkeyman was promoted to that elevation, and he, feeling his new responsibility, got the condenser intake cleared — which was the cause of our stoppage — whilst I was confined to my room, and when I came-to there was the old girl grinding off her eight-point five, with donkey and a fireman standing watch and watch in the machine shop and calling themselves Second and Third Engineers, I'll trouble you, — the unqualified sons of perdition.

' "Missing; believed drowned," was the best we could send home to Goole to the relations and friends of Mr Augustus Pighills.

' "I didn't want you to push off to that couldn't-happen old windjammer as you know, Mr McTodd," says our *Betty Bedford's* old man. "But you being somewhat dazed with that knock" — "Malaria" said I — "dazed with any old thing you like, and hooked it without leave. So did the chief. It was your funeral. I saw you both board her, and those frosty-whiskered Santa Claus pirates bow at you arrival. I saw you both go below. Then for half an hour it was as-you-were, although the damned old ruin got in the trough and tried to roll herself over. But she kept afloat though scuppers spouted, and I wondered what kind of anti-sea-sick mixture they were giving you in the cuddy.

' "Pighills," Captain Brabazon goes on, "I never saw after he went below. But you shot out on to the well deck after about a two-hour wait with a fine tumult at your heels. It looked to me the old tub was settling in the water. But that didn't seem to impede your efforts. You put up a dandy scrap, Mac, and when in the finish they rushed you, and held an inquest, you didn't seem sufficiently dead to suit them. So they hove you over into the boat that was riding alongside, and you wagged hell back at them with that brass belaying pin that you have brought back on board of me here. The *Flying Dutchman* settled down out of sight by the time you'd drifted alongside me. We saw her mast trucks pulled under. I logged her as 'sailing ship, name unknown, sunk with all hands.' "

'There you have it, Mister. Captain Brabazon of the *Betty Bedford* was a man I never liked, he having, like Captain Vanderdecken, too much of the deck manner for the engine-room officer to really cotton to. But there was his evidence hot and new. He saw this brass belaying pin marked *G. van V.* brought aboard the *Betty Bedford*. Here it is now in my best mahogany and panelled parlour in Ballindrochater. What more do you want?'

'Was that the real end of the *Flying Dutchman*?' I asked.

'Do you read Lloyd's shipping list?' Mr McTodd asked.

'Not regularly,' I admitted.

'Well, read it, Mister, and next time you see "*Flying Dutchman*, G. Vanderdecken, Master," reported in those pages, you apply to me, and I will send you three dozen of my best home-brewed whisky. And, Mister, I don't give away valuable liquor like that unless I'm forced, being Scottish myself.'

I had to leave the brass pin marked *G. van V.* behind me, though I tried to annex it. A horrid thought hung in my head all through Mr McTodd's yarn that the master of the *Flying Dutchman* was named *van Straaten*, and I wanted to see if the people at the British Museum could connect that up with the *G. van V.* on the battered belaying pin.

BY THE LIGHT OF THE LANTERNS

Pierre MacOrlan

I

The first lantern scooted over the ship's bridge as though borne on invisible and diminutive legs, for the form of the one who carried it, mingled with the pitch-black of the sky, was indistinguishable. A torch caught up the fugitive gleam, and its light revealed the lantern-bearer as a huge, emaciated figure, whose smoke-dried visage displayed three terrifying apertures, two eyes and a mouth. The nose, so thin as to be imperceptible, appeared to have been eaten away by some abominable malady.

The lantern-bearer raised his light, so that it fell on the one with the torch, and the face of the latter was seen to be very much like that of the other. The three tremendous gaps in each face gave the two a common cadaverous likeness.

By the poop-deck, an ancient structure if there ever was one, other lanterns were changing place, like goblin lights at the entrance of a cemetery. In the starless sky, sombre masses of sails bent over the silent ship like clouds puffed by a tempest. The plash of the ship's stem, ploughing its way, was distinctly audibly. A confused sound of bare feet, their whereabouts revealed by chiefly thuds along the rigging, preceded a sudden flaring of the lanterns, which lighted up, one by one, like luminous flowers in the black fields on the borders of Acheron.

By the light of the lanterns, the night watch was hoisting the rigging and running about in shrouds. This strange spectacle might have passed as a funereal amusement in the land of dead souls. The uproar increased, and the grinding of pulleys mingled confusedly with the cries of curlews, skimming the silvered crest of the restless void.

In order to facilitate the activity of this maritime hive, a seaman raised his torch at arms' length; its gleam rode against the black sky and, on the bridge, cut to shreds the immense and comical shadows which, suddenly elongated, suddenly shortened, gave rise to a fantasy that made it impossible to identify the owner of any shadow — who was, after all, perhaps, but the shadow of his shadow. Occasionally, a bright-coloured cloth, yellow as butter, enveloping a carronade, would light up in a swift flash the brass work of cannon, rudely covered by a tarpaulin. At the foot of the main-mast, a tremulous, broken voice arose. It was that of a man singing:

When I adjusted your cockade
And turned your black neck round,
It was because I then was bound
To see C amar de, the naughty maid.

He stopped short, like a machine that had run down, and another, behind a lantern, chuckled. In a weak voice, the man finished the song.

The little laughter of the old men, like the sound of grain being shelled, spread among the shrouds, from group to group about the cannonry, then in process of being polished.

A commandant with a speaking trumpet was endeavouring to bring order out of the confusion, but on account of the wind, which sang melodiously through the rigging, the only sound to be made out was a sort of 'Oua, oua, ouao.' The boatswain's whistle resembled the lanterns, some of which had gone out. On the horizon, a narrow band of livid light indicated the line of separation between the blackness of sky and sea.

A thin, broken voice, which might have been that of the previous singer, stammered: 'L-l-larboard watch a-a-head.'

There was only one lantern left on the bridge. A man's voice spoke: 'It's another day.'

The glimmer of sunrise and that of a lamp were striving with each other in the cabin of the *Flying Dutchman*. The night watch already had betaken themselves to sleep, now that the sun had come once more to diffuse the gliding rays of the great and ambulant mystery.

Well steered by its masters against those rapid currents which lose themselves about the poles, the big ship, an eternal wanderer, now made for unknown seas, far from the frequented paths of men, in order that its crew might enjoy a daytime repose without being on the alert and without having to listen for the unpleasant sound of a trumpet, calling the dead to their post of combat.

The sailors aboard this good ship, the hardened wood of which had stood the test of time, owed allegiance to a certain perjured captain, who, like the land-holder, Juan Espera-en-Dios or Bouttedieu, roamed the seas, the paths across the plains, the woods and villages of the world with no new sight ever to greet his eye.

The captain bore the name of Peter Maus. He was a native of Düsseldorf and had been immobilized by death under the aspect of a skeleton-like old dotard, wearing for two hundred years the identical costume he had worn as a living being, at the time he had traded for Holland. He had been a good spender, then, with the sons of Amsterdam, who were skilled in the practice of a wholesome and peaceable debauchery, accompanied by numerous divertissements of a more or less gross nature.

The love of women, so far from being able to save him from his destiny, had not been able to triumph over that other destiny which impelled him incessantly toward new adventures, which he always hoped would be more thrilling than any gone before; and now, alone with his secret, in the company of his crew, he was sailing the seas with a hundred outlawed rascals and a handful of imbeciles who had been shanghaied aboard the big ship freighted with despair.

The lieutenant belonged to the same generation as the captain. He was a Norman of Dieppe, Pierre Radet by name, commonly known as Little Pierre. He knew Peter Maus' secret and, like the latter, aspired feverishly to a repose for which he dared not hope. In the solitude of the cabin, populated with world-maps and compasses of a form long since fallen into desuetude, these two would sit, their heads between their hands, studying the charts and keeping a sharp lookout for the reef they longed to strike, which should plunge them once more into a real death, a death which should be no mere legend but an eternal rest. But in spite of the precision of their manoeuvrings, the bewitched currents always kept the *Flying Dutchman* far from shipwreck and destruction.

The day watch having been told off, while the remainder of the crew took such repose as they could in the ship's broadsides, under the pale light of the northern sun, which spread a great cloth of golden spangles over the sea, Peter Maus and Little Pierre would experience an envious desire to eat and drink. Their mummified organisms, however, could serve them no longer; their needs did not correspond to their desires. They were animated by a ferocious hatred of the earth and of the old life they had led among the living; and accordingly, they would clench their fists and amuse themselves in the patient and edifying contemplation of the punishments which they proposed to visit upon the living, if, some day, divine grace should permit them to share once more in life.

In their sacrilegious ignorance, these two old madmen, without being aware of the fact, would be praying to heaven.

'O God,' they would groan, 'grant that we may meet upon our way but one living being, fat and chubby, and grant, in thy all-powerful kindness, that we may torture him and make him suffer to suit our pleasure.'

And they would add, childishly: 'Grant, O God, that we may make a meal of bread and sausages, just once more.'

Then, Pierre Radet, known as Little Pierre, would take from the cupboard an empty bottle and two glasses. He would place them dreamily on the table, brushing them off with the flap of his round-jacket. Then he would go through the motions of pouring wine, and first one and then the other would put the glass to his withered old lips and pretend to drink.

Madness would shake them, suddenly, and the bottle would be hurled to the floor. The bottle would break.

Little Pierre would lament his luck and begin whimpering: 'Don't break the damned bottle, for the love of God. Soon, or we shan't have any more bottles, and then, we'll not be able to pretend that we're drinking.'

Sometimes they would suck on a long empty white-clay pipe, and then, with their eyes sunken in their emaciated sockets, they would recall the good old days and hate life to their hearts' content, that life so fertile in pleasures, that life the gestures of which they sought, in their distress, to reconstruct by means of a sterile and imaginative parody.

'After thinking it over well,' said Little Pierre, 'it is better to be dead. For the weak point with us, when we were sailors, was putting into port; in one night, the result of six or seven months' labour would run aground in the purse of Ninon la Bretonne.'

'You forget Angela Cecchi of Palerma,' said Peter Maus.

'Ah, yes, Angela Cecchi and her little place at the foot of the Pellegrino.'

Once more, they would plunge into their memories. Each

of them, in his fleshless head, under its cover of dried skin, would launch forth upon a weird sea of images, at once naïve and perverse, at times vague, at times endowed with the perfection of absolute design.

'There is a God,' Peter Maus would declare. 'Who could doubt it, seeing that we have been damned by Him for all eternity? It was different when I was a child — I don't care to recall how many years ago that was — I believed in God then, all right, but I wasn't sure of anything. I said my prayers like the other children, as a matter of precaution, and in order to put all the chances on my side. Since then, I have acquired the absolute certainty of a divine providence.'

'Well, Maus,' Little Pierre would speak up in his turn, 'does that mean that we're going to have to sail the long stretch without putting in for all eternity?'

'I could eat an orange,' Maus would remark, clacking his skinny mouth, which was like an old leather purse.

'Imbecile,' Little Pierre would reply, shrugging his shoulders.

He would reach out his hand for the bottle, and the two again would go through the motions of drinking. Their shoulders would shake in foolish laughter. Clinking their glasses, they would repeat a tremulous toast:

'Here's to you, youngster.'

'Same to you, sailor.'

Whereupon, Little Pierre would arise and, stumbling like a drunken man, would begin to curse roundly the sea, mankind, and everything under the sun.

In the broadsides, the crew listened with the smiles of veteran connoisseurs to the vociferations of the two old dotards. Swinging in their hammocks, they were not asleep. They, too, pretended — pretended to sleep, though sleep was an unimportant matter to them, since they were dead; all day long, they dreamed madly, haunted by life-like images of unfulfilled desires.

The sun dived once more into the cold waters of the Antarctic sea, and with the first stars, the watch came down. Their coarse boots clattered on the gunroom ladder, and the night life of the ship began again. As a precaution against meeting a vessel manned by living beings, the tarpaulins covering the cannon were removed, and, on the bridge at the foot of the mainmast, guns and long-bladed knives with handles of rough wood were stacked. A whistle from the captain of the watch called the men to their posts. Some of the crew, who were litde more than skeletons, hardly could stand against the wind, which filled the sails like leather bags, while others, twisted into pitiful shapes, looked like grapevines in a storm.

Towards midnight, the blind lookout, who had been stationed at his post as a jest, gave a long raucous blast upon his horn. Already, however, the crew of the *Flying Dutchman* were leaning over the gunrails, regarding with open mouths a terrifying and luminous apparition, which was bearing down upon them with the regular, rhythmic breathing of a good healthy beast.

A long row of lamps adorned the sombre mass of an enormous vessel. The crew of the *Flying Dutchman* contemplated, without a word, this magnificent craft, which was, perhaps, to be their liberator, and which seemed even more phantom-like than their own.

'It's the end!' cried Peter Maus, all of a sudden. 'Lads, we're really going to die this time. Down on your knees, lads, and thank God, as you see me doing.'

All fell to their knees and beat their heads on the deck, in the hope of a catastrophe which should put an end to their cruise.

They did not raise their heads at the sound of a distant and rather dull detonation. Suddenly, a great sheaf of flames spurted up from the brilliantly lighted vessel, and a shower of débris of all sorts fell on the deck of the *Flying Dutchman*. Instinctively, since they had nothing to fear, the crew raised their elbows, protectingly.

When they opened their eyes, the sea was deserted. In place of the huge ship, there was nothing but an expanse of smooth water.

Peter Maus shook his fist in the face of heaven, and the blind lookout, high among the shrouds, laughed.

It was then that a feeble cry from the sea caused every mother's son to pick up his ears. It was, without doubt, the wail of a little child. The voice was small and hoarse. One could picture a baby, with its wry and rumpled face, shaking its chubby fists and kicking up its little feet.

'Let down the long boat,' ordered Peter Maus.

The ancient pulleys groaned, as, not far away on the bosom of the sea, the cry of an infant arose, unmistakably, on the air.

II

In a violent odour of iodine, seaweed, and wet wood, the long boat was drawn up, and with it, a very small baby in a three-piece hood, with a red face and little fingers perpetually in motion. It might have been some ten or twelve months old. Its big round eyes surveyed without fright the funereal visages of the dead seamen who crowded about it.

'Faith,' said Little Pierre, 'it's really a live baby. It is round and well formed.'

All about the infant, the ghostly figures pressed, gazing upon their prey with eager eyes. They examined it with great exaltation, but their glances revealed nothing of what was in their inmost thoughts.

At daybreak, Peter Maus and Little Pierre, who had installed the child in the ship's cabin, began considering how they were going to contrive to bring it up. A ship peopled by dead men who did not eat naturally contained no provisions.

'This child is alive,' said Peter Maus. 'There can be no doubt of that. Can a live being go on living among dead men? I do not think so. We might kill the brat, and perhaps, a little dead one like him would liven things up a bit aboard ship, with his pretty little ways and all that sort of thing, which one expects to find in a child of good bringing-up.'

'This child is too small to give us much amusement,'

replied Little Pierre. "Let's bring him up till he's ten; at that age, on the day of his first communion' (and Little Pierre crossed himself) 'we will kill him; and then, we shall have a little dead cabin boy to lighten our labours.'

'Your plan is adopted,' said Peter Maus, 'and we shall look about among the hulks of this craft we have frightened into shipwreck to see if we can find some sort of nourishment for this little milk-lapper.'

A leading French newspaper carried in its columns the following information, which is curious enough in its way:

Shanghai, July 10, 1921.

The Japanese cruiser, *Nogi*, returning from target practice, recently encountered, in the offing of the bay of Along, a vessel which, with its fires extinguished, was making in a southerly direction. Having given the usual signals, the commodore gave the order to stop the ship and fitted out a whale-boat to board the mysterious craft.

It was found that the vessel in question, a Swedish freighter, had been completely plundered and abandoned. It contained no provisions of any sort. There was one curious detail. In the officers' cabin, the cover had been laid, and a few morsels of food were in the last stages of putrefaction.

It is difficult to imagine the motives which had forced the crew of this ship instantly to abandon their occupations. The affair has the appearance of a Bolshevik atrocity.

This dispatch, read by thousands, did not catch the attention of the crowd. It conveyed a superficial hint of romantic adventures, but it was not detailed enough to be highly interesting. Strictly speaking, the discovery made by the cruiser, *Nogi*, had in it the elements of a romance of rare perversity, but one, of course, which could lay no claim to the approving interest of serious folk.

There was no one in the world, not even the most credulous sailor, but would have had his doubts, had he been told that at the bottom of this mysterious drama was to be found a tiny infant, picked up by one of the crew of damned souls aboard the eternal *Phantom Ship*. One survivor of the adventure there was who, after a few glasses in a tavern swept by seaside breezes, had a tale to tell: of how, one night in the Pacific, his ship had been assailed by an invisible crew, by the light of innumerable lanterns. His tale was listened to with the respect commonly accorded a *raconteur* of quality, without any one's believing a word of the narrative.

The *Flying Dutchman*, commanded by its skipper, Peter Maus, continued on its endless tack and ran up the black flag in place of the one it originally had flown. Frequently, in the middle of the night, the harsh sound of à trumpet would give the signal to clear the decks for action, and fifty lanterns would scamper over the bridge. And the *Flying Dutchman*, rising in all its haughtiness out of the darkness, would hurl forth its adventurers to plunder the goods of the living.

The child prospered among the dead. Little Pierre patiently fattened it up with the aid of bottles of preserved milk. Sometimes, they would spread a coverlet on the bridge, and every one would come to look at the baby, wallowing in its bed of soft wool. The dead men, clustered about the rosy infant, would take on the appearance of stones and old marbles. Part of their skeletons at times showed through their dry, cracked skins. They called the child 'the Rosy King'; and as a matter of fact, he did resemble those roses, at once fragile and robust, which flourish in little village churchyards.

The Rosy King grew and learned to repeat docilely the words which were taught him. He expressed himself a little in all languages, speaking all of them in an antiquated form.

During the night, he would play about, leaping like a familiar demon over the lanterns and climbing up to the lookout to tease the blind old salt who was always so restless. He would roll on his back like a cat, catching the dead men round their pins and crying: 'Come on, now, you old beast, give me my stick.' And the crew would find much amusement in it all, and think, 'What a pretty little dead boy Rosy King will make. For all eternity, we shall be able to refresh our souls with his gestures, his words, his cries and his little hurts.'

In the cabin, between the map of the world and the maritime charts, among the piles of preserve-bottles and biscuit-packages, which had been taken aboard from plundered cargoes, the young Rosy King would listen benevolently, with his knees on a stool, to the monotonous counsels of the captain and the second officer.

'How is it,' the child would ask, 'that you are so different from me? And besides, you have such a funny odour. And you don't eat like me nor drink milk and sweet water.'

'That,' Peter Maus would reply, 'is because you are now living in the kingdom of the dead. Here, on this ship, we are all dead ones.'

'What is a dead one?' Rosy King would inquire.

'You don't understand.'

'Ah, I want to be dead like you, like Little Pierre, like Gruida, the boatswain, and like Loiselet who plays the flute. I want to be dead like you, so I can have a pretty brown skin, and so I can crack the bones in my hands. I'd like to run over the bridge with a little lantern.'

'We were just like you, fat and chubby youngsters, when we were alive.'

'Where do the alive people live,' the child would ask, 'on the English coast?'

Peter Maus gave up trying to explain the double mystery

215

of life and death, but each day, Rosy King would listen to the former's curses against those enigmatic beings, the living, whom the captain held responsible for his own damnation.

Certain nights, under the diabolical light of the lanterns, the dead crew would dance, hurling abominable threats at the living. Having gone through the motions of drinking, they would imitate the excesses of drunken men; and then, they would light a fire in their empty pipe-bowls, and their mouths would suck in, voluptuously, the green and yellow flames.

The young Rosy King was now twelve years old. He presided at these celebrations, playing horseback with a cannon. He would clap his hands, ravished by the spectacle, which for him was the most amusing one he could dream of.

'One day, I shall be dead like them,' he thought, and his little bosom would heave with pride.

III

Clad in a coat of scarlet cloth, which formerly had belonged to Peter Maus, and which an ingenious spectre had retailored, after a half-way fashion, Rosy King had further obtained from Little Pierre, who was inclined to spoil the child, a tiny lantern, which he would brandish by night as he galloped over the worm-eaten deck of the *Flying Dutchman*.

He loved this life by one's wits aboard the famous ghost-ship, and he was vastly amused by the terror-stricken faces of poor mariners, surprised in mid-sea by the rapid passage of the vessel, the crew of which were the victims of so wondrous a punishment. But he loved, above all, to stand against the poop-house and listen to the dead as they took vengeance on the living. The child had come to consider these living beings as mysterious, cruel, perverted in character, and with unsavoury pasts behind them — as a people from whom he must guard himself at all costs.

Later, thanks to the conversation of Little Pierre, he had created for himself a conception of life that was all his own, one that the infernal environment in which he had been reared only tended to strengthen. Life impressed him as being a distant catastrophe, so distant that he was unable precisely to estimate its dimensions; but he had a frightful chill, every time he thought of it at all attentively. His youth, however, did not permit of any but the briefest meditations. And so, he grew up, in the broadsides of this legendary ship, without any point of comparison which would give him a chance for a reasonable appraisement of his exceptional situation.

Then, one day, Peter Maus, contemplating the childish grace of the lad, who had grown to quite a size on a diet of fishes, which he now caught with considerable skill, conceived the idea of redeeming past sins by one good deed. So he said to Little Pierre:

'Lieutenant, the more I think of it, the more I am struck with the idea that Providence, in sending us, upon a wreck, this little living creature, was merely trying us out. Don't you believe that we would be acting in accordance with the ends of Providence, if we were to give the child back to life? True enough, the presence among us to a little rascal of a dead lad could not help relieving the bitterness of our fate; but I do not think that God has placed him in the path of the *Flying Dutchman* to meet that same fate. What do you think?'

Little Pierre brought the long bones of his hands together over his knees.

'I think the same as you,' he replied, 'that it would be best to set the child ashore; and perhaps, if we did so, it would bring us a little divine favour.'

'Very well, we'll set him ashore, along the coast, tomorrow night; yes, we'll set him ashore along the Breton coast, near Auray, on holy ground. Let's be sure to put all the chances on our side.'

'You old villain,' remarked Little Pierre.

Whereupon, Peter Maus straightened himself and yelped: 'Cross yourself! You swine! Cross yourself! You blasphemer! You Judas, you! Youjudas!'

They fought, and the clashing of their arms was like the sound of wooden sticks.

The following day, shortly before nightfall, Peter Maus called Rosy King to him and, pointing out with one finger a grey band on the horizon, said to him: 'There is the land from which you came to which you are going to return. You cannot stay with us any longer. God will not permit it . . . I have spoken to you angrily about God sometimes, but I was wrong; I spoke as all the damned do, as you will understand, too late, if you ever come to this state . . . Almighty God has given you life, and we cannot make a dead one out of you.'

The child began to cry: 'Let me die by your side, O Peter Maus, and I will make you laugh by imitating old Gruida when he plays the flute.'

But Peter Maus shook his head, and the lad, shrivelled up with despair, threw himself down on the bridge and set up a weird wail that was enough to tear the heart out of any man.

'Of course, you couldn't have avoided this,' grumbled

Little Pierre. 'It would have been better to set him ashore without telling him all that.'

Night came, and the Southern Cross shone in the sky. With all sails filled, the *Flying Dutchman* soon left the tropics behind, in a supernatural effort to take advantage of the favouring winds. Soon, the quiet harbours of old Europe hove into view.

The skeleton crew, drawn up on deck, gazed at the lad as he stood, shivering with fright, in his scarlet coat of ancient cut. The lanterns on the bridge outlined the dark shadow of each man, but all the light streamed on Rosy King's white face and chattering teeth. Then, there came a noise like the rustling of wings, and the sound of the yawl, brushing the ship's sides, was heard.

'Come, Rosy King,' said the captain, 'say good-bye and pray for us. Here's a little silver to buy candles. The first woman you meet will tell you what you should do for the repose of our souls.'

'I don't want to live!' screamed Rosy King. 'Let me be, Peter Maus, let me be!'

They lowered the lad down into the yawl, and Peter Maus took the tiller. The oars ground in their tholes. Soon, a black line hollowed itself out into a semi-circle.

'Attention,' commanded Peter Maus, 'back water all around.'

The yawl snapped throughout its frame.

'Pull to the larboard,' directed Peter Maus.

The bottom of the yawl grated on the shingles, and Peter Maus carefully stepped overboard. The water came up to his thighs. He took Rosy King in his arms and made for land.

A frightful whistling filled the night.

'Don't be afraid,' said Peter Maus, 'it's only the wind in the trees!'

He deposited Rosy King at the foot of a white path that ran back into the land; then, with great strides, he regained the long boat.

Rosy King, paralyzed with fright, stood still, without a whimper; but as the long boat receded farther and farther from shore, in order to regain the *Flying Dutchman* as quickly as possible, as is the law of dead souls, the cry of a child might have been heard. It was the cry of a dying soul, lamenting its fate.

'Good-bye, Rosy King,' cried Peter Maus once more, from the long boat.

MAREDATA AND GIULIO

OR

THE OCEAN SPIRIT

The sun, ere he sank on the bosom of the ocean, brightened the coast of Calabria with his farewell rays. A sweet twilight shed its softening influence over the earth; the ocean flamed in gold and purple, and seemed adorned like the bed of a royal bridegroom, to receive its glorious guest. The gentle breeze of the west floated warm and mild through the air; and the heat of a bright day had given way to a refreshing balm. With her mysterious veil the approaching night covered the surrounding objects. A new world appeared to have risen on the well-known shore, and new charms were added to its original grandeur. Yet still this beautiful scene was lifeless, no human form broke its solitude. One might fancy the ocean and sky enamoured of their own beauty, wished to disclose their charms only to each other, free from the profaning gaze of man.

At length a youth arrives to enjoy the silent wonders of nature; a youth worthy of seeing the goddess without her girdle; — Giulio, the only son of the rich and powerful Count of Monte-fuoco. He delighted in swimming through the gende waves flowing along the flowery shore. The heat of the season heightened the pleasure he took in those exercises, and soon the stormy element owned his power; for the water seemed gratefully to yield to his efforts, and proud of bearing his god-like form: never, he thought, the floods had played so warmly, so lovingly, round his limbs. It was as if out of every little wave, there arose a flattering voice; the waters, sparkling in changing colours in the last rays of the sun, appeared to him like a thousand mirrors, presenting smiling eyes and divine forms to his enchanted soul. But, lo! how he started, when suddenly he beheld close to him a woman of such heavenly beauty, that if he at first in his dreams had taken the phantoms of his imagination for beings of substance, he now mistook reality for a vision. But the idea of the dangerous situation wherein the fair one was placed recalled his senses; he clasped his arms round her slender limbs, a grateful fascinating glance gave him strength, he swam towards the shore, where he soon beheld his delightful burthen in safety; here he left her in order that he might procure his garments. Having thrown his mantle over his shoulder, he rejoined the fair being, who had, in the mean time, repaired the disorder of her dress, which, in the splendour and brightness of its appearance, seemed to consist of the silver foam of the sea. On his approach, she fell on her knees and embraced his feet, with looks full of gratitude and love. He raised her hastily, and full of respect, asked to know whom he had the happiness to save, and whence she came? A fear clouded her eye; she shook her head, laid her finger on her mouth, as if to say she was deprived of the power of speech, and pointed in answer to his question with her white hand to the sea. He addressed her in different languages, but although she seemed to understand him perfecdy well, she remained silent.

Giulio led the unknown lady to the Castle. The family received her with politeness; but the Countess and her daughters, envious of the more than human beauty of the stranger, treated her with a degree of reserve bordering on coolness. They contrived, nevertheless, to give her the assistance her misfortune seemed to require. Giulio's heart was now the seat of the most ardent passion; the image of the silent lady never left his fancy for a moment. He endeavoured, in a thousand different, ways, to induce her to utter a single sound, but all in vain; neither was she able to answer to his questions, written in different idioms. 'Do you write no language?' asked he. — 'No!' was the sense of her replying gesture. The mother of Giulio made some contemptuous reflections respecting the education of the mysterious lady: but she by her gentle and humble behaviour, attempted to soften the haughty spirit of the Countess, and succeeded. She even gave proof of a more refined education, in once taking a lute, and drawing from it the most celestial tones. All the deep feelings, which her eyes expressed, seemed now to have found a corresponding language. The sounds fell on the listeners' ears like an unknown mysterious harmony of a better world, and filled their hearts with delight and rapture. Inclining over her lute, she often fixed her eyes, full of the tenderest love, on Giulio, and a tear stole slowly over her cheek. As still she remained silent, it became necessary to give her a name, and Giulio called her MAREDATA, which, in Italian, signifies 'given by the sea'.

From the first moment, the old Count, partial to beauty, had been the declared champion of the silent lady. Nevertheless, he was strangely surprised when once the youth declared, with a fire and vehemence that would admit of no contradiction, that he could no longer exist without the possession of Maredata. The wise Count knew that passion would become more violent by opposition, and, therefore, did not withhold his consent to their union. The church sanctified their love, and Giulio, in the possession of Maredata, thought himself the happiest mortal. A sweet boy soon increased their mutual felicity. Giulio accustomed himself in time to her silence, and understood so perfectly well her eloquent gestures, that he almost imagined her inaudible language to be the true idiom of love.

Once, as he returned from the chase, his sister Manuela met him, and with an appearance of great anxiety, drew him into her lonely closet. 'My dear brother,' said she, 'I tremble to impart to you a discovery I have made, for it may prove destructive to your happiness, but the fear of seeing you in the snares of some supernatural and malicious being overcomes all other considerations. Know, then, that about an hour ago I passed Maredata's apartment, when I heard a tuneful voice singing to the accents of the lute. I entered suddenly, and found Maredata, who seemed extremely embarrassed, and relapsed immediately into her accustomed silence. 'Now,' added Manuela, 'what a false heart must hers be, if she, able to speak, can be silent to you — to you, the founder of all her happiness! What can be her aim, but to destroy your body and your soul?'

Giulio, deeply affected, hastened to Maredata, requesting an explanation of this extraordinary event, and conjured her to break her long silence. But Maredata, with tears in her eyes, presented him their child, and seemed by the sweetest caresses to make her amends for disobedience. Her loving husband was soon appeased. He entreated her to accompany him on a walk, and, perhaps without intention, he led her to the sea-coast. The ocean lay before them, brightened by all the lustre of an Italian moon-light. The effect which the sight of the element made upon Maredata was as unexpected as it was wonderful. Her eyes sparkled with delight, she spread out her arms, uttered a cry of joy, and threw herself into the waves. Giulio stood amazed, but soon he beheld her rise smiling and nodding at him, and swimming with an astonishing agility and grace. Her slender form appearing through the floods and the silver light of the moon, seemed not to be that of a mortal. Love and anxiety filled her husband's bosom, and he followed her into the sea to protect her in the dangerous element. If ever the waters had appeared sweet to him, it was now. He thought a soft music sounded from the depths, alluring voices invited the couple to sink in the mysterious bosom of the floods, and indeed, in the arms of Maredata, he sunk deeper, till he almost lost his senses, when Maredata suddenly threw out a cry of despair, and seizing him with both her arms, moved towards the shore, where she deposited him on the very spot where he had once placed her. Soon her endeavours and her caresses called him again to life. 'Who art thou?' cried he, 'wonderful being, who art thou?' But Maredata, taking his hand, fled with quick steps, and encircled her veil fast round her ears, as if to avoid the seducing sound of the roaring waves, which rose higher and higher, pursuing the beautiful fugitive. Arrived at the casde, he repeated his entreaties to her to solve this mystery. But Maredata clasped her lily arms round him, and her soft expressive eye asked him, 'Am I not thine? Art thou not happy? Why askest thou more?' And indeed Giulio seemed to be satisfied; he even promised, he never would ask her again, and consented to lead her shortly to another castle in the heart of the country, where she would not be troubled by the sight of the sea. The joy which sparkled at this assurance in her eyes was his sweet reward, and once more a happy husband, he pressed his happy wife to his heart.

But the next day his parents requested his company, and his father addressed him thus: 'My son, we were walking yesterday on the border of the sea, when we beheld the extraordinary scene which happened with Maredata. You easily see that you never saved her out of the waves, since she possesses such a wonderful power over the element. Manuela has told us that she had heard her sing, and notwithstanding your entreaties, she maintains an obstinate silence. This must be broken for the sake of your immortal soul; conjure her — command her to speak, and if she still remains silent, you must separate.' Giulio, on the contrary, after having discoursed a long time with his parents, asserted that he was himself perfectly happy, — that such a soft affectionate being as Maredata could never endanger his soul, and finished by asking his parents' leave to go with his family to their castle in the interior of the country. After some reflection, the Count granted his request: 'But,' added he, 'before you depart for the country, you will accompany me to Naples, where I want to present you to the King.' Giulio promised to obey, and in the space of a few days the Count and his family, Giulio, Maredata, and their child proceeded to Naples.

Soon after their arrival, Giulio was presented to the King. The old Count, seeing that he could not prevail on his son to force Maredata to disclose her secret, discovered the whole to the King.

He therefore received Giulio with hard words, reproaching him with a sinful alliance with a fairy, and commanded him, under pain of disgrace, to learn immediately the truth from Maredata, and threatened even to burn his wife, as a being devoted to the demon. At these words of the King, Giulio lost his patience; a spirit of rage seemed to have taken possession of his soul. He hastened home, rushed into the apartment of his wife, whom he found playing with her child in her arms. He brandished his sword over her head, and exclaimed, 'Thou cursed witch, who art thou? Speak, or instant death' — but he could not finish his sentence, for she fell into his arms, and cried out, 'Now indeed it is time to speak! Now indeed we must part, and part for ever!' A flood of tears checked her words, but she overcame her emotion, and with a sweet voice she entreated her amazed husband, who, at the first sound of her voice, had lost his rage, to sit down near her, and she then proceeded: 'Know then, my only love, that I was born in the depth of the ocean. Once, as thou wert swimming near the shore, — I beheld — I loved thee. But our laws will not permit us to speak to any mortal, or, if we do, his life is forfeited to the powerful spirits of the deep. Oh! how difficult is it to be mute when love fills the heart! The word would part from my lips, yet I was silent, and now, that have once spoken to thee, I must depart, and my child too. For the revenge of the spirits is dreadful, and all of us would soon be sacrificed to their wrath should I delay any longer. Farewell, Giulio from this moment, I take leave of joy, of love and happiness! Farewell!' She embraced him, and would depart, but Giulio, trembling like a murderer at the sight of the gory wound of his victim, rose suddenly, and seizing the child, cried out, 'Never! never, shalt thou carry off my child!' But she gazed on him with a long, deep look, that chilled his blood to his very heart; then she began to sing in such mournful pensive sounds, that he lost his senses.

When he recovered, she was gone. The inmates of the castle had seen her proceed towards, and leap into the sea. From that moment a still melancholy preyed upon Giulio. He said not a single word to his amazed parents. Long time elapsed before he was able to leave the room, till he one evening walked down to the coast to his accustomed bathing-place. His anxious parents beheld him swimming, when suddenly the sea glowed in a thousand colours, and Giulio disappeared. The beautiful phenomenon lasted for hours, but Giulio was seen no more. A tradition prevailed among the people, that the lustre of the sea had been a signal of the re-union of the faithful lovers.

THE HAUNTED PAMPERO

William Hope Hodgson

[I]

'Great news!' cried young Tom Pemberton, as he threw open the door and came quickly into the room where his newly wed wife was busily employed about some sewing. 'They've given me a ship — What ho!' and he threw his peaked uniform-cap down on the table with a bang.

'A ship, Tom?' said his wife, letting her sewing rest idly on her lap.

'The *Pampero*!' said Tom proudly.

'What! The "Haunted *Pampero*"?' cried his wife, in a voice expressive of more dismay than elation.

'That's what a lot of fools call her,' admitted Tom, unwilling to hear a word against his new kingdom. 'It's all a lot of rot! She's no more haunted than I am!'

'And you've accepted?' asked Mrs Tom anxiously, rising to her feet with a sudden movement which sent the contents of her lap to the floor.

'You bet I have!' replied Tom. 'It's not a chance to be thrown away, to be master of a vessel before I've jolly well reached twenty-five.'

He went towards her, holding out his arms happily, but stopped suddenly as he caught sight of the dismayed look upon her face.

'What's up, little girl?' he asked. 'You don't look a bit pleased.' His voice denoted that her lack of pleasure in his news hurt him.

'I'm not, Tom. Not a bit. She's a dreadful ship! All sorts of horrible things happen to her—'

'Rot!' interrupted Tom decisively. 'What do you know about her, anyway? She's one of the finest vessels in the company.'

'Everybody knows,' she said, with a note of tears in her voice. 'Oh, Tom, can't you get out of it?'

'Don't want to,' he replied crossly.

'Why didn't you come and ask me before deciding?'

'Wasn't any time,' Tom said gruffly, 'It was "Yes" or "No".'

'Oh, why didn't you say "No"?'

'Because I'm not a fool!' he answered, growing savage.

'I shall never be happy again,' she said, sitting down abruptly and beginning to cry.

Tears had their due effect, and the next instant Tom was

kneeling beside her, libelling himself heartily. Presently, after sundry passages, her nose — a little pink — came out from the depths of his handkerchief.

'I shall come with you!' The words were uttered with sufficient determination to warn him that there was real danger of her threat being put into execution, and Tom — who was not entirely free from the popular superstition regarding the *Pampero* — began to feel uneasy as she combated every objection which he put forward. It was all very well going to sea in her himself, but to take his little girl — well, that was another thing. And so, like a sensible, loving fellow, he fought every inch of ground with her; the natural result being that at the end of an hour he retired — shall we say 'retreated' — to smoke a pipe in his den and meditate on the perversity of womankind in general and his own wife in particular.

And she — well, she went to her bedroom and turned out all her pretty summer dresses, and for a time was quite happy. No doubt she was thinking of the tropics. Later, under Tom's somewhat despairing guidance, she made a selection from among her more substantial frocks. And, in short, three weeks later saw her at sea in the 'Haunted *Pampero*' along with her husband.

[II]

The first ten days, aided by a fresh, fair wind, took them well clear of the Channel, and Mrs Tom Pemberton was beginning to find her sea legs. Then, on the thirteenth day out, they ran into dirty weather. Hitherto the *Pampero* had been lucky — for her — nothing special having occurred, save that one of the men was 'laid up' through the starboard fore crane-line having given way under him, letting him down on deck with a run. Yet, because the man was alive and no limbs broken, there was a general feeling that the old packet was on her good behaviour.

Then, as I have said, they ran into bad weather, and were hove-to for three weary days under bare poles. On the morning of the fourth, the wind moderated sufficiently to allow their setting the main topsail, storm foresail, and staysail, and running her off before the wind. During that day the weather grew steadily finer, the wind dropping and the sea going down, so that by evening they were bowling along before a comfortable six-knot breeze. Then, just before sunset, they had evidence once again that the *Pampero* was on her good behaviour, and that there were other ships less lucky than she, for out of the red glare of sunset, to starboard, there floated to them the water-logged shell of a ship's lifeboat.

In passing, one of the men caught a glimpse of something

235

crumpled up on a thwart, and sang out to the mate, who was in charge. He, having obtained permission from the skipper, put the ship in irons, and lowered a boat. Reaching the wrecked craft, it was discovered that the something on the thwart was the still-living form of a seaman, exhausted and scarcely in his right mind. Evidently the rescue had been only just in time, for hardly had they removed him to their own boat before the other, with a slow, oily roll, disappeared from sight.

They returned with him to the ship, where he was made comfortable in a spare bunk, and on the next day, being sufficiently recovered, told how that he had been one of the A.B.s in the *Cyclops*, and how that she had broached-to while running before the gale two nights previously, and gone down with all hands. He had found himself floating beside the battered lifeboat, which had evidently been torn from its place on the skids as the ship capsized; he had managed to get hold of the lifelines and climb into her, and since then how he had managed to exist he could not say.

Two days later the man who had fallen through the breaking of the crane-line expired, at which some of the 'crowd' were aggrieved, declaring that the old packet was going back on them.

'It's as I said,' remarked one of the ordinaries, 'she's er bloomin' 'aunted tin kettle, an' if it weren't better being 'aunted 'n 'ungry, I'd bloomin' well stayed ashore!' Wherein he may be said to have voiced the general sentiments of the crew.

With this man dying, Captain Tom Pemberton offered to sign on Tarpin — the man they had picked up — in his place. Tarpin thankfully accepted, and took the dead man's place in the fo'cas'le, for, though undeniably an old man, he was, as he had already shown on a couple of occasions, a smart sailor.

And now it appeared that the ship's bad genius was determined to prove that it was by no means as black as it had been painted, for matters went on quietly and evenly for two complete weeks, during which the ship wandered across the line into the Southern Tropics, and there slid into one of those hateful calms which lurk there remorselessly awaiting their prey.

For two days Captain Tom Pemberton whistled vainly for wind; on the third he swore — under his breath when his wife was about, otherwise when she was below. On the evening of the fourth day he ceased to say naughty words about the lack of wind, for something happened, something altogether inexplicable and frightening, so much so that he was careful to tell his wife nothing concerning the matter, she being below at the time.

The sun had set some minutes and the evening was

dwindling rapidly into night, when from for'ard there came a tremendous uproar of pigs squealing and shrieking.

Captain Tom and the second mate, who were pacing the poop together, stopped in their promenade and listened.

'Damnation!' exclaimed the captain. 'Who's messing with the pigs?'

The second mate was proceeding to roar out to one of the 'prentices to jump forward and see what was up, when a man came running aft to say that there was something in the pigsty getting at the pigs, and would he come forward.

On hearing this, the captain and the second mate went forward at a run. As they passed along the deck and came nearer to the scene of action they distinctly heard the sound of savage snarling mingled with the squealing of the pigs.

'What the devil's that!' gasped the second, as he tried to keep pace with the skipper. Then they were by the pigsty, and, in the gathering gloom, found the crew grouped in a semicircle foreside the sty.

'What's up?' roared Captain Tom Pemberton. 'What's up here?' He made a way through the men, and stooped and peered through the iron bars of the sty; but it was too dark to make anything out with certainty. Then, before he could take away his face, there came a deeper, fiercer growl, and something snapped between the bars. The captain gave out a cry and jumped back among the men, holding his nose.

'Hurt, sir?' asked the second mate anxiously.

'N-no,' said the captain in a scared, doubtful voice. He fingered his nose for a further moment or two. 'I don't think so.'

The second mate turned and caught the nearest man by the shoulder.

'Bring out one of your lamps; smart, now!'

Yet even as he spoke, one of the ordinaries came running out with one ready lighted. The second snatched it from him and held it towards the pigsty. In the same instant something wet and shiny struck it from his hand. The second mate gave a shout, and then there was an instant's quietness, in which all caught a sound of something slithering curiously along the decks to leeward. Several of the men made a run to the fo'cas'le, but the second was on his knees groping for the lantern. He found it and struck a light. The pigs had stopped squealing, but were still grunting in an agitated manner. He held the lantern near the bars and looked.

Two of the pigs were huddled up in the starboard corner of the sty; they were bleeding in several places. The third, a big fellow, was stretched upon his back; he had been bitten terribly about the throat and was quite dead.

The captain put his hand on the second's shoulder and stooped forward to get a better view.

'Good heavens, Mister Kasson, what's been here!' he

muttered with an air of utter consternation.

The men had drawn up close behind and around, and were now looking on, almost too astonished to venture opinions. Then a man's voice broke the momentary silence:

'Looks as if they 'ad been 'avin' a 'op with a cussed great shark!'

The second mate moved the light along before the bars.

'The door's shut and the toggel's on, sir,' he said in a low voice.

The skipper grasped his meaning, but said nothing.

'S'posin' it 'ad been one o' us?' muttered a man behind him.

From the surrounding 'crowd' there came a murmur of comprehension and some uneasy glancing from side to side and behind.

The skipper faced round upon them.

He opened his mouth to speak; then shut it as though a sudden idea had come to him.

'That light, quickly, Mister Kasson!' he exclaimed, holding out his hand.

The second passed him the lamp, and he held it above his head. He was counting the men. They were all there, watch below and watch on deck; even the man on the 'lookout' had come running down. There was only absent the man at the wheel.

He turned to the second mate.

'Take a couple of the men aft with you, Mister Kasson, and pass out some lamps. We must make a search!'

In a couple of minutes they returned with a dozen lighted lamps, which were quickly distributed among the men; then a thorough search of the decks was commenced. Every corner was peered into, but nothing found, and so at last they had to give it up, unsuccessful.

'That'll do, men,' said Captain Tom. 'Hang one of those lamps up foreside the pigsty, and shove the others back in the locker.' Then he and the second mate went aft.

At the bottom of the poop steps the skipper stopped abruptly and said, 'Hush!' For the half of a minute they listened, but without being able to say that they had heard anything definite. Then Captain Tom Pemberton turned and continued his way up on to the poop.

'What was it, sir?' asked the second, as he joined him at the top of the ladder.

'I'm hanged if I know!' replied Captain Tom. 'I feel all adrift. I never heard there was anything — anything like this!'

'And we've no dogs aboard!'

'Dogs! More like tigers. Did you hear what one of the shellbacks said?'

'A shark, you mean, sir?' said the second mate, with some

remonstrance in his tone.

'Have you ever seen a shark-bite, Mister Kasson?'

'No, sir,' replied the second mate.

'Well, I have.'

'But — but —' began the second mate.

'Those are shark-bites, Mister Kasson! God help us! Those are shark-bites!'

[III]

After this inexplicable affair a week of stagnant calm passed without anything unusual happening, and Captain Tom Pemberton was gradually losing the sense of haunting fear which had been so acute during the nights closely following the death of the porker.

It was nearly night, and Mrs Tom Pemberton was sitting in a deck-chair on the weather side of the saloon skylight, near the for'ard end. The captain and the first mate were walking up and down, passing and repassing her. Presently the captain stopped abruptly in his walk, leaving the mate to continue along the deck. Then, crossing quietly to where his wife was sitting, he bent over her.

'What is it, dear?' he asked. 'I've seen you once or twice looking to leeward as though you heard something. What is it?'

His wife sat forward and caught his arm.

'Listen!' she said in a sharp undertone. 'There it is again! I've been thinking it must be my fancy, but it isn't. Can't you hear it?'

Captain Tom was listening, and just as his wife spoke his strained sense caught a low, snarling growl from among the shadows to leeward. Though he gave a start he said nothing; but his wife saw his hand steal to his side pocket.

'You heard it?' she said eagerly. Then, without waiting for

243

an answer: 'Do you know, Tom, I've heard that sound three times already. It's just like an animal growling somewhere over there.' And she pointed among the shadows. She was so positive about having heard it that her husband gave up all idea of trying to make her believe that her imagination had been playing tricks with her. Instead, he caught her hand and raised her to her feet.

'Come below, Annie,' he said, and led her to the companion-way. There he left her for a moment, and ran across to warn the first mate to be on the look-out; then back to her, and led her down the stairs. In the saloon she turned and faced him.

'What was it, Tom? You're afraid of something, and you're keeping it from me. It's something to do with this horrible vessel!'

The captain stared at her with a puzzled look. He did not know how much or how little to tell her. Then, before he could speak, she had stepped to his side and thrust her hand into the side pocket of his coat on the right.

'You've got a pistol!' she cried, pulling the weapon out with a jerk. 'That shows it's something you're frightened of! It's something dangerous, and you won't tell me. I shall come up on deck with you again!'

She was almost tearful, and very much in earnest, so much so that the captain turned to her and told her everything, which was, after all, the wisest thing he could have done under the circumstances.

'Now,' he said, when he had made an end, 'you must promise never to come up on deck at night without me — now promise!'

'I will, dear, if you will promise to be careful and — and not run any risks. Oh, I wish you hadn't taken this horrible ship!' And she commenced to cry.

Later she consented to be quieted, and the captain left her, after having exacted a promise from her that she would 'turn in' right away and get some sleep.

The first part she fulfilled without delay, but the latter was more difficult, and at least an hour went by tediously before, at last growing drowsy, she fell into an uneasy sleep. From this she was awakened some little time later with a start. She had seemed to hear some noise. Her bunk was up against the side of the ship, and a glass port opened right above it, and it was from this port that the noise proceeded. It was a queer, slurring sort of noise, as though something were rubbing up against it, and she grew frightened as she listened, for though she had pushed-to the port on getting into her bunk, she was by no means certain that she had slipped the screw-catch on properly. She was, however, a plucky little woman, and wasted no time, but made one jump to the floor, slipping on a gown, and ran to the lamp. Turning it up she glanced towards the port. Behind the thick circle of glass she made out something that seemed to be pressed up against it. A queer, curved indentation ran right across it. Abruptly, as she stared, it gaped, and teeth flashed into sight. The whole thing started to move up and down across the glass, and she heard again that queer slurring noise which had frightened her into wakefulness. The thought leapt across her mind, as though it were a revelation, that it was something living, and it was grubbing at the glass, trying to get in. She put a hand down on to the table to steady herself, and tried to think.

Behind her the cabin door opened softly, and someone came into the room. She heard her husband's voice say: 'Why, Annie—' in a tone of astonishment, and then stop dead. The next instant a sharp report filled the little cabin with sound, and the glass of the port was starred all across, and there was no more anything of which to be afraid, for Captain Tom's arms were round her.

From the door there came a noise of loud knocking and the voice of the first mate:

'Anything wrong, sir?'

'It's all right, Mr Stennings. I'll be with you in half a minute.'

He heard the mate's footsteps retreat, and go up the companion ladder. Then he listened quietly as his wife told him her story. When she had made an end they sat and talked a while gravely, with an infinite sense of being on the borders of the Unknown. Suddenly a noise out upon the deck interrupted their talk, a man crying aloud with terror, and then a pistol shot and the mate's voice shouting. Captain Pemberton leapt to his feet simultaneously with his wife.

'Stay here, Annie!' he commanded, and pushed her down on to her seat.

He turned to the door; then an idea coming to him, he ran back and thrust his revolver into her hands.

'I'll be with you in a minute,' he said assuringly; then, seizing a heavy cutlass from the rack on the bulkhead, he opened the door and made a run for the deck.

His wife, on her part, at once hurried to make sure that the port catch was properly on. She saw that it was, and made haste to screw it up tightly. As she did so she noticed that the bullet had passed clean through the glass on the left-hand side, low down. Then she returned to her seat with the revolver, and sat listening and waiting.

On the main deck the captain found the mate and a couple of men just below the break of the poop. The rest of the watch were gathered in a clump a little foreside of them, and between them and the mate stood one of the 'prentices, holding a binnacle lamp. The two men with the mate were Coalson and Tarpin. Coalson appeared to be saying something. Tarpin was nursing his jaw, and seemed to be in considerable pain.

'What is it, Mr Stennings?' sang out the skipper quietly.

The first mate glanced up.

'Will you come down, sir,' he said. 'There's been some infernal devilment going on!'

Even as he spoke the captain was in the act of running down the poop ladder. Reaching the mate and the two men, he put a few questions rapidly, and learnt that Coalson had been on his way aft to relieve the 'wheel', when all at once something had leapt out at him from under the lee pinrail. Fortunately he had turned just in time to avoid it, and then, shouting at the top of his voice, had run for his life. The mate had heard him, and thinking he saw something behind, had fired. Almost directly afterwards they heard Tarpin calling out further for'ard, and then, he, too, had come running aft; but just under the skids he had caught his foot in a ringbolt, and come crashing to the deck, smashing his face badly against the sharp corner of the after-hatch.

He, too, it would appear, had been chased; but by what he could not say. Both the men were greatly agitated, and could only tell their stories jerkily and with some incoherence.

With a certain feeling of the hopelessness of it all, Captain Pemberton gave orders to get lanterns and search the decks; but, as he anticipated, nothing unusual was found. Yet the bringing out of the lanterns suggested a wise precaution; for he told them to keep out a couple, and carry them about with them when they went to and fro along the decks.

[IV]

Two nights later, Captain Pemberton was suddenly aroused from a sound sleep by his wife.

'Shush!' she whispered, putting her fingers on his lips. 'Listen!'

He rose on his elbow, but otherwise kept quiet. The berth was full of shadows, for the lamp was turned rather low. A minute of tense silence followed; then, abruptly, from the direction of the door, he heard a slow, gritty, rubbing noise. At that he sat upright, and sliding his hand beneath his pillow, brought out his revolver; then remained silent — waiting.

Suddenly he heard the latch of the door snicked softly out of its catch, and an instant later a little breath of air swept through the berth, stirring the draperies. By that he knew that the door had been opened, and he leant forward, raising his weapon. A moment of intense stillness followed; then, all at once, something dark slid between the little glimmer of flame in the lamp and him. Instantly he aimed and fired, once — twice. There came a hideous howling, which seemed to be retreating towards the door, and he fired in the direction of the noise. He heard it pass into the saloon. Then came a quick slither of steps upon the companion stairway, and the noise died away into silence.

Immediately afterwards the skipper heard the mate

250

bellowing for the watch to lay aft, then his heavy tread came tumbling down into the saloon, and the captain, who had left his berth to turn up the lamp, met him in the doorway. A minute sufficed to put the mate in possession of such facts as the skipper himself had gleaned, and after that they lit the saloon lamp and examined the floor and companion stairs. In several places they found traces of blood, which showed that one, at least, of Captain Tom's shots had got home. They were also found to lead a little way along the lee side of the poop, but ceased altogether nearly opposite the end of the skylight.

As may be imagined, this affair had given the captain a big shaking up, and he felt so little like attempting further sleep that he proceeded to dress, an action which his wife imitated, and the two of them passed the rest of the night on the poop; for, as Mrs Pemberton said:

'You felt safer up in the fresh air. You could at least feel that you were near help.' A sentiment which, probably, Captain Tom felt more distinctly than he could have put into words. Yet he had another thought, of which he was much more acutely aware, and which he did manage to formulate in some shape to the mates during the course of the following day. As he put it:

'It's my wife that I'm afraid for! That Thing — whatever it is — seems to be making a dead set for her!'

His face was anxious and somewhat haggard under the tan. The two mates nodded.

'I should keep a man in the saloon at night, sir,' suggested the second mate, after a moment's thought. 'And let her keep with you as much as possible.'

Captain Tom Pemberton nodded with a slight air of relief. The reasonableness of the precaution appealed to him. He would have a man in the saloon after dark, and he would see that the lamp was kept going; then, at least, his wife would be safe, for the only entrance to his cabin was through the saloon. As for the shattered port, it had been replaced the day after he had broken it, and now every dog watch he saw to it himself that it was securely screwed up, and not only that but the iron storm-cover as well; so that he had no fears in that direction.

That night at eight o'clock, as the roll was being called, the second mate turned and beckoned respectfully to the captain, who immediately left his wife and stepped up to him.

'About the man who will stand guard in the saloon, sir?' said the second. 'I'm up here till twelve o'clock. Who would you care to have out of my watch?'

'Just as you like, Mister Kasson. Who can you best spare?'

'Well, sir, if it comes to that, there's old Tarpin. He's not been much use on a rope since that tumble he got the other night. He hurt his arm as well, for he's not able to use it.'

'Very well, Mister Kasson. Tell him to step up.'

This the second mate did, and in a few moments old Tarpin stood before them. His face was bandaged up, and his right arm was slipped out of the sleeve of his coat.

'You seem to have been in the wars, Tarpin,' said the skipper, eyeing him up and down.

'Yes, sir,' replied the man, with a touch of grimness.

'I want you down in the saloon till twelve o'clock,' the captain went on. 'If you — er — hear anything, call me. Do you hear?'

The man gave out a gruff 'Ay, ay, sir,' and went slowly aft.

'I don't expect he's best pleased, sir,' said the second, with a slight smile.

'How do you mean, Mister Kasson?'

'Well, sir, ever since he and Coalson were chased, and he got that tumble, he's taken to waiting round the decks at night. He seems a plucky old devil, and it's my belief he's waiting to get square with whatever it was that made him run.'

'Then he's just the man I want in the saloon,' said the skipper. 'It may just happen that he gets his chance of coming to close quarters with this infernal hell-thing that's knocking about. And, by Jove, if he does, he and I'll be friends for evermore!'

At nightfall Captain Tom Pemberton and his wife went below. They found old Tarpin sitting on one of the benches. At their entrance he rose to his feet and touched his cap awkwardly to them. The captain stopped a moment and spoke to him.

'Mind, Tarpin, the least sound of anything about, and you call me! And see you keep the lamp bright.'

'Ay, ay, sir,' said the man quietly; and the skipper left him, and followed his wife into their cabin.

[V]

The captain had been asleep over an hour, when, abruptly, something roused him. He reached for his revolver, and then sat upright. Yet, though he listened intently, no sound came to him save the gentle breathing of his wife. The lamp was low, but not so low that he could not make out the various details of the cabin. His glance roved swiftly round and showed him nothing unusual, until it came to the door; then, in a flash, he noted that no light from the saloon lamp came under the bottom.

He jumped swiftly from his bunk, with a sudden gust of anger. If Tarpin had gone to sleep and allowed the lamp to go out, well . . . His hand was upon the key. He had taken the precaution to turn it before going to sleep. How providential this action had been he was soon to learn. In the very act of unlocking the door he paused, for all at once a low, grumbling purr came to him from beyond the door. Ah, that was the sound that had come to him in his sleep, and wakened him. For a moment he stood, a multitude of frightened fancies coming to him. Then, realising that now was such a chance as he might not have again, he turned the key with a swift movement, and flung the door open.

The first thing he noticed was that the saloon lamp had burned down and was flickering, sending uncomfortable slashes of light and darkness across the place. The next, that

255

something lay at his feet across the threshold, something that started up with a snarl, and turned upon him. He pushed the muzzle of his revolver against it, and pulled the trigger twice. The Thing gave out a queer roar, and flung itself from him half-way across the saloon floor; then it rose to a semi-upright position, and darted, howling, through the doorway leading to the companion stairs.

Behind him he heard his wife crying out in alarm, but he did not stay to answer her; instead, he followed the Thing voicing its pain so hideously. At the bottom of the stairs he glanced up and saw something outlined against the stars. It was only a glimpse, and he saw that it had two legs, like a man; yet he thought of a shark. It disappeared, and he leapt up the stairs. He stared to leeward and saw something by the rail. As he fired the Thing leapt, and a cry and a splash came almost simultaneously. The second mate joined him breathlessly as he raced to his side.

'What was it, sir?' gasped the officer.

'Look!' shouted Captain Tom, pointing down into the dark sea.

He stared down into the glassy darkness. Something like a great fish showed below the surface. It was dimly outlined by the phosphorescence. It was swimming in an erratic circle, leaving an indistinct trail of glowing bubbles behind it. Something caught the second mate's eyes as he stared, and he leaned further out so as to get a better view. He saw the Thing again. The fish had two tails, or — they might have been legs. The Thing was swimming downwards. How rapidly, he could judge by the speed at which its apparent size diminished. He turned and caught the captain by the wrist.

'Do you see its — its tails, sir?' he muttered excitedly.

Captain Tom Pemberton gave an unintelligible grunt, but kept his eyes fixed on the deep. The second glanced back. Far below him he made out a little moving spot of phosphorescence. It grew fainter, and vanished in the immensity beneath them.

Someone touched the captain on the arm. It was his wife.

'Oh, Tom, have you — have you —' she began; but he said 'Hush!' and turned to the second mate.

'Call all hands, Mister Kasson!' he ordered; then, taking his wife by the arm, he led her down with him into the saloon. Here they found the steward in his shirt and trousers, trimming the lamp. His face was pale, and he started to question as soon as they entered; but the captain quieted him with a gesture.

'Look in all the empty cabins,' the skipper commanded, and while the steward was doing this the skipper himself made a search of the saloon floor.

In a few minutes the steward came up to say that the cabins were as usual; whereupon the captain led his wife on deck. Here the second mate met them.

'The hands are mustered, sir,' he said.

'Very good, Mister Kasson. Call the roll.'

The roll was gone over, each man answering his name in turn. The second mate reached the last three on the list.

'Jones!'

'Sir!'

'Smith!'

'Yessir!'

'Tarpin!'

But from the waiting crowd below, in the light of the second mate's lantern, no answer came. He called the name again, and then Captain Tom Pemberton touched him on the arm. He turned and looked at the captain, whose eyes were full of an incredible realisation.

'It's no good, Mister Kasson,' the captain said. 'I had to make quite sure—'

He paused, and the second mate took a step towards him.

'But — but where is he?' he asked, almost stupidly.

'You saw him go, Mister Kasson!' he said in a low voice.

The second mate stared back; but he did not see the captain. Instead, he saw again in his mind's eye two things that looked like legs — human legs!

There was no more trouble that voyage; no more strange happenings; nothing unusual; but Captain Tom Pemberton had no peace of mind until he reached port and his wife was safely ashore again.

The story of the *Pampero*, her bad reputation, and this latest extraordinary happening got into the papers. Among the many articles which the tale evoked was one which held certain interesting suggestions.

The writer quoted from an old manuscript, entitled 'Ghosts', the well-known legend of the sea-ghoul, which, as will be remembered, asserts that those who 'die by ye sea, live of ye sea, and do come upward upon lonely shores, and do eate, biting like ye shark or ye deyvel-fishe, and are dreydful in hunger for ye fleyshe of man, and, moreover, do strive in mid sea to board ye ships of ye deep water, that they shall saytisfy theire dreydful hunger'.

The author of the article suggested seriously that the man Tarpin was some abnormal thing out of the profound deeps; that had destroyed those who had once been in the whale-boat, and afterwards, with dreadful cunning had been taken aboard the *Pampero* as a castaway, afterwards indulging its monstrous appetite. What form of life the creature possessed the writer frankly could not indicate, but set out the uncomfortable suggestion that the case of the *Pampero* was not the first; nor would it be the last. He reminded the public of the many ships that vanish. He pointed out how a ship, thus dreadfully bereft of her crew, might founder and sink when the first heavy storm struck her.

He concluded his article by asserting his opinion that he did not believe the *Pampero* to be 'haunted'. It was, he held, simple chance that had associated a long tale of ill-luck with the vessel in question, and that the thing which had happened could have happened as easily to any other vessel which might have met and picked up the grim occupant of the derelict whale-boat.

Whatever may be the correctness of the writer's suggestions, they are at least interesting, in endeavouring to sum up this extraordinary and incomprehensible happening.

THE DIVER

A. J. Alan

For some reason or other the BBC are always asking me to tell a ghost story — at least, they don't ask me, they tell me I've got to. I say, 'What kind of a ghost story?' and they say, 'Any kind you like, so long as it's a personal experience and perfectly true.'

Just like that; and it's cramped my style a bit. Not that my personal experiences aren't true. Please don't think that. But it's simply this: that when it comes to supernatural matters my luck hasn't been very good. It isn't that I don't believe in such things on principle, but I do like to be present when the manifestations actually occur, instead of just taking other people's word for them; and, somehow or other, as I've said before, my luck has not been very good.

Lots of people have tried to convert me. There was one young woman in particular. She took a lot of trouble about it — quite a lot. She used to dra — take me to all sorts of parties where they had séances — you know the kind: table-turning, planchette, and so on — but it wasn't any good. Nothing ever happened when I was there. Nothing spiritual, that is. People always said:

'Ah, my boy, you ought to have been here last night. The table fairly got up and hit us in the face.'

Possibly very wonderful — but, after all, the ground will do that if you let it.

Well, as I say, they took me to several of these parties, and we used to sit for hours round tables, in a dim light, holding hands. That was rather fun sometimes — it depended on who one sat next to — but apart from that, the nights they took me, no manifestations ever occurred. Planchette wouldn't spell a word, and the table might have been screwed to the floor. To begin with they used to put it down to chance, or the conditions not being favourable. But after a time they began to put it down to me — and I thought: 'Something will have to be done about it.' It's never amusing to be looked upon as a sort of Jonah.

So I invented a patent table-tapper. It was made on the same principle as lazy tongs. You held it between your knees, and when you squeezed it a little mallet shot up (it was really a cotton reel stuck on the end of a pencil) and it hit the underneath of the table a proper biff. It was worked entirely with the knees, so that I could still hold the hands of the people on either side of me. And it was a success from the word 'Go'.

At the very next séance, as soon as the lights were down, I gave just a gentle tap. Our host said:

'Ah, a powerful force is present!' and I gave a louder — ponk! Then he said:

'How do you say "Yes"?' — and I said:

'Ponk!' Then he said:

'How do you say "No"?' And I said:

'Ponk, ponk!'

So far so good. Communication established. Then people began asking questions and I spelt out the answers. Awful hard work ponking right through the alphabet, but quite worth it. I'm afraid some of my answers made people sit up a bit. They got quite nervous as to what was coming next. Needless to say, this was some years ago.

Then someone said:

'Who's going to win the Derby?' (I don't know *who* said that) and I laboriously spelt out Signorinetta. This was two days before the race. I don't know *why* I said Signorinetta, because there were several horses with shorter names, but it just came into my head. The annoying thing was that I didn't take my own tip and back it. You may remember it won at 100 to 1 by I don't know how many lengths — five lengths dividing second and third. However, it's no use crying over the stable door after the horse has spilt the milk, and it has nothing whatever to do with the story.

The amusing thing was that when the séance was over various people came round to me and said:

'*Now* will you believe in spiritualism?' 'What more proof do you want?' and so on and so forth. It struck me as rather rich that they should try to convert me with my own false evidence. And I don't mind betting you that if I'd owned up to the whole thing being a spoof, not a soul would have believed me. That's always the way.

I've told you all this to show that I'm not exactly dippy on the subject of spiritualism — at any rate, not the table-turning variety — very largely because it *is* so easy to fake your results.

But when something *genuinely* uncanny comes along — why, then I'm one of the very first to be duly thrilled and mystified and — what not. It's one of those *genuine* cases I want to tell you about. It happened to me personally. But first of all you must know that there's a swimming bath at my club. Very good swimming bath, too. Deep at one end and shallow at the other. There's a sort of hall-place adjoining it, and in this hall there's a sandwich bar — very popular. It's much cheaper than lunching upstairs. Quite a lot of people seem to gravitate down there — especially towards the end of the month. Everything's quite informal. You just go to the counter and snatch what you want and take it to a table and eat it. Then when you've done, you go and tell George what you've had. George runs the show, and he says 'one-and-ninepence', or whatever it is, and that's that.

Personally, I usually go to a table in a little recess close to the edge of the swimming bath itself. You have to go down a few steps to get to it. But you are rather out of the turmoil and not so likely to get anything spilt over you. It's quite dangerous sometimes, people darting in and out like a lot of sharks — which reminds me: a member once wrote in to the secretary complaining that the place wasn't safe — I shan't say who it was, but you'd know his name if I told you; I managed to get hold of a copy of his letter. This is what he says, speaking of the sandwich bar:

'I once saw an enormous shark, at least five feet ten inches long, go up to the counter and seize a sausage roll — itself nearly four inches long — and take it away to devour it. When he had bitten off the end, which he did with a single snap of his powerful jaws, he found that it was empty. The sausage, which ought to have been inside, had completely vanished. It had been stolen by another shark even more voracious and ferocious than himself.

'Never shall I forget the awful spectacle of the baffled and impotent rage of this fearful monster. He went back to the counter, taking the empty sarcophagus with him, and said: "George, I have been stung!"

'In order to avoid such scenes of unparalleled and revolting cruelty' — after that he is rather inclined to exaggerate, so I shan't read any more — I usually go late, when the rush is over and it's fairly quiet. People come and practise diving, and sometimes they are worth watching — and sometimes not.

That's the sort of place it is, and if you know of anywhere less likely to be haunted I should like to see it. Very well, then.

One day I was just finishing lunch when there was a splash. I was reading a letter and didn't look up at once, but when I did I was rather surprised to see no ripples on the water, and no one swimming about, so I went on with my letter and didn't think any more about it. That was all that happened that day.

Two or three weeks later, at about the same time, I was again finishing lunch, and there was another splash. This time I looked up almost at once and saw the ripples, and it struck me *then* that it must have been an extraordinarily clean dive, considering that whoever it was must have gone in off the top. One could tell that from where the ripples were — well out in the middle. So I waited for him to come up. But he didn't come up. Then I thought that he must be doing a length under water, and I got up and went to the edge of the bath to watch for him. But still he didn't come

266

up and I got a bit worried. He might have bumped his head on the bottom, or fainted, or anything, and I saw myself having to go in after him with all my clothes on.

I sprinted right round the bath, but there was undoubtedly no one in it. The attendant came out of one of the dressing-rooms and evidently thought I'd gone cracked, so I went to the weighing-machine and weighed myself — eleven stone eight — but I don't think he believed me.

That was the second incident. The third came about a fortnight later. This time I saw the whole thing clearly. I was sitting at my usual table and I saw a man climbing up the ladder leading to the top diving-board. When he got up there he came out to the extreme end of the plank and stood for a few seconds rubbing his chest and so on — like people often do.

He was rather tall and muscular — dark, with a small moustache — but what particularly caught my eye was a great big scar he had. It was about nine inches long and it reached down from his left shoulder towards the middle of his chest. It looked like a bad gash with a bayonet. It must have hurt quite a lot when it was done.

I don't know why I took so much notice of him, but I just did, that's all. And, funnily enough, he seemed to be just as much interested in me as I was in him. He gave me a most meaningful look. I didn't know what it meant, but it was undoubtedly a meaningful look.

As soon as he saw that he'd got me watching him he dived in, and it was the most gorgeous dive I've ever seen. Hardly any noise or splash — just a gentle sort of plop as though he'd gone into oil rather than water — and the ripples died away almost at once. I thought, if only he'll do that a few more times it'll teach me a lot, and I waited for him to come up — and waited — and waited — but not a sign.

I went to the edge of the bath, and then I walked right round it. But, bar the water, it was perfecdy empty. However, to make absolutely certain — I mean that he couldn't have got out without my seeing him — I dug out the attendant and satisfied myself that no towels and — er — costumes had been given out since twelve o'clock — and it was then half-past two — and he, the attendant, he'd actually seen the last man leave.

The thing was getting quite serious. My scarred friend couldn't have melted away in the water, nor could he have dived slap through the bottom of the bath — at least, not without leaving some sort of a mark. So it was obvious that either the man had been a ghost, which was absurd — who's ever heard of a ghost in a swimming bath? — I mean the idea's too utterly — er — wet for anything — or that there was something wrong with the light lager I was having for lunch.

I went back to my table and found I'd hardly begun it, and in any case let me tell you it was *such* light lager that a gallon of it wouldn't have hurt a child of six — and — I'm *not* a child of six. So I ruled that out, and decided to wait and see if it happened again. It wouldn't have done to say anything about it. One's friends are apt to be a bit flippant when you tell 'em things like that. However, I made a point of sitting at the same table for weeks and weeks afterwards, but old stick-in-the-mud didn't show up again.

A good long time after this — it must have been eighteen months or more — I got an invitation to dine with some people called Pringle. They were old friends of mine, but I hadn't seen them for a long time because they'd mostly lived in Mexico, and one rather loses touch with people at that distance. Anyway, they were going back there in a few days, and this was a sort of farewell dinner.

They'd given up their flat and were staying at an hotel. They'd got another man dining with them. His name was Melhuish, and he was, with one exception, the most offensive blighter I've ever come across. Do you know those people who open their mouths to contradict what you are going to say before you've even begun to say it? Well, he did that, among other things. It was rather difficult to be entirely civil to him. He was travelling back to Mexico with the Pringles, as he'd got the job of manager to one of their properties.

Something to do with oil, but I didn't quite grasp what, my mind was so taken up with trying to remember where on earth I'd seen the man before.

Of course *you* all know. You know he was the man who dived into the swimming bath. It sticks out about a mile, naturally; but I'd only seen him once before in a bad light, and it took me till half-way through the fish to place him. Then it came back with a rush, and my interest in him became very lively. He was an American, and he'd come over to England two months before, looking for a job — so he said. I asked him why he'd left America, and he didn't hear; but it did seem fairly certain that he'd never been in Europe before. So when we got to dessert I proceeded to drop my brick.

I said: 'Do you mind telling me whether you have a scar on your chest like this?' And I described it. The Pringles just stared, but Melhuish looked as if he were going to have a fit. Then he pulled himself together and said: 'Have you ever been in America?' And I said: 'No, not that I know of.' Then he said: 'Well, it's a most extraordinary thing, but I *have* a scar on my chest,' and he went on to explain how he'd got it.

Funnily enough, he'd gone in for high diving a lot when he was younger, and taken any amount of prizes, and on one occasion he'd found a sharp stake at the bottom of a river.

He gave us full particulars. Very messy. But what they all wanted to know was how the — how I knew anything about it. Of course, it was a great temptation to tell 'em, but they'd only have thought I'd gone off my rocker, so I started a hare about perhaps having seen a photograph of his swimming club in some newspaper or other. They caught on to that idea quite well, so I left them to it.

The whole thing was by way of being rather a problem, and it kept me awake that night. Without being up in such matters, it did occur to me that it might be a warning of some kind. Is it likely that anyone — even a ghost — would take the trouble to come all the way from America simply to show me how well he could dive? Of course not, and I sort of thought that a man who was in the habit of going in off the deep end and *not* coming up again was no fit travelling companion for any friends of mine. I'm not superstitious, goodness knows! Of course, I don't walk under ladders, or light three matches with one cigarette, or any of those things, but that's because they're unlucky — not because I'm superstitious.

Anyhow, in case the Pringles might be, I went round next day and saw them. At least, I saw her — he was out — and told her all about the apparition at the club, and so on. That did it. She fairly went off pop. It was a portent, a direct intervention of Providence; nothing would induce her to travel with Melhuish after what she'd heard — and all the rest of it.

I left her to carry on the good work. I don't know how she managed it, but the fact remains that the Pringles did *not* start for Mexico, as arranged, and Melhuish did.

And now you are expecting me to say that the ship in which he sailed was never heard of again. But that wouldn't be strictly true. He got to the other side all right. But the train in which he was travelling through Mexico had to cross a bridge over a river. A steel bridge, it was. Now some months previously there'd been a slight scrap between two local bands of brigands, in the course of which the bridge had been blown up.

When the quarrel was patched up the bridge was patched up, too, but not with the meticulous care it might have been. The result was that in the daytime, when the sun was hot and the steelwork fully expanded, it was a perfectly good bridge, but at night, when it was cold and the girders had shrunk a bit — well, it didn't always quite meet in the middle.

It so happened that the train in question tried to cross this wretched bridge at the very moment when it was having rather a job to make both ends meet — and it simply couldn't bear it. The middle span carried away and the engine and two carriages crashed through into the river, and fourteen people were killed. It was very sad about thirteen of them, but the fourteenth was Mr Melhuish.

There must be a moral to this story, if I could only think of it; but I can't, so perhaps some of you can help me by suggesting one . . .

THE RED STOCKADE

WE WAS ON THE southern part of the China station, when the *George Ranger* was ordered to the Straits of Malacca, to put down the pirates that had been showing themselves of late. It was in the forties, when ships was ships, not iron-kettles full of wheels, and other devilments, and there was a chance of hand-to-hand fighting — not being blown up in an iron cellar by you don't know who. Ships was ships in them days!

There had been a lot of throat-cutting and scuttling, for them devils stopped at nothing. Some of us had been through the straits before, when we was in the *Polly Phemus*, seventy-four, going to the China station, and although we had never come to quarters with the Malays, we had seen some of their work, and knew what kind they was. So, when we had left Singapore in the *George Ranger*, for that was our saucy, little thirty-eight-gun frigate — the place wasn't in them days what it is now — many and many's the yarn was told in the fo'c'sle, and on the watches, of what the yellow devils could do, and had done. Some of us took it one way, and some another, but all, save a few, wanted to get into hand-grips with the pirates, for all their kreeses, and their stinkpots, and the devil's engines what they used. There was some that didn't mind cold steel of an ordinary kind, and would have faced cutlasses and boarding-pikes, any day, for a holiday, but that didn't like the idea of those knives like crooked flames, and that sliced a man in two, and hacked through the bowels of him. Naturally, we didn't take much stock of this kind; and many's the joke we had on them, and some of them cruel enough jokes, too.

You may be sure there was good stories, with plenty of cutting, and blood, and tortures in them, told in their watches, and nigh the whole ship's crew was busy, day and night, remembering and inventing things that'd make them gasp and grow white. I think that, somehow, the Captain and the officers must have known what was goin' on, for there came tales from the ward-room that was worse nor any of ours. The midshipmen used to delight in them, like the ship's boys did, and one of them, that had a kreese, used to bring it out when he could, and show how the pirates used it when they cut the hearts out of men and women, and ripped them up to the chins. It was a bit cruel, at times, on them poor, white-livered chaps — a man can't help his liver, I suppose — but, anyhow, there's no place for them in a warship, for they're apt to do more harm by living where there's men of all sorts, than they can do by dying. So there wasn't any mercy for them, and the Captain was worse on them than any. Captain Wynyard was him that commanded the corvette *Sentinel* on the China station, and was promoted to the *George Ranger* for cutting up a fleet of junks that was hammering at the *Rajah*, from Canton, racing for Southampton with the first of the season's tea. He was a man, if you like, a bulldog full of hell-fire, when he was on for fighting; he wouldn't have a white liver at any price. 'God hates a coward,' he said once, 'and under Her Britannic Majesty I'm here to carry out God's will. Trice him up, and give him a dozen!' At least, that's the story they tell of him when he was round Shanghai, and one of his men had held back when the time came for boarding a fire-junk that was coming down the tide. And with that he went in, and steered her off with his own hands.

Well, the Captain knew what work there was before us, and that it weren't no time for kid gloves and hair-oil, much less a bokey in your buttonhole and a top-hat, and he didn't mean that there should be any funk on his ship. So you take your davy that it wasn't his fault if things was made too pleasant aboard for men what feared fallin' into the clutches of the Malays.

Now and then he went out of his way to be nasty over such folk, and, boy or man, he never checked his tongue on a hard word when anyone's face was pale before him. There was one old chap on board that we called 'Old Land's End', for he came from that part, and that had a boy of his on the

Billy Ruffian, when he sailed on her, and after got lost, one night, in cutting out a Greek sloop at Navarino in 1827. We used to chaff him when there was trouble with any of the boys, for he used to say that his boy might have been in that trouble, too. And now, when the chaff was on about bein' afeered of the Malays, we used to rub it into the old man; but he would flame up, and answer us that his boy died in his duty, and that he couldn't be afeered of nought.

One night there was a row on among the midshipmen, for they said that one of them. Tempest by name, owned up to being afraid of being kreesed. He was a rare bright litde chap of about thirteen, that was always in fun and trouble of some kind; but he was soft hearted, and sometimes the other lads would tease him. He would own up truthfully to anything he thought, or felt, and now they had drawn him to own something that none of them would — no matter how true it might be. Well, they had a rare fight, for the boy was never backwards with his fists, and by accident it came to the notice of the Captain. He insisted on being told what it was all about, and when young Tempest spoke out, and told him, he stamped on the deck, and called out: 'I'll have no cowards in this ship,' and was going on, when the boy cut in: 'I'm no coward, sir; I'm a gentleman!'

'Did you say you were afraid? Answer me — yes, or no?'

'Yes, sir, I did, and it was true! I said I feared the Malay kreeses; but I did not mean to shirk them, for all that. Henry of Navarre was afraid, but, all the same, he –'

'Henry of Navarre be damned,' shouted the Captain, 'and you, too! You said you were afraid, and that, let me tell you, is what we call a coward in the Queen's navy. And if you are one, you can, at least, have the grace to keep it to yourself! No answer to me! To the masthead for the remainder of the day! I want my crew to know what to avoid, and to know it when they see it!' and he walked away, while the lad, without a word, ran up the maintop.

Some way, the men didn't say much about this. The only one that said anything to the point was Old Land's End, and says he: 'That may be a coward, but I'd chance it that he was a boy of mine.'

As we went up the straits and got the sun on us, and the damp heat of that kettle of a place — Lor' bless ye! ye steam there, all day and all night like a copper at the galley — we began to look around for the pirates, and there wasn't a man that got drowsy on the watch. We coasted along as we went up north, and took a look into the creeks and rivers as we went. It was up these that the Malays hid themselves; for the fevers and such that swept off their betters like flies, didn't seem to have any effect on them. There was pretty bad bits, I tell you, up some of them rivers through the mango groves, where the marshes spread away, mile after mile, as far as you could see, and where everything that is noxious, both beast, and bird, and fish, and crawling thing, and insect, and tree, and bush, and flower, and creeper, is most at home.

But the pirate ships kept ahead of us; or, if they came south again, passed us by in the night, and so we ran up till about the middle of the peninsula, where the worst of the piracies had happened. There we got up as well as we could to look like a ship in distress; and, sure enough, we deceived the beggars, for two of them came out one early dawn and began to attack us. They was ugly-looking craft, too — long, low hull and lateen-sails, and a double crew twice told in every one of them.

But if the crafts was ugly the men was worse, for uglier devils I never saw. Swarthy, yellow chaps, some of them, and some with shaven crowns and white eyeballs, and others as black as your shoe, with one or two white men, more shame, among them, but all carrying kreeses as long as your arm, and pistols in their belts.

They didn't get much change from us, I tell you. We let them get close, and then gave them a broadside that swept their decks like a hailstorm; but we was unlucky that we didn't grapple them, for they managed to shift off and ran for it. Our boats was out quick, but we daren't follow them where they ran into a wide creek, with mango swamps on each side as far as the eye could reach. The boat came back after a bit and reported that they had run up the river which was deep enough but with a winding channel between great mud-banks, where alligators lay in hundreds. There seemed some sort of fort where the river narrowed, and the pirates ran in behind it and disappeared up the bend of the river.

Then the preparations began. We knew that we had got two craft, at any rate, caged in the river, and there was every chance that we had found their lair. Our Captain wasn't one that let things go asleep, and by daylight the next morning we was ready for an attack. The pinnace and four other boats started out under the first lieutenant to prospect, and the rest that was left on board waited, as well as they could, till we came back.

That was an awful day. I was in the second boat, and we all kept well together when we began to get into the narrows of the mouth of the river. When we started, we went in a couple of hours after the flood-tide, and so all we saw when the light came seemed fresh and watery. But as the tide ran out, and the big black mud-banks began to show their heads above everywhere, it wasn't nice, I can tell you. It was hardly possible for us to tell the channels, for everywhere the tide raced quick, and it was only when the boat began to touch the black slime that you knew that you was on a bank. Twice our boat was almost caught this way, but by good luck we pulled and pushed off in time into the ebbing tide; and hardly a boat but touched somewhere. One that was a bit out from the rest of us got stuck at last in a nasty cut between two mud-banks, and as the water ran away the boat turned over on the slope, despite all her crew could do, and we saw the poor fellows thrown out into the slime. More than one of them began to swim toward us, but behind each came a rush of something dark, and though we shouted and made what noise we could, and fired many shots, the alligators was too close, and with shriek after shriek they went down to the bottom of the filth and slime. Oh, man! it was a dreadful sight, and none the better that it was new to nigh all of us. How it would have taken us if we had time to think about it, I hardly know, but I doubt that more than a few would have grown cold over it; but just then there flew amongst us a hail of small shot from a fleet of boats that had stolen down on us. They drove out from behind a big mud-bank that rose steeper than the others and that seemed solider, too, for the gravel of it showed, as the scour of the tide washed the mud away. We was not sorry, I tell you, to have men to fight with, instead of alligators and mud-banks, in an ebbing tide, in a strange tropical river.

We gave chase at once, and the pinnace fired the twelve-pounder which she carried in the bows, in among the huddle of the boats, and the yells arose as the rush of the alligators turned to where the Malay heads bobbed up and down in the drift of the tide. Then the pirates turned and ran, and we after them as hard as we could pull, till round a sharp bend of the river we came to a narrow place, where one side was steep for a bit and then tailed away to a wilderness of marsh, worse than we had seen. The other side was crowned by a sort of fort, built on the top of a high bank, but guarded by a stockade and a mud-bank which lay at its base. From this there came a rain of bullets, and we saw some guns turned towards us. We was hardly strong enough to attack such a position without reconnoitring, and so we drew away; but not quite quick enough, for before we could get out of range of their guns a round shot carried away the whole of the starboard oars of one of our boats.

It was a dreary pull to the ship, and the tide was agin us, for we all got thinking of what we had to tell — one boat and crew lost entirely, and a set of oars shot away — and no work done.

The Captain was furious; and, in the ward-room, and in the fo'c'sle that night, there was nothing that wasn't flavoured with anger and curses. Even the boys, of all sorts, from the cabin-boys to the midshipmen, was wanting to get at the Malays. However, sharp was the order; and by daylight three boats was up at the stockaded fort, making an accurate survey. I was again in one of the boats; and, in spite of what the Captain had said to make us all so angry — and he had a tongue like vitriol, I tell you — we all felt pretty down and cold when we got again amongst those terrible mud-banks and saw the slime that shone on them bubble up, when the grey of the morning let us see anything.

We found that the fort was one that we would have to take if we wanted to follow the pirates up the river, for it barred the way without a chance. There was a gut of the river between the two great ridges of gravel, and this was the only channel where there was a chance of passing. But it had been staked on both sides, so that only the centre was left free. Why, from the fort they could have stoned anyone in the boats passing there, only that there wasn't any stone, that we could see, in their whole blasted country!

When we got back, with two cases of sunstroke among us, and reported, the Captain ordered preparations for an attack on the fort, and the next morning the ball began. It was ugly work. We got close up to the fort, but, as the tide ran out, we had to sheer away somewhat so as not to get stranded. The whole place swarmed with those grinning devils. They evidently had some way of getting to and from their boats behind the stockade. They did not fire a shot at us — not at first — and that was the most aggravating thing that you can imagine. They seemed to know something that we did not, and they only just waited. As the tide sank lower and lower, and the mud-banks grew steeper, and the sun on them began to fizzle, a steam arose that nigh turned our stomachs. Why, the sight of them alone would make your heart sink!

The slime shimmered in all kinds of colours, like the water when there's tarring work on hand, and the whole place seemed alive with all that was horrible. The alligators kept off the boats and the banks close to us, but the thick water was full of eels and water-snakes, and the mud was alive with water-worms and leeches, and horrible, gaudy-coloured crabs. The very air was filled with pests — flies of all kinds, and a sort of big-striped insect that they call the 'tiger mosquito', which comes out in the daytime and bites you like red-hot pincers. It was bad enough, I tell you, for us men with hair on our faces, but some of the boys got very white and pale, and they was all pretty silent for a while. All at once the crowd of Malays behind the stockade began to roll their eyes and wave their kreeses and to shout. We knew that there was some cause for it, but couldn't make it out, and this exasperated us more than ever. Then the Captain sings out to us to attack the stockade; so out we all jumped into the mud. We knew it couldn't be very deep just there, on account of the gravel beneath. We was knee-deep in a moment, but we struggled, and slipped, and fell over each other; and, when we got to the top of that bank, we was the queerest, filthiest-looking crowd you ever see. But the mud hadn't took the heart out of us, and the Malays, with their necks craned over the stockade, and with the nearest thing to a laugh or a smile that the Devil lets them have, drew back and fell, one on another, when they heard our cheer.

Between them and us there was a bit of a dip where the water had been running in the ebb-tide, but which seemed now as dry as the rest, and the foremost of our men charged down the slope, and then we knew why they had kept silent and waited! We was in a regular trap. The first ranks disappeared at once in the mud and ooze in the hollow, and those next were up to their armpits before they could stop. Then those Malay devils opened on us, and while we tried to pull our chaps out, they mowed us down with every kind of small arm they had — and they had a queer assortment, I tell you.

It was all we could do to get back over the slope and to the boats again — what was left of us — and, as we hadn't hands enough left even to row with full strength, we had to make for the ship as far as we could, for their boats began to pass out in a cloud through the narrow by the stockade. But before we went we saw them dragging the live and dead out of the mud with hooks on the end of long bamboos; and there was terrible shrieks from some poor fellows when the kreeses gashed through them. We daren't wait; but we saw enough to make us swear revenge. When we saw them devils stick the bleeding heads of our comrades on the spikes of the stockade, there was nigh a mutiny because the Captain wouldn't let us go back and have another try for it. He was cool enough now; and those of us that knew him and understood what was in his mind, when the smile on him showed the white teeth in the corners of his mouth, felt that it was no good day's work that the pirates had done for themselves.

When we got back to the ship and told our tale, it wasn't long till the men was all on fire; and nigh every man took a turn with the grindstone at his cutlass, till they was all like razors. The Captain mustered everyone on board, and detailed every man to his work in the boats, ready for the next time; and we knew that, by daylight, we were to have another slap at the pirates. We got six-pounders and twelve-pounders in most of the boats, for we was to give them a dose of big shot before we came to close quarters.

When we got up near the stockade, the tide had turned, and we thought it better to wait till dawn, for it was bad work among the mud-banks at the ebb in the dark. So we hung on a while, and then when the sky began to lighten, we made for the fort. When we got nigh enough to see it, there wasn't a man of us who didn't want to have some bloody revenge, for there, on the spikes of the stockade, were the heads of all the poor fellows that we had lost the day before, with a cloud of mosquitoes and flies already beginning to buzz around them in the dawn. But beyond that again, they had painted the outside of the stockade with blood, so that the whole place was a crimson mass. You could smell it as the sun came up!

Well, that day was a hard one. We opened fire with our guns, and the Malays returned it, with all they had got. A fleet of boats came out from beyond the fort, and for a while we had to turn our attention to these. The small guns served us well, and we made a rare havoc among the boats, for our shot went crashing through them, and quite a half of them were sunk. The water was full of bobbing heads; but the tide carried them away from us, and their cries and shrieks came from beyond the fort and then died away. The other boats recognized their danger, and turned and ran in through the narrow, and let us alone for hours after. Then we went at the fort again. We turned our guns at the piles of the stockade, and, of course, every shot told — but their fire was at too close quarters, and with their rifles and matchlocks, and the rest, they picked us off too fast, and we had to sheer off where our heavy metal could tell without our being within their range. Before we sheered off, we could see that the hole we had knocked in the stockade was only in the outer work, and that the real fort was within. We had to go down the river, as we couldn't go far enough across without danger from the banks, and this only gave us a side view, and, do what we would, we couldn't make an impression — at least any that we could see.

That was a long and awful day! The sun was blazing on us like a furnace, and we was nigh mad with heat, and flies, and drouth, and anger. It was that hot that if you touched metal it fairly burned you. When the tide was near the flood, the Captain ordered up the boats in the wide water now opposite the fort: and there, for a while, we got a fair chance, till, when the ebb began, we should have to sheer off again. By this time our shot was nearly run out, and we thought that we should have to give over; but all at once came order to prepare for attack, and in a few minutes we was working for dear life across the river, straight for the stockade. The men set up a cheer, and the pirates showed over the top of the stockade and waved their kreeses, and more than one of them sliced off pieces of the heads on the spikes, and jeered at us, as much as to say that they would do the same for us in our turn! When we got close up, every one of them had disappeared, and there was a silence of the grave. We knew that there was something up, but what the move was we could not tell, till from behind the fort came rushing again a fleet of boats. We turned on them, and, like we did before, we made mincemeat of them. This time the tide made for us, and the bobbing heads went by us in dozens. Now and then there was a wild yell, as an alligator pulled some one down into the mud. This went on for a little, and we had beaten them off enough to be able to get our grappling-irons ready for climbing the stockade, when the second lieutenant, who was in the outer boat, called out: 'Back with the boats! Back, quick, the tide is falling!' and with one impulse we began to shove off. Then, in an instant, the place became alive again with the Malays, and they began firing on us so quickly that before we could get out into the whirl of tide there was many a dead man in our boats.

There was no use trying to do any more that day, and after we had done what could be done for the wounded, and patched up our boats, for there was plenty of shot-holes to plug, we pulled back to the ship. The alligators had had a good day, and as we went along, and the mud-banks grew higher and higher with the falling of the tide, we could see them lie out lazily, as if they had been gorged. Aye! And there was enough left for the ground-sharks out in the offing; for the men on board told us that every while on the ebb something would go along, bobbing up and down in the swell, till presently there would be a swift ripple of a fin, and then there was no more pirate.

Well! when we got aboard, the rest was mighty anxious to know what had been done; and when we began, with the heads on spikes of the red stockade, the men ground their teeth, and Old Land's End up, and says he: 'The Red

Stockade! We'll not forget the name! It'll be our turn next, and then we'll paint it inside this time.'

And so it was that we came to know the place by that name. That night the Captain was like a man that would do murder. His face was like steel, and his eyes was as red as flames. He didn't seem to have a thought for any one; and everything he did was as hard as though his heart were brass. He ordered all that was needful to be done for the wounded, but he added to the doctor: 'And, mind you, get them well as soon as you can. We're too short-handed already!'

Up to now, we all had known him treat men as men, but now he only thought of us as machines for fighting! True enough, he thought the same of himself. Twice that very night he cut up rough in a new way. Of course, the men was talking of the attack, and there was lots of brag and chaff, for all they was so grim earnest, and some of the old fooling went on about blood and tortures. The Captain came on deck, and as he walked along, he saw one of the men that didn't like the kreeses, and he didn't evidently like the looks of him, for he turned on his heel and said savagely: 'Send the doctor here!'

So the doctor came, and the Captain he says to him, cold as ice, and as polite as you please: 'Dr Fairbrother, there is a sick man here! Look at his pale face. Something wrong with his liver, I suppose. It's the only thing that makes a seaman's face white when there's fighting ahead. Take him down to sick bay, and do something for him. I'd like to cut the accursed white liver out of him altogether!' and with that he went down to his cabin.

Well if we was hot for fighting before, we was boiling after that, and we all came to know that the next attack on the Red Stockade would be the last, one way or the other! We had to wait two more days before that could come off, for the boats and tackle had to be made ready, and there wasn't going to be any mistakes made this time.

It was just after midnight when we began to get ready. Every man was to his post. The moon was up, and it was lighter nor a London day, and the Captain stood by and saw every man to his place, and nothing escaped him. By-and-by, as no. 6 boat was filling, and before the officer in charge of it got in, came the midshipman, young Tempest, and when the Captain saw him he called him up and hissed out before all the crew: 'Why are you so white? What's wrong with you, anyway? Is your liver out of order, too?'

True enough, the boy was white, but at the flaming insult the blood rushed to his face and we could see it red in the starlight. Then in another moment it passed away and left him paler than ever, and he said with a gentle voice, though standing as straight as a ramrod: 'I can't help the blood in my face, sir. If I'm a coward because I'm pale, perhaps you are right. But I shall do my duty all the same!' and with that he pulled himself up, touched his cap, and went down into the boat.

Old Land's End was behind me in the boat with him, number five to my six, and he whispered to me through his shut teeth: 'Too rough that! He might have thought a bit that he's only a child. And he came all the same, even if he was afeer'd!'

We stole away with muffled oars, and dropped silently into the river on the flood-tide. If any man had had any doubts as to whether we was in earnest at other times, he had none then, anyhow. It was a pretty grim time, I tell you, for the most of us felt that whether we won or not this time, there would be many empty hammocks that night in the *George Ranger*; but we meant to win even if we went into the maws of the sharks and crocodiles for it. When we came up close on the flood we lost no time but went slap at the fort. At first, of course, we had crawled up the river in silence, and I think that we took the beggars by surprise, for we was there before the time they expected us. How-somever, they turned out quick enough and there was soon music on both sides of the stockade. We didn't want to take any chance on the mud-banks this time, so we ran in close under the stockade at once and hooked on. We found that they had repaired the breach we had made the last time. They fought like devils, for they knew that we could beat them hand to hand, if we could once get in, and they sent round the boats to take us on the flank, as they had done each time before. But this time we wasn't to be drawn away from our attack, and we let our boats outside tackle them, while we minded our own business closer home.

It was a long fight and a bloody one. They was sheltered inside, and they knew that time was with them, for when the tide should have fallen, if we hadn't got in we should have our old trouble with the mud-banks all over again. But we knew it, too, and we didn't lose no time. Still, men is only men, after all, and we couldn't fly up over a stockade out of a boat, and them as did get up was sliced about dreadful — they are handy workmen with their kreeses, and no doubt! We was so hot on the job we had on hand that we never took no note of time at all, and all at once we found the boat fixed tight under us.

The tide had fallen and left us on the bank under the Red Stockade, and the best half of the boats was cut off from us. We had some thirty men left, and we knew we had to fight whether we liked it or not. It didn't much matter, anyhow, for we was game to go through with it. The Captain, when he seen the state of things, gave his orders to take the boats out into mid-stream, and shell and shot the fort, whilst we was to do what we could to get in. It was no use trying to bridge over the slobs, for the masts of an old seventy-four wouldn't have done it. We was in a tight place, then, I can tell you, between two fires, for the guns in the boats couldn't fire high enough to clear us every time, without going over the fort altogether, and more than one of our own shots did some of us a harm. The cutter came into the game, and began sending the war-rockets from the tubes. The pirates didn't like that, I tell you, and more betoken, no more did we, for we got as much of them as they did, till the Captain saw the harm to us, and bade them cease. But he knew his business, and he kept all the fire of the guns on the one side of the stockade, till he knocked a hole that we could get in by. When this was done, the Malays left the outer wall and went within the fort proper. This gave us some protection, since they couldn't fire right down on us, and our guns kept the boats away that would have taken us from the riverside. But it was hot work, and we began dropping away with stray shots, and with the stinkpots and hand-grenades that they kept hurling over the stockade on to us.

So the time came when we found that we must make a dash for the fort, or get picked out, one by one, where we stood. By this time some of our boats was making for the opening, and there seemed less life behind the stockade; some of them was up to some move, and was sheering off to make up some other devilment. Still, they had their guns in the fort, and there was danger to our boats if they tried to cross the opening between the piles. One did, and went down with a hole in her within a minute. So we made a burst inside the stockade, and found ourselves in a narrow place between the two walls of piles. Anyhow, the place was drier, and we felt a relief in getting out of up to our knees in steaming mud. There was no time to lose, and the second lieutenant, Webster by name, told us to try to scale the stockade in front.

It wasn't high, but it was slimy below and greasy above, and do what we would, we couldn't get no nigher. A shot from a pistol wiped out the lieutenant, and for a moment we thought we was without a leader. Young Tempest was with us, silent all the time, with his face as white as a ghost, though he done his best, like the rest of us. Suddenly he called out: 'Here, lads! take and throw me in. I'm light enough to do it, and I know that when I'm in you'll all follow.'

N'er a man stirred. Then the lad stamped his foot and called again, and I remember his young, high voice now: 'Seamen to your duty! I command here!'

At the word we all stood at attention, just as if we was at quarters. Then Jack Pring, that we called the Giant, for he was six feet four and as strong as a bullock, spoke out: 'It's no duty, sir, to fling an officer into hell!' The lad looked at him and nodded.

'Volunteers for dangerous duty!' he called, and every man of the crowd stepped out.

'All right, boys!' says he. 'Now take me up and throw me in. We'll get down that flag, anyhow,' and he pointed to the black flag that the pirates flew on the flagstaff in the fort. Then he took the small flag of the float and put it on his breast, and says he: 'This'll suit better.'

'Won't I do, sir?' said Jack, and the lad laughed a laugh that rang again.

'Oh, my eye!' says he, 'has anyone got a crane to hoist in the Giant?' The lad told us to catch hold of him, and when Jack hesitated, says he: 'We've always been friends, Jack, and I want you to be one of the last to touch me!' So Jack laid hold of him by one side, and Old Land's End stepped out and took him by the other. The rest of us was, by this time, kicking off our shoes and pulling off our shirts, and getting our knives open in our teeth. The two men gave a great heave together and they sent the boy clean over the top of the stockade. We heard across the river a cheer from our boats, as we began to scramble. There was a pause within the fort for a few seconds, and then we saw the lad swarm up the bamboo flagstaff that swayed under him, and tear down the black flag. He pulled our own flag from his breast and hung it over the top of the post. And he waved his hand and cheered, and the cheer was echoed in thunder across the river. And then a shot fetched him down, and with a wild yell they all went for him, while the cheering from the boats came like a storm.

We never knew quite how we got over that stockade. To this day I can't even imagine how we done it! But when we leaped down, we saw something lying at the foot of the flagstaff all red — and the kreeses was red, too! The devils had done their work! But it was their last, for we came at them with our cutlasses — there was never a sound from the lips of any of us — and we drove them like a hailstorm beats down standing corn! We didn't leave a living thing within the Red Stockade that day, and we wouldn't if there had been a million there!

It was a while before we heard the shouting again, for the boats was coming up the river, now that the fort was ours, and the men had other work for their breath than cheering.

Between us, we made a rare clearance of the pirates' nest that day. We destroyed every boat on the river, and the two ships that we was looking for, and one other that was careened. We tore down and burned every house, and jetty, and stockade in the place, and there was no quarter for them we caught. Some of them got away by a path they knew through the swamp where we couldn't follow them. The sun was getting low when we pulled back to the ship. It would have been a merry enough home-coming, despite our losses

— all but for one thing, and that was covered up with a Union Jack in the Captain's own boat. Poor lad! when they lifted him on deck, and the men came round to look at him, his face was pale enough now, and, one and all, we felt that it was to make amends, as the captain stooped over and kissed him on the forehead.

'We'll bury him tomorrow,' he said, 'but in blue water, as becomes a gallant seaman.'

At the dawn, next day, he lay on a grating, sewn in his hammock, with the shot at his feet, and the whole crew was mustered, and the chaplain read the service for the dead. Then he spoke a bit about him — how he had done his duty, and was an example to all — and he said how all loved and honoured him. Then the men told off for the duty stood ready to slip the grating and let the gallant boy go plunging down to join the other heroes under the sea; but Old Land's End stepped out and touched his cap to the Captain, and asked if he might say a word.

'Say on, my man!' said the Captain, and he stood, with his cocked hat in his hand, whilst Old Land's End spoke.

'Mates! ye've heerd what the chaplain said. The boy done his duty, and died like the brave gendeman he was! And we wish he was here now. But, for all that, we can't be sorry for him, or for what he done, though it cost him his life. I had a lad once of my own, and I hoped for him what I never wanted for myself — that he would win fame and honour, and become an admiral of the fleet, as others have done before. But, so help me God! I'd rather see him lying under the flag as we see that brave boy lie now, and know why he was there, than I'd see him in his epaulettes on the quarter-deck of the flagship! He died for his Queen and country, and for the honour of the flag! And what more would you have him do!'

EDGAR ALLAN POE

THE LIGHTHOUSE

January 1, 1796

This day — my first on the lighthouse — I make this entry in my diary, as agreed on with DeGrät. As regularly as I *can* keep the journal, I will — but there is no telling what may happen to a man all alone as I am — I may get sick or worse . . .

So far, well! The cutter had a narrow escape — but why dwell on that, since I am *here*, all safe? My spirits are beginning to revive already, at the mere thought of being — for once in my life at least — thoroughly *alone*; for, of course, Neptune, large as he is, is not to be taken into consideration as 'society'. Would to heaven I had ever found in 'society' one half as much *faith* as in this poor dog; in such case I and 'society' might never have parted — even for a year . . .

What most surprises me is the difficulty DeGrät had in getting me the appointment — and I a noble of the realm! It could not be that the Consistory had any doubt of my ability to manage the light. *One* man has attended it before now —

and got on quite as well as the three that are usually put in. The duty is a mere nothing; and the printed instructions are as plain as possible. It would never have done to let Orndoff accompany me. I should never have made any way with my book as long as he was within reach of me, with his intolerable gossip — not to mention that everlasting meerschaum. Besides, I wish to be *alone* . . .

It is strange that I never observed, until this moment, how dreary a sound that word has — 'alone'! I could half fancy there was some peculiarity in the echo of these cylindrical walls — but oh, no! — that is all nonsense. I do believe I am going to get nervous about my insulation. *That* will never do. I have not forgotten DeGrät's prophecy. Now for a scramble to the lantern and a good look around to 'see what I can see.' . . . To see what I can see indeed! — not very much. The swell is subsiding a little, I think — but the cutter will have a rough passage home, nevertheless. She will hardly get within sight of the *Norland* before noon tomorrow — and yet it can hardly be more than 190 or 200 miles.

January 2

I have passed this day in a species of ecstasy that I find it impossible to describe. My passion for solitude could scarcely have been more thoroughly gratified. I do not say *satisfied*; for I believe I should never be satiated with such delight as I have experienced today . . .

The wind lulled after daybreak, and by the afternoon the sea had gone down materially . . . Nothing to be seen with the telescope even, but ocean and sky, with an occasional gull.

January 3

A dead calm all day. Toward evening, the sea looked very much like glass. A few seaweeds came in sight; but besides them absolutely *nothing* all day — not even the slightest speck of cloud . . . Occupied myself in exploring the lighthouse . . . It is a very lofty one — as I find to my cost when I have to ascend its interminable stairs — not quite 160 feet, I should say, from the low-water mark to the top of the lantern. From the bottom *inside* the shaft, however, the distance to the summit is 180 feet at least: thus the floor is twenty feet below the surface of the sea, even at low tide. . . .

It seems to me that the hollow interior at the bottom should have been filled in with solid masonry. Undoubtedly the whole would have been thus rendered more *safe*: but what am I thinking about? A structure such as this is safe enough under any circumstances. I should feel myself secure in it during the fiercest hurricane that ever raged — and yet I have heard seamen say that, occasionally, with a wind at southwest, the sea has been known to run higher here than anywhere, with the single exception of the western opening of the Straits of Magellan.

No mere sea, though, could accomplish anything with this solid iron-riveted wall — which, at fifty feet from high-water mark, is four feet thick, if one inch. The basis on which the structure rests seems to me to be chalk . . .

January 4

I am now prepared to resume work on my book, having spent this day in familiarizing myself with a regular routine.

My actual duties will be, I perceive, absurdly simple — the light requires little tending beyond a periodic replenishment of the oil for the six-wick burner. As to my own needs, they are easily satisfied, and the exertion of an occasional trip down the stairs is all I must anticipate.

At the base of the stairs is the entrance room; beneath that is twenty feet of empty shaft. Above the entrance room, at the next turn of the circular iron staircase, is my storeroom, which contains the casks of fresh water and the food supplies, plus linens and other daily needs. Above that — again another spiral of those interminable stairs! — is the oil room, completely filled with the tanks from which I must feed the wicks. Fortunately, I perceive that I can limit my descent to the storeroom to once a week if I choose, for it is possible for me to carry sufficient provisions in one load to supply both myself and Neptune for such a period. As to the oil supply, I need only to bring up two drums every three days and thus ensure a constant illumination. If I choose, I can place a dozen or more spare drums on the platform near the light and thus provide for several weeks to come.

So it is that in my daily existence I can limit my movements to the upper half of the lighthouse; that is to say, the three spirals opening on the topmost three levels. The lowest is my 'living room' — and it is here, of course, that Neptune is confined the greater part of the day; here, too, that I plan to write at a desk near the wall slit that affords a view of the sea without. The second-highest level is my bedroom and kitchen combined. Here the weekly rations of food and water are contained in cupboards for that purpose; here, too, is the ingenious stove fed by the selfsame oil that lights the beacon above. The topmost level is the service room giving access to the light itself and to the platform surrounding it. Since the light is fixed, and its reflectors set, there is no need for me ever to ascend to the platform, save when replenishing the oil supply or making a repair or adjustment as per the written instructions — a circumstance which may well never arise during my stay here.

Already I have carried enough oil, water, and provender to the upper levels to last me for an entire month — I need stir from my two rooms only to replenish the wicks.

For the rest, I am free! Utterly free — my time is my own, and in this lofty realm I rule as king. Although Neptune is my only living subject, I can well imagine that I am sovereign o'er all I see — ocean below and stars above. I am master of the sun that rises in rubicund radiance from the sea at dawn, emperor of wind and monarch of the gale, sultan of the waves that sport or roar in roiling torrents about the base of my palace pinnacle. I command the moon in the heavens, and the very ebb and flow of the tide does homage to my reign.

But enough of fancies — DeGrät warned me to refrain from morbid or from grandiose speculation — now I shall take up in all earnestness the task that lies before me. Yet this night, as I sit before the window in the starlight, the tides sweeping against these lofty walls can only echo my exultation: I am free — and, at last, alone!

January 11

A week has passed since my last entry in this diary, and as I read it over, I can scarce comprehend that it was I who penned those words.

Something has happened — the nature of which lies un-fathomed. I have worked, eaten, slept, replenished the wicks twice. My outward existence has been placid. I can ascribe the alteration in my feelings to nought but some inner alchemy; enough to say that a disturbing change has taken place.

Alone! I, who breathed the word as if it were some mystic incantation bestowing peace, have come — I realize it now — to loathe the very sound of the syllables. And the ghastliness of meaning I know full well.

It is a dismaying, it is a dreadful thing, to be alone. Truly alone, as I am, with only Neptune to exist beside me and by his breathing presence remind me that I am not the sole inhabitant of a blind and senseless universe. The sun and stars that wheel overhead in their endless cycle seem to rush across the horizon unheeding — and, of late, unheeded, for I cannot fix my mind upon them with normal constancy. The sea that swirls or ripples below me is nought but a purposeless chaos of utter emptiness.

I thought myself to be a man of singular self-sufficiency, beyond the petty needs of a boring and banal society. How wrong I was! — for I find myself longing for the sight of another face, the sound of another voice, the touch of other hands whether they offer caresses or blows. Anything, anything for reassurement that my dreams are indeed false and that I am *not*, actually, alone.

And yet I *am*. I am, and I will be. The world is 200 miles away; I will not know it again for an entire year. And it in turn — but no more! I cannot put down my thoughts while in the grip of this morbid mood.

January 13

Two more days — two more centuries! — have passed. Can it be less than two weeks since I was immured in this prison tower? I mount the turret of my dungeon and gaze at the horizon; I am not hemmed in by bars of steel but by columns and pillars and webs of wild and raging water. The sea has changed; gray skies have wrought a wizardry so that I stand surrounded by a tumult that threatens to become a tempest.

I turn away, for I can bear no more, and descend to my room. I seek to write — the book is bravely begun, but of late I can bring myself to do nothing constructive or creative — and in a moment I fling aside my pen and rise to pace, to endlessly pace the narrow, circular confines of my tower of torment.

Wild words, these? And yet I am not alone in my affliction — Neptune, Neptune the loyal, the calm, the placid feels it too.

Perhaps it is but the approach of the storm that agitates him so — for Nature bears closer kinship with the beast. He stays constantly at my side, whining now, and the muffled roaring of the waves without our prison causes him to tremble. There is a chill in the air that our stove cannot dissipate, but it is not cold that oppresses him . . .

I have just mounted to the platform and gazed out at the spectacle of gathering storm. The waves are fantastically high; they sweep against the lighthouse in titanic tumult. These solid walls of stone shudder rhythmically with each onslaught. The churning sea is gray no longer — the water is black, black as basalt and as heavy. The sky's hue has deepened so that at the moment no horizon is visible. I am surrounded by a billowing blackness thundering against me . . .

Back below now, as lightning flickers. The storm will break soon, and Neptune howls piteously. I stroke his quivering flanks, but the poor animal shrinks away. It seems that he fears even my presence; can it be that my own features betray an equal agitation? I do not know — I only feel that I am helpless, trapped here and awaiting the mercy of the storm. I cannot write much longer.

And yet I will set down a further statement. I must, if only to prove to myself that reason again prevails. In writing of my venture up to the platform — my viewing of the sea and sky — I omitted to mention the meaning of a single moment. There came upon me, as I gazed down at the black and boiling madness of the waters below, a wild and willful craving to become one with it. But why should I disguise the naked truth? — I felt an insane impulse to hurl myself into the sea!

It has passed now; passed, I pray, forever. I did not yield to this perverse prompting and I am back here in my quarters, writing calmly once again. Yet the fact remains — the hideous urge to destroy myself came suddenly, and with the force of one of those monstrous waves.

And what — I force myself to realize — was the meaning of my demented desire? It was that I sought escape, escape from loneliness. It was as if by mingling with the sea and the storm I would no longer be *alone*.

But I defy the elements. I defy the powers of the earth and of the heavens. Alone I am, alone I *must* be — and come what may, I shall survive! My laughter rises above all your thunder!

So — ye spirits of the storm — blow, howl, rage, hurl your watery weight against my fortress — I am greater than you in all your powers. But wait! Neptune . . . something has happened to the creature — I must attend him.

January 16

The storm is abated. I am back at my desk now, alone — truly alone. I have locked poor Neptune in the storeroom below; the unfortunate beast seems driven out of his wits by the forces of the storm. When last I wrote he was worked into a frenzy, whining and pawing and wheeling in circles. He was incapable of responding to my commands and I had no choice but to drag him down the stairs by the scruff of his neck and incarcerate him in the storeroom where he could not come to harm. I own that concern for *my* safety was involved — the possibility of being imprisoned in this lighthouse with a mad dog must be avoided.

His howls, throughout the storm, were pitiable indeed, but now he is silent. When last I ventured to gaze into the room I perceived him sleeping, and I trust that rest and calm will restore him to my full companionship as before.

Companionship!

How shall I describe the horrors of the storm I faced *alone?*

In this diary entry I have prefaced a date — *January 16* — but that is merely a guess. The storm has swept away all track of time. Did it last a day, two days, three — as I now surmise — a week, or a century? I do *not* know.

I know only an endless raging of waters that threatened, time and again, to engulf the very pinnacle of the lighthouse. I know only an eternity of ebony, an aeon of billowing black composed of sea and sky commingled. I only know that there were times when my own voice outroared the storm — but how can I convey the cause of *that?* There was a time, perhaps a full day, perhaps much longer, when I could not bear to rise from my couch but lay with my face buried in the pillows, weeping like a child. But mine were not the pure tears of childhood innocence — call them, rather, the tears of Lucifer upon the realization of his eternal fall from grace. It seemed to me that I was truly the victim of an endless damnation; condemned forever to remain a prisoner in a world of thunderous chaos.

There is no need to write of the fancies and fantasies which assailed me through those unhallowed hours. At times I felt that the lighthouse was giving way and that I would be swept into the sea. At times I knew myself to be a victim of a colossal plot — I cursed DeGrät for sending me, knowingly, to my doom. At times (and these were the worst moments of all), I felt the full force of loneliness, crashing down upon me in waves higher than those wrought by water.

But all has passed, and the sea — and myself — are calm again. A peculiar calmness, this; as I gaze out upon the water there are certain phenomena I was not aware of until this very moment.

Before setting down my observations, let me reassure myself that I am, indeed, *quite* calm; no trace of my former tremors or agitation yet remains. The transient madness induced by the storm has departed and my brain is free of phantasms — indeed, my perceptive faculties seem to be sharpened to an unusual acuity.

It is almost as though I find myself in possession of an additional sense, an ability to analyze and penetrate beyond former limitations superimposed by Nature.

The water on which I gaze is placid once more. The sky is only lightly leaden in hue. But wait — low on the horizon creeps a sudden flame! It is the sun, the Arctic sun in sullen splendor, emerging momentarily from the pall to incarnadine the ocean. Sun and sky, sea and air about me, turn to blood.

Can it be I who but a moment ago wrote of returned, regained sanity? I, who have just shrieked aloud, 'Alone!' — and half-rising from my chair, heard the muffled booming echo reverberate through the lonely lighthouse, its sepulchral accent intoning 'Alone!' in answer? It may be that I am, despite all resolution, going mad; if so, I pray the end comes soon.

January 18

There will be no end! I have conceived a notion, a theory which my heightened faculties soon will test. I shall embark upon an experiment . . .

January 26

A week has passed here in my solitary prison. Solitary? — perhaps, but not for long. The experiment is proceeding. I must set down what has occurred.

The sound of the echo set me to thinking. One sends out

one's voice and it comes back. One sends out one's thoughts and — can it be that there is a response? Sound, as we know, travels in waves and patterns. The emanations of the brain, perhaps, travel similarly. And they are not confined by physical laws of time, space, or *duration*.

Can one's thoughts produce a reply that *materializes* just as one's voice produces an echo? An echo is a product of a certain vacuum. A thought . . .

Concentration is the key. I have been concentrating. My supplies are replenished, and Neptune — visited during my venture below — seems rational enough, although he shrinks away when I approach him. I have left him below and spent the past week here. Concentration, I repeat, is the key to my experiment.

Concentration, by its very nature, is a difficult task: I addressed myself to it with no little trepidation. Strive but to remain seated quietly with a mind 'empty' of all thought, and one finds in the space of a very few minutes that the errant body is engaged in all manner of distracting movement — foot tapping, finger twisting, facial grimacing.

This I managed to overcome after a matter of many hours — my first three days were virtually exhausted in an effort to rid myself of nervous agitation and assume the inner and outer tranquillity of the Indian fakir. Then came the task of 'filling' the empty consciousness — filling it completely with *one* intense and concentrated effort of will.

What echo would I bring forth from nothingness? What companionship would I seek here in my loneliness? What was the sign or symbol I desired? What symbolized to me the whole absent world of life and light?

DeGrät would laugh me to scorn if he but knew the concept that I chose. Yet I, the cynical, the jaded, the decadent, searched my soul, plumbed my longing, and found that which I most desired — a simple sign, a token of all the earth removed: a fresh and growing flower, *a rose!*

Yes, a simple rose is what I have sought — a rose, torn from its living stem, perfumed with the sweet incarnation of life itself. Seated here before the window I have dreamed, I have mused, I have then concentrated with every fiber of my being upon a *rose.*

My mind was filled with redness, not the redness of the sun upon the sea, or the redness of blood, but the rich and radiant redness of the rose. My soul was suffused with the scent of a rose: as I brought my faculties to bear exclusively upon the image, these walls fell away, the walls of my very flesh fell away, and I seemed to merge in the texture, the odor, the color the actual *essence* of a rose.

Shall I write of this, the seventh day, when seated at the window as the sun emerged from the sea, I felt the commanding of my consciousness? Shall I write of rising, descending the stairs, opening the iron door at the base of the lighthouse and peering out at the billows that swirled at my very feet? Shall I write of stooping, of grasping, of holding?

Shall I write that I have indeed descended those iron stairs and returned here with my waveborne trophy — *that this very day, from waters 200 miles distant from any shore, I have reached down and plucked a fresh rose?*

January 28

It has not withered! I keep it before me constantly in a vase on this table, and it is a priceless ruby plucked from dreams. It is real — as real as the howls of poor Neptune, who senses that something odd is afoot. His frantic barking does not disturb me; nothing disturbs me, for I am master of a power greater than earth or space or time. And I shall use this power, now, to bring me the final boon. Here in my tower I have become quite a philosopher: I have learned my lesson well and realize that I do not desire wealth, or fame, or the trinkets of society. My need is simply this — Companionship. And now, with the power that is mine to control, I shall have it!

Soon, quite soon, I shall no longer be alone!

January 30

The storm has returned, but I pay it no heed; nor do I mark the howlings of Neptune, although the beast is now literally dashing himself against the door of the storeroom. One might fancy that his efforts are responsible for the shuddering of the very lighthouse itself, but no; it is the fury of the northern gale. I pay it no heed, as I say, but I fully realize that this storm surpasses in extent and intensity anything I could imagine as witness to its predecessor.

Yet it is unimportant; even though the light above me flickers and threatens to be extinguished by the sheer velocity of wind that seeps through these stout walls; even though the ocean sweeps against the foundations with a force that makes solid stone seem flimsy as straw; even though the sky is a single black roaring mouth that yawns low upon the horizon to engulf me.

These things I sense but dimly, as I address myself to the appointed task. I pause now only for food and a brief respite — and scribble down these words to mark the progress of resolution toward an inevitable goal.

For the past several days I have bent my faculties to my will, concentrating utterly and to the uttermost upon the summoning of a Companion.

This Companion will be — I confess it! — a woman; a woman far surpassing the limitations of common mortality.

For she is, and must be fashioned, of dreams and longing, of desire and delight beyond the bounds of flesh.

She is the woman of whom I have always dreamed, the One I have sought in vain through what I once presumed, in my ignorance, was the world of reality. It seems to me now that I have always known her, that my soul has contained her presence forever. I can visualize her perfectly — I know her hair, each strand more precious than a miser's gold; the riches of her ivory and alabaster brow, the perfection of her face and form are etched forever in my consciousness. DeGrät would scoff that she is but the figment of a dream — but DeGrät did not see the rose.

The rose — I hesitate to speak of it — has gone. It was the rose which I set before me when I first composed myself to this new effort of will. I gazed at it intently until vision faded, senses stilled, and I lost myself in the attempt of conjuring up my vision of a Companion.

Hours later, the sound of rising waters from without aroused me. I gazed about, my eyes sought the reassurance of the rose and rested only upon a *foulness*. Where the rose had risen proudly in its vase, red crest rampant upon a living stem, I now perceived only a noxious, utterly detestable strand of ichorous decay. No rose this, but only seaweed; rotted, noisome, and putrescent. I flung it away, but for long moments I could not banish a wild presentiment — was it

317

true that I had deceived myself? Was it a weed, and only a weed I plucked from the ocean's breast? Did the force of my thought momentarily invest it with the attributes of a rose? Would anything I called up from the depths — the depths of sea or the depths of consciousness — be *truly* real?

The blessed image of the Companion came to soothe these fevered speculations, and I knew myself saved. There *was* a rose; perhaps my thought had created it and nourished it — only when my entire concentration turned to other things did it depart, or resume another shape. And with my Companion, there will be no need for focusing my faculties elsewhere. She, and she alone, will be the recipient of everything my mind, my heart, my soul possesses. If will, if sentiment, if love are needed to preserve her, these things she shall have in entirety. So there is nothing to fear. Nothing to fear . . .

Once again now I shall lay my pen aside and return to the great task — the task of 'creation', if you will — and I shall not fail. The fear (I admit it!) of loneliness is enough to drive me forward to unimaginable brinks. She, and she alone, can save me, shall save me, *must* save me! I can see her now — the golden glitter of her — and my consciousness calls to her to rise, to appear before me in radiant reality. Somewhere upon these storm-tossed seas she *exists*, I know it — and wherever she may be, my call will come to her and she will respond.

January 31

The command came at midnight. Roused from the depths of the most profound innermost communion by a thunderclap, I rose as though in the grip of somnambulistic compulsion and moved down the spiral stairs.

The lantern I bore trembled in my hand; its light wavered in the wind, and the very iron treads beneath my feet shook with the furious force of the storm. The booming of the waves as they struck the lighthouse walls seemed to place me within the center of a maelstrom of ear-shattering sound, yet over the demoniacal din I could detect the frenzied howls of poor Neptune as I passed the door behind which he was confined. The door shook with the combined force of the wind and of his still desperate efforts to free himself — but I hastened on my way, descending to the iron door at the base of the lighthouse.

To open it required the use of both hands, and I set the lantern down at one side. To open it, moreover, required the summoning of a resolution I scarcely possessed — for beyond that door was the force and fury of the wildest storm that ever shrieked across these seething seas. A sudden wave might dash me from the doorway, or conversely, enter and inundate the lighthouse itself.

But consciousness prevailed; consciousness drove me forward.

I *knew*, I thrilled to the certainty that *she* was without the iron portal — I unbolted the door with the urgency of one who rushes into the arms of his beloved.

The door swung open — blew open — roared open — and the storm burst upon me; a ravening monster of black-mouthed waves capped with white fangs. The sea and sky surged forward as if to attack, and I stood enveloped in chaos. A flash of lightning revealed the immensity of utter nightmare.

I saw it not, for the same flash illumined the form, the lineaments of *she* whom I sought.

Lightning and lantern were unneeded — her golden glory outshone all as she stood there, pale and trembling, a goddess arisen from the depths of the sea!

Hallucination, vision, apparition? My trembling fingers sought, and found, their answer. Her flesh was real — cold as the icy waters from whence she came, but palpable and permanent. I thought of the storm, of doomed ships and drowning men, of a girl cast upon the waters and struggling toward the succor of the lighthouse beacon. I thought of a thousand explanations, a thousand miracles, a thousand riddles or reasons beyond rationality. Yet only one thing mattered — my Companion was here, and I had but to step forward and take her in my arms.

No word was spoken, nor could one be heard in all that inferno. No word was needed, for she smiled. Pale lips parted as I held out my arms, and she moved closer. Pale lips parted — and I saw the pointed teeth, set in rows like those of a shark. Her eyes, fishlike and staring, swam closer. As I recoiled, her arms came up to cling, and they were cold as the waters beneath, cold as the storm, cold as death.

In one monstrous moment I *knew*, knew with uttermost certainty, that the power of my will had indeed summoned, the call of my consciousness *had* been answered. But the answer came not from the living, for nothing lived in this storm. I had sent my will out over the waters, but the will penetrates all dimensions, and my answer had come from *below* the waters: *She* was from below, where the drowned dead lie dreaming, and I had awakened her and clothed her with a horrid life. A life that thirsted, and must drink . . .

I think I shrieked, then, but I heard no sound. Certainly, I did not hear the howls from Neptune as the beast, burst from his prison, bounded the stairs and flung himself upon the creature.

His furry form bore her back and obscured my vision; in an instant she was falling backward, away, into the sea that spawned her. Then, and only then, did I catch a glimpse of the final moment of animation in that which my consciousness

321

had summoned. Lightning seared the sight inexorably upon my soul — the sight of the ultimate blasphemy I had created in my pride. The rose had wilted . . .

The rose had wilted and become seaweed. And now, the golden one was gone and in its place was the bloated, swollen obscenity of a thing long-drowned and dead, risen from the slime and to that slime returning.

Only a moment, and then the waves overwhelmed it, bore it back into the blackness. Only a moment, and the door was slammed shut. Only a moment, and I raced up the iron stairs, Neptune yammering at my heels. Only a moment, and I reached the safety of this sanctuary.

Safety? There is no safety in the universe for me, no safety in a consciousness that could create such horror. And there is no safety here — the wrath of the waves increases with every moment, the anger of the sea and its creatures rises to an inevitable crescendo.

Mad or sane, it does not matter, for the end is the same in either case. I know now that the lighthouse will shatter and fall. I am already shattered, and must fall with it.

There is time only to gather these notes, strap them securely in a cylinder and attach it to Neptune's collar. It may be that he can swim, or cling to a fragment of debris. It may be that a ship, passing by this toppling beacon, may stay and search the waters for a sign — and thus find and rescue the gallant beast.

That ship shall not find me. I go with the lighthouse and go willingly, down to the dark depths. Perhaps — is it but perverted poetry? — I shall join my Companion there forever. Perhaps . . .

The lighthouse is trembling. The beacon flickers above my head and I hear the rush of waters in their final onslaught. There is — yes — a wave, bearing down upon me. It is higher than the tower, it blots out the sky itself, everything . . .